The Musubi Murder

The Musubi Murder

Frankie Bow

FIVE STAR
A part of Gale, Cengage Learning

GALE
CENGAGE Learning

Farmington Hills, Mich • San Francisco • New York • Waterville, Maine
Meriden, Conn • Mason, Ohio • Chicago

Five Star™ Publishing, a part of Cengage Learning, Inc.

LIBRARY OF CONGRESS CATALOGING-IN-PUBLICATION DATA

Bow, Frankie.
The musubi murder / Frankie Bow. — First edition.
pages cm
ISBN 978-1-4328-3074-8 (hardback) — ISBN 1-4328-3074-0 (hardcover) — ISBN 978-1-4328-3085-4 (ebook) — ISBN 1-4328-3085-6 (ebook)
1. College teachers—Fiction. 2. Murder—Investigation—Fiction. I. Title.
PS3602.O8953M68 2015
813'.6—dc23 2015008334

First Edition. First Printing: July 2015
Find us on Facebook– https://www.facebook.com/FiveStarCengage
Visit our website– http://www.gale.cengage.com/fivestar/
Contact Five Star™ Publishing at FiveStar@cengage.com

Printed in the United States of America
1 2 3 4 5 6 7 19 18 17 16 15

The Musubi Murder

Chapter One

Our guest of honor, Jimmy Tanaka, may have been "The Most Hated Man in Hawaii," but he was also the biggest donor in the history of the College of Commerce. We were in no position to be picky about the moral character of our benefactors. Not after the latest round of budget cuts.

I had never seen the cafeteria this dressed up: white tablecloths, a wall-length refreshment table laden with stainless chafing dishes and platters, and extra security. I felt out of place, a drab little sparrow (and a sweaty one) in my dark wool suit. Everyone else sported Aloha Friday wear, cool cotton prints with colorful hibiscus or monstera designs. Something was making my neck itch. It was either the humidity or the plumeria-spiked floral centerpiece.

I was the only professor at the table. We had been evenly dispersed around the cafeteria to encourage (force) us to mingle with our Friends in the Business Community. The arrangement had the added benefit of keeping Hanson Harrison and Larry Schneider separated. Our two most senior professors are like fighting fish, flaring their gills at each other when they get too close.

I'm constantly telling my students how important it is to network. What I don't tell them is that I, personally, hate doing it, and, furthermore, I'm not very good at it. Mercedes Yamashiro, the only person at the table I knew, was deep in conversation with the woman next to her.

Bill Vogel appeared at our table, looking even more sour-faced than usual. Put him in a lace mantilla, and my dean could do a passable impression of Queen Victoria. "Mercedes," he barked. "Do you have any idea why Mr. Tanaka would be delayed this morning?"

"Oh, hello, Bill. No, I haven't seen Jimmy since he checked in last night."

He gave Mercedes a curt nod and stalked off without so much as a glance in my direction. I was the only person at the table who actually worked for him, but I was of no immediate use. Vogel would remember my name well enough when it was time to delegate some unpleasant task.

The good-looking man on my right was studying the contents of a manila folder. Even if I had the nerve to interrupt him, I couldn't imagine what I would say. I certainly couldn't open a conversation by telling him how much I liked the way he smelled, although that would have been the truth. He had a pleasant aroma of soap and cedar. Maybe I could comment on the weather. *Hey, have you noticed it's raining outside, ha ha, what are the chances? It only does that like three hundred days a year in Mahina.* He looked familiar, but I couldn't quite place him, and I certainly didn't want to volunteer the fact that I had forgotten his name. I wished that whoever had planned this breakfast had thought of providing name tags. I stared at the exit sign over a side door.

Exit. I dearly wished I could.

A flicker of motion under the sign caught my eye. I thought I saw a flash of baseball caps and sunglasses. I blinked at the empty doorway, and wondered if I had seen anything at all.

A shriek, followed by a metallic crash, startled the entire cafeteria into silence. At the refreshment table, two black-aproned servers stood wide-eyed, staring down at the wreckage of the dropped fruit platter. One held his hands over his mouth; the other clutched a round, stainless steel cover. Something round and white rolled to a halt on the floor, where it rocked gently among the translucent pineapple wedges and flabby melon chunks. Security guards converged on the object, conferred briefly, and sent the skinniest one sprinting out.

"It's okay, Molly." Mercedes Yamashiro patted my arm. "This kine stuff follows Jimmy around. I cannot even remember how many times he's had blood thrown at him, or people make one human chain to keep him out of somewhere. Not your guys' fault that people can be so rude. What *was* that thing? Not a bomb, I hope."

"Look over there," I said. "Our dean seems really upset. This is very unfortunate."

I had been secretly hoping for a minor disruption like this—something that would let me get out of there and back to work as quickly as possible. I could see Vogel now across the room, shouting into his cell phone, his jowly face wobbling like an enraged blancmange.

"Eh, this is late, even for Mr. Big Shot Jimmy Tanaka." Mercedes glanced around, then lowered her voice to a whisper that only a few tables around us could hear. "I wen' knock on his door this morning to see if he wanted to drive up with me but no answer. I left him alone 'cause I thought he got a ride with someone else, but now I think he was probably hungover in his room."

I glanced over at the refreshment table. The spilled food was being swept up, and a replacement fruit platter had already been set out.

"Do you want to call Mr. Tanaka and check on him?" I asked.

"Too late." She shook her wrist to clear a tangle of gold and jade bracelets out of the way, and checked her slender watch. "Even if he left now, he wouldn't get here till after ten. Probably for the best. Eh, Molly, you no like the food?"

Mercedes gestured at the Spam musubi congealing on my plate.

The Spam musubi, Hawaii's favorite snack and Merrie Musubis's signature dish, is a cube of sticky rice topped with a slice of fried Spam, and then wrapped in a strip of dried seaweed. From a distance, musubis look a lot like oversized pieces of sushi. Up close, they're delicious.

Unfortunately, my appetite had been damped by the stench of our ancient air conditioning mixed with the greasy breakfast smells and cloying plumeria scent. Also, I'm a little self-conscious about stuffing my face in front of attractive strangers.

"Of course I like the food," I said. I stole a sidelong glance at the nice-smelling man, and wondered if I could pocket the musubi without anyone noticing. I could eat it later, in my office. "It's just, I'm not usually up to breakfast this early."

That was a dumb thing to say. This town still runs on plantation time, and no one around here thinks nine in the morning is early. The Farmers' Market opens before sunrise, or so I hear.

The handsome man closed his manila folder and tucked it into the briefcase next to his chair.

"Good idea to have Jimmy Tanaka's restaurant cater the breakfast," he said, with an easy smile. *Who was he?* He seemed to know Mercedes, which wasn't any help. Mercedes knows everyone.

"I do like Merrie Musubis," I said. "I think their food is actually pretty decent. Especially compared to most of what you find around—"

"Oh, Molly!" Mercedes interrupted me. "Speaking of food! When are you going to invite Donnie to come talk to your class about the restaurant business?"

Donnie! Now I remembered who he was. I was sitting next to Donnie Gonsalves, owner of Donnie's Drive-Inns, Home of the Lolo Lunch Plate, and the Sumo Saimin Bowl. Merrie Musubis' main competitor.

"Oh!" I squeaked, "That's a great idea! You know my students really—"

"Shh!" Mercedes waved her hand to quiet me. "Here's your dean. He's gonna say something now."

Chapter Two

The room hushed as we watched Bill Vogel stride up to the podium. Vogel was tall, as deans tend to be, and his gleaming mahogany coif added extra height. He thanked everyone for coming, expressed his regret that our guest of honor had been unavoidably detained, and apologized for the unfortunate incident and for any inconvenience. He reaffirmed the university's commitment to both free speech and civility, and assured the guests that while we welcome diverse voices, the unfortunate demonstration that had just occurred in no way represented the views of the College of Commerce. He finished up by inviting our Friends from the Business Community to stay and enjoy breakfast and coffee, which was apparently everyone's cue to get up and clear out as quickly as possible.

As Vogel stepped down from the podium, he caught my eye and motioned to me. I looked around and behind me, and realized that he really did want to speak to me. I excused myself from the table and trudged up to meet him.

"Molly," Bill Vogel said, "Security wants to interview all of the faculty. And then I need to see you when you're done."

Officer Medeiros, with his dewy complexion and faint moustache, looked barely old enough to be a student here, much less head of the security department. He was big, even taller than Bill Vogel, and about twice as broad.

"I thought I saw some people in black in the doorway over there," I said, "but I'm not really sure. I couldn't tell you who they were." I stepped back so that I could look Officer Medeiros in the eye without craning my neck. "Was it a bomb?" I asked.

"Follow me," he said. Officer Medeiros's voice was surprisingly high-pitched. I realized I had expected a booming bass, like a cartoon giant. He led me through the swinging double doors back into the kitchen. On the stainless steel counter, nestled in a white dishtowel, sat something that looked like a replica of a human skull.

"Oh!" I said. "Is that the thing that was on the ground?"

"Someone put it in the fruit tray," he said. "Had to have been some time this morning. Do you remember seeing anything unusual?"

"I bet it came from the prop room," I said.

"You know where this came from?"

"Well. I can make an educated guess. I'm sure if you check with the theater department, you'll find a missing Yorick."

"A missing what?"

"A prop skull," I started to explain, but Officer Medeiros cut me off. "Oh yah, Yorick. The churchyard scene from *Hamlet.* How come you think it came from there?"

"The theater department chair, Stephen Park?" I said. "He never locks it. He's supposed to, but he always forgets. Last year when they put on the *Vagina Monologues,* some frat boys went in and stole this giant—well, anyway, yeah. You guys should talk to Stephen Park."

I gave Officer Medeiros Stephen's cell phone number. I still knew it by heart. I tried to slip back to my table without attracting Bill Vogel's attention, but he intercepted me.

"Molly. I have an opportunity for you."

"An opportunity?" I repeated, without enthusiasm. Oh, good. Next comes the part where he tells me to be a "team player," and then dumps some tedious task on me.

"It's a chance for you to show that you can be a team player," Bill Vogel said.

"Wonderful," I said. "What is it?"

"As you saw, Mr. Tanaka was unavoidably detained today, and was unable to join us."

"Well, it was probably for the best, considering what happened with the fruit tray."

"I'm in dialogue with our security department about that. This event was supposed to be limited to invited guests." He shot a glance at Officer Medeiros, who was on his walkie-talkie. "Anyway, we need to keep the momentum going on this. I'm asking you to write up the press release announcing Mr. Tanaka's gift to the college."

"Me? A press release? You know, that's not really my area of expertise."

I glanced around at the thinning crowd, hoping that Donnie Gonsalves had stuck around. It was easy to spot Mercedes in her brightly flowered muumuu, chatting with a pair of men in reverse-print, tucked-in aloha shirts. Bankers, probably. I didn't see Donnie Gonsalves.

"You teach business writing," Vogel said.

"I *used* to teach business communication," I said. "But I haven't—"

"You'll need to get in touch with Mr. Tanaka before you write it. Get one or two quotes from him. You have until next week."

"I have a *week*?"

The Campus Dining Center was nearly empty. The refreshment table had been cleared. Only the bases of the chafing dishes remained.

"You can email it to Serena," he said.

The last thing I needed at the beginning of the fall semester was one more thing on my to-do list. But the other last thing I needed was to antagonize my dean.

"Sure," I sighed. "No problem. Something like, controversial donor sparks anonymous protest?"

"This is not the time for humor, Molly. Please approach this assignment with some maturity and do not mention the incident."

"What? I wasn't trying to be—fine. I'll get right on it."

I couldn't bring myself to call him either "Bill," which would signal friendly familiarity, or "Dr. Vogel," which would imply respect.

Too bad that skull wasn't yours, I thought.

Emma Nakamura and Patrick Flanagan were already in my office when I got back. They were drinking what I assume was my coffee. The Arts and Sciences building is on the other side of campus, but Emma and Pat manage to turn up here on a regular basis. That's what I get for setting up an espresso machine. They may look different—Emma is short, brown, and solidly built, while Pat is gangly and fish-belly white—but when it comes to mooching my coffee, they are as one.

"Well, that's over, finally." I slammed the door shut behind me.

"Oh, poor thing," Emma pouted. "Had to go to one fancy catered breakfast with all the high makamaka movers and shakers."

"Ugh," Pat grimaced and hunched over in the plastic visitor chair as if he was going to be sick. "You couldn't pay me enough to hang out with those corporate weasels."

"They're not corporate weasels, Pat. They're our Friends in the Business Community. Except for my terrible dean. He—hey, what is *that*?"

"What do you mean? We thought it was yours," Pat said.

"It's not?" Emma added.

"No. I've never seen it before."

Pat and Emma exchanged glances. Pat shrugged.

Chapter Three

The suitcase was shabby, black, and—except for the fact that it had suddenly materialized in my office—unremarkable. I edged past it to get behind my desk, doing my best not to touch it, and picked up my phone. Serena, the dean's secretary, would know what was going on. Unfortunately, Serena wasn't answering. I left a message.

"Open it!" Emma demanded.

"What? Ew. No."

I plopped down on my yoga ball. We don't have any budget for office furniture, so when my old office chair collapsed, I replaced it with an off-brand yoga ball from Galimba's Bargain Boyz. It's the nicest piece of furniture in my office. My desk is a hand-me-down of rusted metal and peeling walnut-grain veneer. We removed half of the fluorescent light tubes in the building last year to save on our electric bill, so it's now too dim in my office to see where my particle-board bookshelf has swollen and split from the humidity.

"Hey, speaking of things turning up in my office," I said, "how did *you* guys get in here?"

"Your door was unlocked," Emma said.

"I'm pretty sure it wasn't—"

"We tried to catch you before you went to the breakfast," Pat said, "but Serena said you were in a meeting with your dean. Was it about your online ratings? Sorry about that."

"No," I said, "I think we're the only ones who read those.

No, it was about my cheaters."

"Expelled?" Emma asked hopefully.

"Not even close. Vogel is making me give them a do-over. Without any penalty."

"What?" Emma's eyes widened. "Auwe! Your dean is making you reward them for cheating!"

"I know! What can I do, Emma? If I try to make a report to the Office of Student Conduct, Vogel won't sign it. You know what else he said? 'Consider it a teachable moment.' "

Pat laughed. "A teachable moment? Right. Don't upset the 'customers' and don't bother the dean. There's your lesson. Did he talk about silos?"

"Of course he did," I said. "We have to break down the silos that separate the academic side of the house from the Student Retention Office, apparently."

Emma wrinkled her nose. "Why is it a good thing to break silos? All that happens when you break a silo is that the grain spills out. Or the missile falls over. Pilau, your dean."

"I know," I said. "I'm going to try to talk to my department chair again. Maybe he can do something. Anyway, let me tell you what *else* happened at breakfast—"

"What's Jimmy Tanaka like?" Emma interrupted. "Does he walk funny cause of his cloven hooves?"

"No idea," I said. "He never showed. It's probably for the best, actually."

Before Emma could interrupt again, I told them about the skull turning up in the fruit platter.

"Weren't you hoping the breakfast was going to be a disaster?" Pat said.

"No, Pat, I was not hoping for it to be a disaster. How petty do you think I am?"

"Was it a real skull?" Emma asked.

"Nah. It looked fake to me. I bet it'll turn out to be from

Stephen's prop room. He always forgets to lock up."

"Oh, yah!" she exclaimed. "Remember last year—"

"I know," I said. "So guess who I was sitting next to? Donnie Gonsalves! From Donnie's Drive-Inn!"

"Donnie Gonsalves! Ooh, I think he's single, Molly!"

"So I guess you're over Stephen now," Pat said. "That didn't take long."

"Oh, shut up, Pat. You *hated* Stephen. Don't pretend you feel sorry for him. Anyway, Molly, you get his number?"

"No. Things got kind of hectic."

"Aw, girl." Emma shook her head. "We gotta work on your game."

Emma nudged the suitcase with her toe.

"Emma, stop that!"

"Come on," Emma said. "Let me open it."

"No! It might have bedbugs."

"That's gross," said Emma.

"Molly's right though," said Pat.

"Yah," Emma conceded, "does look kinda junk."

My office phone rang. I hoped it was Serena calling me back about the suitcase. It wasn't.

"Hi, Betty!" I hoped my tone of voice didn't betray the fact that I had forgotten my appointment with my coauthor. "Yes, of course I'm here. Ready to go. See you soon." I hung up the phone, moved my stack of unopened mail from my desk to a shelf, and pulled down a milk crate labeled "Rapport—Relationship Building/SF Conference." It was full of article reprints, manila folders, and loose papers.

"Sorry, guys," I said, pulling out folders and sorting them into piles on the desk. "I have to kick you out. Betty's going to be here in a couple of minutes."

"You still haven't finished your presentation?" Emma said. "Isn't your conference pretty soon?"

I closed my eyes and pressed my fingertips to my temples.

"Yes, it is. Plus I have papers to grade, I'm behind on my Student Retention Office reports, and now I have to write this stupid—"

"Hey, Molly," Pat said. "You want come to the Hanohano with me after work?"

"The Hanohano?" I opened my eyes. "That's one of Jimmy Tanaka's properties, isn't it? I wonder if he'll be there."

"Why do you wanna meet Jimmy Tanaka so bad?" Emma asked.

"Oh yeah, I didn't tell you. Vogel 'tasked' me with writing the press release about the donation. He wants me to get in touch with Tanaka first."

"How come Vogel's making *you* write it?" Emma asked. "Don't we have a marketing office?"

"Why should he bother putting in a request and waiting his turn when he can just make an untenured faculty member do it? Just another one of the indignities routinely heaped upon the junior faculty in my college. At least he's not making me pick up his dry cleaning. Poor Serena gets stuck doing that. Anyway, Pat, what's happening at the Hanohano Hotel?"

"I can't go," Emma said. "I have to get home right after my lab, otherwise Yoshi gets grumpy."

"That's okay," Pat said. "No offense, Emma, but I was really hoping Molly would come with me. I need someone who looks like a tourist."

"Thanks," I said. "What exactly are we supposed to be doing there?"

"If I tell you in advance, it won't work as well."

"I'll think about it," I said.

Chapter Four

The third floor was as high as we could go. The buttons for floors four and five glowed through the duct tape covering them. The elevator heaved and shuddered to our stop, and then paused for an unnerving length of time before the metal doors creaked open to let us out.

I followed Pat down the dim hallway, doing my best to ignore the squelch of the damp carpet. By the time I caught up to him, he had disappeared into one of the guest rooms.

"Are you sure it's okay for us to be here?" I called into the room.

"No wonder the TV crew didn't find anything." Pat emerged from behind rust-mottled vertical blinds, brushing something off his face. "What kind of unfabulous ghost would ever want to haunt this place?"

"It smells horrible up here," I said. "Can we go back downstairs now?"

"Let me take a couple of pictures first."

"Pictures? Of this? Are you kidding? Why?"

Watercolor blotches of peach and salmon adorned the bedspreads. The couch picked up the theme with an abstract pastel print and whitewashed oak arms. The wallpaper was a faded peach and aqua stripe, peeling away at the seams.

"I think all this stuff was already out of date the day it was put in," Pat said, pulling up the edge of the carpet. He stood back up and started snapping pictures of the floor.

Pat Flanagan and I were on the third floor of Jimmy Tanaka's New Hanohano Hotel, a grim concrete box that had been built out to the edge of the property, blocking the light and the view of its more modestly sized neighbors on Hotel Drive. The original Hanohano had been a picturesque single-story sugar plantation house, with a generous porch and nine-foot ceilings. The only things the original landmark had in common with its successor were the location and the name.

We took the emergency stairwell back downstairs (I refused to get back on the elevator). Pat paused at the fire door that led to the lobby and tugged his flannel shirt straight.

"Do I look like a friendly lifestyle reporter?" he asked.

"Friendly? If you were going for 'friendly,' you shouldn't have shaved your head. You look like an IRA gunrunner."

"Paying someone to cut my hair is wasteful," he said. He pushed the stairwell door open. "Your cell phone's buzzing," he called back to me.

It was a text message from Stephen. It must have been a misdial. Why would he try to get in touch now, after all this time? I swiped the message to delete it and followed Pat into the lobby.

"Who was it?" he asked.

"Wrong number."

We approached the receptionist, the only living soul we had seen so far. Purple orchids adorned her lacquered black up-do and complemented her purple hibiscus-print uniform. She beamed at us as we drew closer. In her situation I suppose even I would have been grateful for human contact.

Pat introduced himself and started asking her questions about the legendary ghosts of the Hanohano. Did the ghosts leave when the old building was torn down? Had she ever heard mysterious footsteps? Felt the presence of night marchers?

She laughed at the mention of ghosts. She confirmed what Pat had already told me, that the advance crew from one of those ghost hunter reality shows had come to check out the Hanohano. The scouts had found no paranormal activity and had left disappointed. I hovered at the edge of the conversation, listening, nodding, and (thanks to the mildewy stench that permeated the building) taking the shallowest breaths I could manage.

Pat glanced at her name tag. "So, Moana, what's it like to work for The Most Hated Man in Hawaii?"

"We don't call him that," she giggled and lowered her voice. "Not to his face, anyway."

She had worked at the old Hanohano, she told us, and she felt lucky to get her job back after Jimmy Tanaka bought the hotel. She glanced around the empty lobby. "Most of my friends were not hired back. Sandy Medeiros, her and me was best friends, and she was a single mom. And then when Sal was killed . . ." She blinked. "He had a wife and a young boy, you know. It was terrible."

"Sal?" Pat repeated. He was committing the conversation to memory.

"Salvador Pung. You probably never saw it in the paper. Just one small story when it happened."

I watched a pinkish-tan gecko scamper up the wall behind the reception desk. It looked like the ones that hang out on the ceiling of my carport and gobble up termites. There seemed to be plenty of insect life to feast on at the Hanohano. Lucky gecko.

"My husband was a foreman," Moana said. "He always come home grumbling about how the building is going up too fast. They wasn't giving the workers their breaks or nothing. And then they brought in the crane . . ."

By the time she got to the part where the ambulance arrived, I was ready to pass out. I excused myself from the conversation and wandered over to the closest couch. Close up, I could see black specks on the flowered pillows. They were not part of the original design. I sat on the white fiberglass cube that served as an end table, rested my elbows on my knees, and took out my phone to check my email.

The top item in my inbox was from someone claiming to be my student, although he had not yet shown up to class.

Hey proffeser, I need to make up the assignment I missed. I couldn't get the textbook cuz the bookstore is totaly sold out. Thx, Joshua

The bookstore still had plenty of my assigned textbooks in stock, and I had placed copies on reserve in the library as well. I'm a patient person, regardless of what Emma might tell you, but I take exception to being lied to. I considered a number of crisply worded replies before my better angels prevailed. I wrote,

Dear Joshua,

Please refer to the course syllabus for the policy on late work.

The next email was from our Student Retention Office. The subject line read, "Use Social Media to Connect with Your Students!"

I deleted it unread, and walked outside to get some air.

The Hanohano didn't look any nicer on the outside. Black mildew streaked down the white stucco below the windows like runny mascara. I turned away from the hotel to watch the ocean roll and sparkle in the sun. Poor Salvador Pung. Why did the name sound so familiar? I knew there must be a word for this. You hear about something for the first time, and next thing you know it seems like you're seeing it everywhere.

I found Pat in the gift shop, taking pictures of the ceiling. There was no one behind the counter to guard the neon plastic flowers, odd-smelling straw hats, tiki key chains, or the plastic stick-on soul patch and eyebrow package, which was the only item I thought might be worth buying.

"Ready to go?" he asked.

"Very. Are you going to tell me what we supposedly accomplished here? There sure wasn't any sign of Jimmy Tanaka."

"Sure," he said. "Let's get out of here first."

Chapter Five

I took a deep breath as soon as we stepped outside. The air was warm and dense, and mercifully free of the sour, moldy smell that had pervaded the interior of the Hanohano. Drops of drizzle spattered the broken asphalt of the parking lot.

"I hope we don't track the odor into my interior," I said, as we made our way back to my car.

"Why didn't you let me drive?" Pat asked.

"I like driving," I lied.

I don't like putting extra miles on my 1959 Thunderbird, especially with gas prices the way they are, but it was worth it not to ride in Pat's car. You'd think that Pat, who lives off the grid twenty miles out of town, would have reliable, sturdy transportation. Especially since his cabin sits at the end of an unpaved private road that turns to muck whenever it rains.

But you would only think that if you didn't know Pat. He likes to find cars that cost less than $500, and then run them until his duct-tape fixes stop working. It's his way of sticking it to the Man. Right now he's driving an oxidized white Plymouth Valiant with one brown door, a missing muffler, and a hole in the passenger-side floorboard big enough to stick both your feet through. The original color of the upholstery is a mystery, obscured by sticky stains and what looks like damage from some kind of burrowing vermin. I won't ride in Pat's car without putting down a clean towel first, and even then I don't feel good about it.

"Pat, that poor man who was killed. In the accident. His last name was Pung, right?" I inched the Thunderbird out of the Hanohano parking lot, steering to avoid protruding roots and clumps of buckled asphalt.

"Yeah," he said. "Same name as on one of your plagiarized papers. You don't have to drive so slow, Molly. Your suspension's not made of toothpicks."

"I just want to get out of here with my muffler still attached. That is where I saw the name! How did you know?"

"I had to help you download the similarity reports, remember? The website wasn't working because you forgot to turn your script blocker off."

"Oh. That's right. Anyway, what's that called when you see something once and then suddenly you're seeing it everywhere?"

"Baader Meinhof phenomenon," Pat said.

"Ah. Thanks! I guess now I'll be seeing 'Baader Meinhof phenomenon' everywhere I look."

"Probably."

"So did you find anything interesting?" I asked. "Ghostwise?"

Pat waited until I pulled out onto Hotel Drive.

"I'm doing a story on the construction of the new Hanohano," he said. "It's even worse than it looks."

"What do you mean? How could it possibly be worse than it looks? And what, the whole ghost thing was just a ruse?"

Pat clicked his lap belt shut and pulled it snug.

"Your car smells weird," he said.

"That's what a clean car smells like."

"Ha ha."

"It's the new upholstery. So you are writing about the Hanohano?"

"The whole thing is really fishy," he said. "How did Tanaka manage to get this thing permitted? I mean, they didn't even try to make it look like it was built to code. There's mold under the carpets and probably inside the walls. There's a utility room downstairs with carpet sitting right on bare dirt. I bet just spending time inside that building is a health hazard."

I glanced back at the monstrous hotel. Construction had begun with great fanfare and no expense spared, but as the project progressed, money had run low. Preposterous, twenty-foot concrete columns flanked a gleaming plate-glass front entrance, but the windows were the cheap aluminum kind. The top floors were never finished. Decayed scaffolding clung to the building, and rusty rebar bristled from raw concrete at the top.

"I can't even imagine what they were going for," I said. "It's aesthetically incoherent."

"Seriously. It looks like a Motel Six designed by Albert Speer."

Pat stretched his long legs out, his gigantic work boots dirtying the new/old stock gray carpet I'd had installed a few months ago. He began to type into his phone.

"That was pretty clever, Pat. Going in asking about the ghost stories."

"Well, if I'd gone after what I really wanted to know, I wouldn't have gotten anywhere. A manager would probably have materialized out of some back office right away and ordered us to leave. But you being there with me, and us asking about the ghost legends—"

"We were just a goofy haole couple chasing a story that had probably been concocted for tourists."

"Exactly! Nice job, by the way. Next time try not holding your nose the whole time, though."

"So are you posting this on *Island Confidential*?" I asked.

"I'm not even close to ready. I'm still finishing up the piece about the telescope protesters."

"What's the latest with that? I've seen some headlines but I haven't really been following it that well."

"The summit of Mauna Kea is over thirteen thousand feet, right?"

"I knew that," I said. "I thought it was closer to fourteen thousand."

"So it's one of the best sites on Earth for ground-based telescopes. But it's also the sacred home of the Divine Ancestors. And home to an endangered species or two. So you have a coalition of environmentalists and native practitioners who don't want the telescope to happen."

"I already knew that too. But that's all been going on for a while, right?"

"Well the latest thing is, they tried to bring Mo'oinanea into a contested case hearing."

"Who is that?" I asked.

"A guardian spirit of Mauna Kea," Pat said. "But the judge ruled that she doesn't have standing because she's not a person."

"Oh, I know the answer to that one. Incorporate. Mo—what was the name?"

"Mo'oinanea."

"Corporations are legal persons. The Mo'oinanea *Corporation* would be recognized as a person, no problem. We're going to cover this in class in a couple of weeks."

My purse hummed from the back seat.

"I'll get it," Pat said. "You're driving."

"No, it's okay, you don't have to—"

But Pat had already pressed the green button.

Chapter Six

"Hi, Molly? It's Serena," said my speakerphone from Pat's huge hand.

"Serena," I shouted over the road noise, "I'm so glad you called back!"

"Hey, Serena." Pat was holding my phone for me as I drove, so I suppose he felt entitled to join the conversation between the dean's secretary and me. "How're you holding up?" he asked her.

"Oh, hello Pat. I guess you heard what happened, yah? And then the guest of honor never even showed up."

"Did they find out who did it?" I asked.

"No," she said. "Security's still looking into it. In fact, they left a message for you, Molly. They want to ask you some questions about it."

"Well, I guess I could talk to them again," I said. "I'm not sure it would help. Listen, Serena, I called earlier because I found a suitcase in my office. Do you know anything about that?"

"What? Oh, the suitcase. You know Mercedes Yamashiro from the Cloudforest Bed and Breakfast, right? Of course you do. You were sitting at her table."

"Right," I said.

"Our college put Jimmy Tanaka up there. At the Cloudforest."

"Mercedes mentioned that. Gee, I wonder why he didn't

want to stay at the Hanohano. There's a real mystery, huh?"

"Mr. Tanaka was supposed to check out this morning. We paid his bill, but Mercedes says she can't store all the property that guests leave behind. She had one of her interns bring his suitcase up right after breakfast. We don't have any storage space, so Dean Vogel wanted me to ask you if you would keep it in your office."

"Ah."

"You weren't in. I hope that was okay," she said.

"Well, do I have a choice?"

"You know, Molly, there isn't much room in there."

"Yes," I said. "I know that. How long do I have to keep it?"

"It shouldn't be for very long. Just until you get a-hold of Mr. Tanaka to interview him. You can give it back to him then."

I don't have room in my office, but I'm also the only person in my department who doesn't have tenure. Vogel wouldn't ask Dan Watanabe to watch the suitcase. Dan's the department chair. And if Vogel had tried to pawn it off on Larry Schneider or Hanson Harrison, he'd get a formal grievance filed against him within the hour.

Rodge Cowper would probably have said, "Sure, no problem" and then left his office door open to let the bag get stolen. That strategic incompetence is exactly how Rodge gets out of doing any committee work, by the way. Either he doesn't bother to show up to the meetings, or he does show up and tells one of his jokes, and then he gets pulled off the committee and sent to sensitivity training.

Rain drummed on the vinyl roof of my car. I pulled Pat's hand closer to my mouth so Serena could hear me.

"Why can't we ship Mr. Tanaka's bag back to his office in Honolulu?" I yelled into Pat's hand.

"I checked, but the College of Commerce can't afford to pay for the interisland shipping."

I twisted the knob to start the windshield wipers. They inched about halfway through their arc and stopped. I already knew how much it would cost to replace the old vacuum wiper motor with an electric one, which was why I hadn't done it yet.

"Okay!" I shouted. "No problem. I'm just driving back from the Hanohano Hotel. I was hoping to find Mr. Tanaka."

"Was he there?" Serena asked.

"No. I'll keep trying though."

Pat slipped my phone back into my bag.

"You're never gonna bring those windshield wipers back to life," he said. "Just buy some Rain-X. Works great."

"My windshield wipers are fine," I squinted at the road ahead through the rivulets on my windshield.

"Hey, why don't you bring the suitcase back to your house?" Pat said.

"I do not want that thing in my house," I said. "You really think it's a lost cause?"

"Your windshield wipers? You remember what Earl said about those old vacuum systems?"

Earl, my mechanic at Miyashiro Motors Autobody, disapproves of squarebirds (referring to model years 1958 to 1960, when Thunderbirds went big and rectangular). He grumbles about their vague handling and self-destructive front-end suspensions, and gives voice to unflattering inferences about the judgment and mental acuity of anyone who would willingly drive one. Earl is also the only mechanic on the island who will even attempt to work on my car.

"Earl's a competent mechanic," I said, "but he has no imagination."

"Why don't you call down to the Cloudforest?" Pat said. "Maybe Mercedes didn't realize you were the one who'd get stuck with the suitcase."

"You know what? I think I will call her. Maybe she'll have

some idea about how I can get hold of Tanaka. Or maybe she'll even take the suitcase back."

Pat pulled the phone out of my purse again and held it up for me to speak to as I drove.

"Aloha, and thank you for calling the Cloudforest."

He sounded young. One of our interns, I assumed. The Cloudforest takes a few of them every semester. I gave my name and asked for Mercedes.

"Oh, hi, Dr. Barda! This is Nate!"

"Oh, Nate. You're doing another internship there?"

"No," he said, "I graduated. I work here now!"

"Oh, that's wonderful!" I gushed. Nate Parsons had been one of my best students. I wondered if answering phones at a bed and breakfast was worth the time and the student loans he had invested. Maybe, if the alternative was unemployment.

"I'll go get Mercedes," he said. "Nice to talk to you, Dr. Barda."

Eventually Mercedes got on the line.

"Oh, Molly. They gave Jimmy's suitcase to you?"

"Yep. Dean Vogel made Serena park it in my office."

Mercedes laughed. "Well, I can't keep everything that guests leave behind. I'd run out of space!"

"I was just at the Hanohano," I said. "Jimmy Tanaka wasn't there. Do you have any idea where he might be?"

"No. And it looks like he didn't even sleep in his room. You know, Molly, we have birria tonight. Come down if you don't have dinner plans. My treat. To make up for the suitcase."

"Is that the goat stew?" Pat whispered.

I nodded.

"Mercedes, that's very nice of you," I said. "But Pat Flanagan is with me, and we—"

"Pat is invited too, of course! Both of you come down!"

"We're on our way," Pat shouted into the phone.

After I hung up, Pat said, "You didn't have anything else planned tonight, did you?"

"Just finishing up my Student Retention Office reports for this week."

"That shouldn't take a lot of time. Just cut and paste from last week's report."

"Can I do that?" I asked.

"Do you think they check to make sure you come up with a brand-new teaching philosophy every week?"

"Mercedes says it looks like Jimmy Tanaka didn't sleep in his room."

"I heard," he said. "I think I'd like to have a look around. There might be another angle to this Hanohano story."

Chapter Seven

I had forgotten how far out of town the Cloudforest Bed and Breakfast was. As we drove south, the road narrowed from two lanes to one as the jungle became denser and taller. Then the road ran out of asphalt. I bit off a swear word and slowed the car to approximately walking speed.

"I don't remember the road being this bad," I said.

"The homeowner's association hasn't gotten around to resurfacing it," Pat said. "Do we have to go *this* slow?"

"Yes, unless *you* want to be the one to pay for my next front-end rebuild. Oh, and listen to the inevitable lecture from Earl? Anyway, what do you mean, the homeowner's association hasn't—"

I caught my breath as the car plunged into a pothole.

"This is a private road," Pat said. "Back when they were building this subdivision, the planning commission let the developers decide what to do with the streets. You know, whether to pave them, put in proper drainage, stuff like that."

"I wonder what the developers decided," I said, steering carefully around a crater in the middle of the road. "Jimmy Tanaka wasn't among these visionaries by any chance, was he?"

"Of course he was," Pat said.

"Ah."

"The developers could afford to sell the individual lots for cheap, 'cause they didn't have to build infrastructure. The rain this summer really did a number, though. The association is still trying to raise the money to do repairs. They can't agree on which part to fix first. Of course you'd know all of this, Molly, if you'd been following my series in *Island Confidential.*"

My bag hummed again.

"Let it go to voice mail," I said, as Pat pulled out my phone.

"Oh, hi, Stephen." Pat grinned broadly and raised his eyebrows at me. I shook my head and mouthed, "No!"

"Sure, she's right here. Hang on. I'll put you on speaker."

I wanted to shoot Pat some serious stinkeye, but I had to keep an eye on the washed-out remnants of the road.

"Hi, Stephen." I tried to project casual insouciance. If my ex was finally going to apologize, I wanted to sound gracious and pleasantly surprised.

"Molly, I need your help," he said.

"You *what*?"

"Want to pull over?" Pat said. "I can drive."

"I'm fine! No one was coming the other way. In fact, look, there's asphalt up ahead. Stephen, what is going on?"

"Someone broke into my prop room. Either last night or this morning. And then—"

"Aaah! Let me guess. One of your props appeared on a dessert tray. At the event that was supposed to honor the biggest donation in our college's history. When you say *broke into* your prop room, do you mean you've started locking it now?"

The silence lasted so long I wondered if I'd lost the connection. Finally, the phone in Pat's hand spoke.

"You don't have to sound so accusing."

"I'm not accusing. I'm just *guessing.* I'm *guessing* that your prop room's still completely disorganized and you never remember to lock it and you have no idea who or what goes in and out of there."

"Molly—"

"Right? What happened to that spreadsheet I spent hours setting up for you? Did you ever even open it?"

"You have no idea how bad this is for me, Molly."

"How bad this is for *you.* Good point. We might have alienated our Friends in the Business Community along with our biggest donor, but let's not lose sight of the most important issue: how does this affect Stephen Park?"

"Road!" Pat was using his free hand to brace himself against the dashboard. I steered back into my lane.

"Look, Stephen, I'm going to give you some helpful advice. You obviously messed up. What you need to do now is apologize. Apologize to the people you need to apologize to—"

"To whom you need to apologize—" Pat interrupted.

I grabbed the phone from Pat.

"Apologize." I pressed the phone to my right ear and batted Pat away with my left hand.

"Steering wheel!" Pat yelled.

"Listen, Stephen, you can argue with me, or you can try to make things right. That's all I can tell you."

"But Molly, I think they—"

I mashed the hang-up button and threw the phone into the back seat.

"Molly, look out!"

"What? I'm fine. Everything's under control." I steered the car off the bumpy forest floor back onto the narrow strip of asphalt. We drove in silence along the rutted thoroughfare until the road widened and smoothed through the town of Kuewa. The termite-eaten boardwalk featured a few New Age shops, a health food store, a couple of restaurants and a tattoo parlor advertising family discounts. Then the Old West–style storefronts thinned out and we were past the town and driving through jungle again.

I finally spotted the glint of solar panels through the trees, in time to turn up a dirt road so narrow and overgrown that it looked like an abandoned driveway. After a few minutes we were approaching the Cloudforest's main building, a single-story house with a green metal roof and a wraparound lanai. I parked the car and we walked to the building.

It took a few seconds for my eyes to adjust to the low light inside. Dark bloodwood floors and koa wainscoting didn't help the visibility. A young woman behind the front desk looked up from her computer and smiled.

"Hi, Margaret," I said. "We're here to see Mercedes."

"Aloha, Dr. Barda, nice to see you! Aloha, Mr. Flanagan. Just a minute, please."

The text alert pinged on Pat's phone.

"It's from Emma," he said. "Last Bon Dance of the season is tonight. I wanted to do a piece on it. I'm glad she reminded me."

"Why didn't she text me too?" I asked.

"She probably did. I think your phone's still in the car. In the back seat."

"Oh, right," I said.

"Where you threw it." He glanced at his watch, an ancient Timex that used to be gold tone. "I shoulda taken my car separately."

"I'll go to the Bon Dance with you," I said. "I can drive. It's on the way back to town, right? I've never been to a Bon Dance."

Chapter Eight

"You sure you want to go with me to the Bon Dance?" Pat said. "I mean, that would be great, but when are you going to do your Student Retention Office paperwork?"

"I'll get it done over the weekend. If it's late I'll just have to fill out a Personal Responsibility Reflection Form."

After a few minutes Mercedes emerged to greet us. Although we had eaten breakfast together that morning, she embraced me like a long-lost sister. Pat got a hug and a kiss too.

"Well," she said. "I was expecting you two a lot sooner."

"Molly's a careful driver," Pat said.

"I forgot how far out of town it was. The trees have grown in a lot. It looks nice. The bougainvillea is gorgeous!"

"It matches your highlights," Pat said to her.

Mercedes dimpled and touched her hair, a sleek burgundy bob streaked with fuchsia. "Oh, the trees need to be cut back. I've been trying to get the boy down here to do that, but he's so busy now. Anyway."

"Can we take a look at where Jimmy Tanaka was supposed to be staying?" Pat asked.

"Couldn't hurt, I suppose. Why not?" She led us out onto the lanai and down the wooden stairs to the pathway.

"Let's go out to the cabin now, before it gets too dark. Terrible, that thing this morning, ah? Good thing Jimmy never saw it. Oh, Molly, I heard your Stephen might be in some trouble over this. Was his responsibility to manage the theater props."

"I heard that too," I said.

As she walked ahead of us, Mercedes paused occasionally to pluck a shriveled bract from the bougainvillea. "Nice, that boy Stephen, but so absent-minded. Molly, I think you can do better. You know, Donnie Gonsalves is single. Remember Donnie? You sat next to him this morning?"

"He seems very nice," I said. I fixed my eyes on the red gravel path in front of me. We followed Mercedes through the double doors and down the walkway to the guest cabins. Hibiscus hedges crowded us on either side, forcing us to walk single-file. I kept my elbows close so the branches wouldn't snag my blouse.

"Mercedes," Pat asked. "Did you actually see Jimmy Tanaka? Are you sure he was ever on-island to begin with?"

"Oh, yes, he was here. I talked to him when he checked in yesterday afternoon. Then he went out to dinner with your dean. I never saw him after that."

She gestured at the wooden frame of a structure being built at the edge of her property. It was going to be a sweat lodge, she explained. "I know. Kind of out of place in Hawaii." She turned her palms upward. "My mainland guests keep asking for it, though, and they get so disappointed when I say no, no sweat lodge anywhere on the island. I already have the crystal bed and the meditation chapel. But"—she shrugged—"the customer is always right, yah Molly?"

"The customer? I guess."

"You repainted the cabins," Pat said. "They look good."

Mercedes frowned as she touched a small, splintered divot in the door casing of Jimmy Tanaka's cabin. She unlocked the door and pushed it open.

"This is just how he left it. Bed still made and everything."

Pat opened and closed each drawer of the simple pine dresser, from top to bottom. Then he disappeared into the bathroom and I heard the medicine cabinet squeak open and then thunk shut. I glanced around the small, simply furnished room. What were we supposed to be looking for? A forwarding address?

When Mercedes had left us, Pat said, "Her hair looks cool with the magenta highlights. You should do something like that to your hair."

"I think that's new," I said. I slid the closet door open, looked around and confirmed that it was empty except for a few wire hangers and a heady fresh paint smell. "I mean, new since breakfast this morning."

The front door opened and my former student Nate Parsons peeked in. Pat emerged from the bathroom wiping his hands on his shirt, introduced himself, and disappeared again.

"Hey, Professor! What are you guys doing down here? I already brought Mr. Tanaka's bag up to the College of Commerce, if that's what you're looking for."

I told Nate that I was trying to find Jimmy Tanaka so that I could write a story about him for our college. Also, I had Tanaka's suitcase in my office and was eager to return it to him.

"Is Pat Flanagan writing a story about it?" Nate asked.

Porcelain clanked in the bathroom. It sounded like Pat was looking inside the toilet tank.

"I don't know," I said. "How do you know Pat? I mean, Mr. Flanagan? Did you take comp from him?"

"I wish. His sections are so popular. They always fill up so fast. I was never able to get in."

"Oh. That must be a terrible problem for him. Being so popular with the students." I sat down on the bed, having exhausted all of the places I could think of looking. Nate pulled over the single chair and sat down on it backwards.

"I read *Island Confidential* every day," he said, glancing back toward the bathroom door. "What did you think of the series on the Kuewa Road?"

"We were just talking about that on the way down," I said.

"Pat told me Jimmy Tanaka was one of the original developers."

Nate shook his head. "It's such a travesty," he said. "I can't believe our college accepted his money. Didn't the faculty protest?"

"We didn't know about it until it was a done deal," I said. "And it's not like we have people lining up to hand us money. Hey, did you see Mr. Tanaka when he was here?"

"Yeah, for a second. I was working that night. I remember someone came to meet him for dinner. Tall haole dude. His hair was real shiny. Kinda like doll hair."

"Probably our dean, Bill Vogel."

"Oh, name's familiar. Never met him though."

"Do you remember them coming back from dinner?" I asked.

"No, but they wouldn't have to come through the main building. If Mr. Tanaka got dropped off he coulda just walked right across to his cabin. I never seen Mr. Tanaka after he checked in. But . . ." Nate trailed off and looked at the floor.

"But?"

"Oh. I dunno. I forgot what I was gonna say."

"By the way, why didn't you send Mr. Tanaka's suitcase back to his address in Honolulu?" I asked.

"Mercedes had me look up how much it would cost to send it over. It's really expensive to ship a big bag like that interisland. That bag's a lot heavier than it looks."

I heard the water shut off in the bathroom, and Pat popped out of the doorway. He shook his head no. Our investigation here was apparently over.

"No gun taped to the inside of the toilet tank?" I asked.

"Nope," Pat said. "Nothing. You guys keep this place nice and clean."

"Thanks," Nate said. "Well, I hope you find Mr. Tanaka. Good to see you again, Professor Barda. Really a pleasure to meet you, Mr. Flanagan. I read *Island Confidential* every day.

I'm a big fan."

"Oh. Well, it's nice to have a loyal reader." Pat directed that last comment at me, not at Nate.

"You guys should hurry. You probably wanna get on the road before it gets dark," Nate said.

"You can't get rid of us that easily," I said. "We're staying for dinner."

Nate lingered in the doorway for a few seconds, looking from me to Pat and back again. Then he turned away and mumbled, "Okay. I better get back to work."

Chapter Nine

After half an hour of bumping down an unlit road, I was convinced that we had taken a wrong turn, and were going to end up either driving into the ocean or, worse, blundering onto someone's well-defended pakololo plantation.

"We should be getting close," Pat said. "Are you okay?"

"I forgot how dark it gets down here, with no streetlights," I said.

Just then, we saw light blazing through the tall trees. The Kuewa Hongwanji Mission was right where the GPS said it would be. Flying termites swarmed in the light from the tall temple windows and clouded around the strings of lanterns in the parking lot. Energetic children, harassed parents, young hippies with tawny dreadlocks, slightly older hippies with gray ponytails, and an assortment of high school and college kids lined up at the concession stands for Styrofoam chili bowls, greasy bags of fried wontons, rainbow shave ice, and paper-wrapped Spam musubis.

The Bon Dance was not an event restricted to the Buddhist faithful. These were now emerging from the temple, having honored their departed in the Obon ceremony. Pat and I sidled up the stairs of the temple against the downward flow of the crowd. Through the wide doorway I could see that it was set up very much like my idea of church—except where it wasn't. A single aisle separated the area into two rows of pews on either side. Racks on the back of the pews held booklets and hymn books. To the right was a church organ, and to the left a pulpit. That's where the similarity ended. In the center sat a golden altar decked with red anthuriums, scrolled brass candelabras and various ceramic and metal vessels. At the top of the altar stood a slender golden Buddha about two feet high, surrounded by a radiant cloud. It reminded me a little of the Virgin of Guadalupe.

"Wow," I said.

"And you thought us Catholics had all the bling," Pat said.

"*We* Catholics, not *us* Catholics. *We* have the bling." I hesitated at the doorway.

"What's the matter, Molly?" he asked.

"I don't feel right just barging into someone's place of worship like a tourist."

"You getting bad juju?"

"I'm sure Emma would feel just as uncomfortable walking into St. Damien," I said.

"*I'm* uncomfortable walking into St. Damien."

"Yeah, well, big surprise there."

Pat nudged me. "Come on, there's Emma."

He started forward over the threshold.

"The incense is bothering my nose. You go in. I'll wait here."

Emma emerged from the temple first. She paused at the threshold, turned around and bowed toward the interior, then turned back out to face me. For someone who had just attended a solemn ceremony, she seemed to be having trouble keeping a straight face.

"Hey Molly, Pat told me you took one look inside and started crossing yourself and backing down the stairs."

Pat sauntered out behind her. I glared at him as he loped past us down the stairs and off into the darkness to take pictures of the last Bon Dance of the summer.

"Don't believe everything Pat says," I said.

"So how was the Hanohano Hotel?" she asked.

Emma and I strolled down the stairs, with the flow of the crowd this time.

"Horrible," I said. "Jimmy Tanaka just threw up that hideous building, and now he's letting it fall apart. It's this awful combination of extravagant waste and ridiculous penny-pinching."

"Oh. Sounds like our university," Emma said.

"At least our university doesn't smell like wet laundry that was forgotten in the washing machine for three days. Pat and I had dinner down at the Cloudforest, though, so that was nice."

We stepped onto damp grass.

"It's so dark out here," I said. "I hope I don't step on a sprinkler head."

"A what?"

"Sprinkler head?"

"That's funny, Molly. How long have you lived here? You know we get like a billion inches of rain a year, right? Hey, by the way, when are you going to get rid of that suitcase in your office? It gets in the way of your coffeemaker."

"As soon as I can find Jimmy Tanaka and give it back to him. I was hoping he'd be there at the Hanohano, but the place seemed to be abandoned, except for one poor lady who was stuck at the front desk. Why do *you* care if the suitcase gets in the way of my coffeemaker?"

"Oh, that reminds me. Jimmy Tanaka. I have something you might be interested in. Just a second." She tipped her chin up and scanned the crowd. I followed her gaze for a few seconds, but it was too dark to see much. The lanterns were more decorative than illuminating.

"Hey!" She socked my arm. "You think that was actually Jimmy Tanaka's skull on the table this morning? Maybe that's why you can't get a-hold of him."

"No," I said. "This isn't one of your low-budget horror movies, Emma. That skull came from Stephen's prop room. Stephen called and confirmed it. Besides, Jimmy Tanaka was just out at dinner with my dean the previous night."

"Wait. Stephen called you? Did he ever apologize?"

"No," I said. "He just wanted me to get him out of trouble, again, as if I could do that. And it sounds like he *is* in trouble."

"You have to stop pining after him, Molly."

"I'm not pining after anyone!"

"Good. That leaves the field clear for Donnie Gonsalves. Know what you should do? You should run into him, accidentally on purpose. Donnie's Drive-Inn is like a five-minute walk from your house, right?"

"It's not *that* close," I said. "But I guess it's walkable."

"And tomorrow is the Farmers' Market. So you have a perfect excuse. Stop for something to eat on your way to shopping. Okay, there's Mrs. Saito. Hang on for a sec. I'll be right back."

Emma disappeared into the crowd. I watched the taiko drummers setting up, and considered the logistics of Emma's plan. If I walked down to the Farmers' Market, it wouldn't be that much out of my way to pass by Donnie's Drive-Inn. And I definitely wanted to stop on the way down, before the lunch rush. Not on the way back up, when I'd be sweaty and laden down with perishables. As my eyes adjusted, I spotted Emma in conversation with a woman I had seen exiting the temple earlier, a slender octogenarian in full kimono.

When she returned, Emma shouted over the booming taiko drums, "That was Mrs. Saito."

"Can we go somewhere quieter?" I shouted back.

Emma led me away from the music and the lights, toward the solitary banyan tree in the center of the lawn. Headlights flashed by on the main road.

"Okay," Emma said, "this all happened a long time ago, way

before you moved here. I was away at school. Mrs. Saito was my parents' neighbor. She worked in the town post office, so she got all the news. Anyway, this was from back when Jimmy Tanaka was still living in Mahina, before he moved his show to Honolulu. Back then he was married."

"Jimmy Tanaka was married? Huh. I guess that's one person who didn't hate him."

"Yeah, well, listen to what happened. One day he doesn't come home. Then the next day? He still doesn't come home. So Jimmy's wife goes to the police station 'cause she wants them to find her missing husband. They assigned this young cop to look for Tanaka."

"And?" I asked.

"Oh, the cop found him. Alive and well, and in a *very* compromising situation."

"What kind of compromising situation?"

"Mrs. Saito wouldn't tell me. She said it wasn't proper conversation for a young lady. I guess she meant me. Anyway, Tanaka's wife divorced him pretty soon after that. And things didn't turn out well for that poor cop."

"What happened?"

"His performance evaluations all got changed, somehow. Even the ones from years earlier. They all went from good to unsatisfactory. Someone got into the records and just rewrote his history. So he had to leave the force. Moral of the story, don't mess with a powerful man like Jimmy Tanaka and expect to keep your job."

"I better write really nice things about him then. Yikes."

"Oh! Becho!" Emma said.

"What?"

"The song! This is the one everyone knows! Come on, you want to come dance?"

"I don't know how to dance to this," I said. "I'll watch."

Emma trotted across the lawn toward the lights and the sound of a flute wheedling over heavy drumbeats. I went to find Pat and tell him I was ready to go home. I wanted to make sure to get my beauty sleep.

Chapter Ten

When I first bought my little plantation-style house, I envisioned myself making the short walk to the Farmers' Market every weekend to buy papayas, purple sweet potatoes, fiddlehead ferns, and other exotic fare that I would learn to prepare. I quickly realized that open-air shopping looks great in photographs, but in real life it's hot and exhausting. Furthermore, I found that I could buy the same mottled papayas and slug-perforated lettuce any day of the week at Natural High Health Foods, which is air-conditioned. And I never did develop a taste for fiddlehead ferns.

But today I was going shopping.

It was only ten in the morning, but I could already feel the heat on my skin. My vintage cotton dress felt tighter around the waist than when I'd bought it, probably because of something the dry cleaner did. I wasn't exactly cool or comfortable—only a climate-controlled astronaut suit could have accomplished that—but I was dressed for the weather and I felt presentable. I trusted that the red-and-white gingham pattern would obscure the sweat stains spreading under my arms.

I'd passed by Donnie's Drive-Inn countless times, but until Emma gave me the idea, it had never occurred to me to eat there. I spotted Donnie wiping down one of the outdoor picnic-style tables. He looked up and grinned. The red Donnie's Drive-Inn polo shirt set off his golden skin and his close-cropped black hair. The bands of the sleeves strained over gleaming, muscular arms.

"Well," he said as I approached, "this is a nice surprise!"

"Nice!" I agreed. "I mean, yes, this *is* a pleasant surprise! I just happened to be on my way to the Farmers' Market!" I brandished my recycled rice bag shopping tote to emphasize my credibility on this point.

"I was going to get something light before the lunch rush," Donnie said. "Would you join me, Molly?"

I accepted his embrace and cheek kiss and then slid onto the bench as gracefully as I could. "Something light" turned out to be a platter of oily Portuguese sausage slices, hard fried chicken katsu strips, and candy-sweet curls of teriyaki beef. I would have preferred a cold salad, but I suppose Donnie wanted to save me the trouble of deciding.

"This is quite a coincidence," he said. "I had a visit from your security folks this morning." He snapped a pair of chopsticks apart and used the large end to transport a sausage slice to his plate.

"Was it about that thing that happened at the breakfast?" I asked.

"Yes. And they were asking me about you."

"About me? What did they want to know?"

"They wanted to know how well I knew you, and if I'd ever heard you talk about Jimmy Tanaka."

I felt uncomfortably warm. I rested the palms of my hands on the tabletop to dissipate the heat. The wood was cool to the touch, freshly painted in the same vibrant red as the staff shirts.

"So what did you tell them?" I asked.

"I said I'd never heard you say anything about Jimmy Tanaka, good or bad. And then they asked, well, they seem to think you're connected with a person of interest. Someone in the theater department."

"I see."

Stephen had given them my name. He was dragging me down into his mess again. I wanted to murder him. *Then* there would be something to investigate.

"Are you?" Donnie asked.

"What? Oh, you mean am I connected to someone in the theater department? No. That's ridiculous. I'm *not* connected to anyone in the theater, and I certainly don't have any motive to sabotage an event that my own college put on."

Donnie touched the back of my hand, a brief gesture of reassurance. "They're just doing their job. Jimmy Tanaka is an important donor, and your university has to do damage control. Are you a vegetarian?"

I glanced down at the platter.

"Oh! No. No, this is very nice." I picked up a hard chunk of chicken katsu and stuffed it into my mouth.

"So what else have you been up to since I saw you last?" Donnie smiled. "Besides drawing the attention of the authorities?"

The question caught me with my mouth full of breaded chicken. "Mm." I chewed hard and swallowed. "You mean since yesterday morning? Here's something. I finally had my first look inside the Hanohano. Have you been?"

"Not since it was remodeled." He shook his head. *"Hanohano,"* he said. "Noble. Praiseworthy. *Dignified.*"

"Sorry, what?"

"I was just thinking. That's what the name of the hotel means." He smiled. "It took me years to get the permits to remodel my kitchen. And Jimmy Tanaka rebuilt an entire hotel in a few weeks. Did you know he ordered the original Hanohano bulldozed just three days before it was going to be listed in the Registry of Historic Places?"

"I remember that," I said. "It didn't win him a lot of friends in the community."

"He didn't have many to begin with. What were you doing down there?"

A puff of cool breeze brushed my cheek. From where I sat I could glimpse the ocean through the tangle of power lines that criss-crossed the narrow street.

"We were looking for ghosts," I felt silly saying it, but I couldn't tell anyone about the real reason for Pat's investigation before Pat published his story.

"Who is *'we'*?" Donnie asked.

"Sorry?"

"You said *'we'* were looking for ghosts."

The part of that sentence that made an impression on him was the "we" part and not the "ghosts" part?

"Do you read *Island Confidential,* the newsblog?" I asked.

"I've heard of it."

"A friend of mine runs it. Pat Flanagan. He used to be a reporter at the *County Courier,* before they had the layoffs. He's working on a piece about the Hanohano Hotel. He went down there to investigate, you know, the ghost stories, and I tagged along."

"How do you know him?" Donnie asked.

"He teaches composition at the university. Part time."

Donnie's expression was neutral, but something in the tone of his voice made me decide not to bring up Pat again. Maybe Donnie had had a bad experience with the news media, or maybe he didn't approve of *Island Confidential*'s anarchist leanings. Or maybe Donnie didn't like the idea of me gadding about with a male person? No, that was impossible. We barely knew each other.

"Do *you* believe in ghosts?" he asked.

"Well, not in the popular sense."

Not in the popular sense? Did I really just say that? *Oh, I used to be into ghosts, before they sold out and went all mainstream.*

"Sorry, that didn't sound right. What I meant is I don't believe in the stereotypical ghost that looks just like the person before they died. There's no reason your immortal soul should look like your former body. Any more than I'd be able to recognize you by looking at your brain."

I glanced down at the glistening heaps of meat.

"Forget I said that. About your brain. I didn't mean to bring up brains over brunch."

What was wrong with me? Whatever interest Donnie may have harbored, I was certain I'd killed it. I'm an evolutionary dead end, I thought. Sorry, Mom and Dad, no grandchildren for you.

"I've heard some of the stories," Donnie said.

"Stories?"

"About the haunted Hanohano. Some of the old-timers talk about things that happened to friends of friends."

"Oh, right. The Hanohano. Like what kinds of things?"

"Liquid dropping on people. The sound of dogs barking. Seaweed smells in the hallways. So, is Pat your boyfriend?"

"Pat? No, of course not. Pat's . . . I don't have a boyfriend.

"Did you find any ghosts? When you went there with *Pat*?"

"Well, there were smells in the hallways, no doubt about that. And I did hear about an accident that happened when they rebuilt the hotel. A worker was killed."

"Salvador Pung," Donnie said.

"Yes! Oh, do you think that could have had anything to do with that incident with the skull? Someone reminding Jimmy Tanaka that he had blood on his hands, something like that?"

"Could be."

"Speaking of Jimmy Tanaka, have you talked to him at all since yesterday?"

"No," he said. "We're not exactly close friends though."

"You know, my friend Emma told me a story about him. She

says he didn't come home one night, and his wife got the police to look for him. She didn't know the details, though. Is there anything to that, do you think?"

Donnie smiled, and instead of answering my question, asked me what I was planning to buy at the Farmers' Market.

I detoured through the Farmers' Market on the way back, still hungry after my stop at Donnie's Drive-Inn. The air was hotter under the shade tarps than out on the street. I bought a few avocados, a couple of dented papayas, and a bag of bedraggled greens from a young couple with ratty blond dreadlocks and a cardboard sign advertising 100% organic produce. The walk home was so steep I had to lean forward as I trudged uphill. It had grown much hotter in the past couple of hours. By the time I got home, the handles of my shopping bags had cut red marks into both wrists.

I turned on my ceiling fans full blast, called in an order for a pizza, and poured myself a glass of wine. My "accidental" meeting with Donnie had gone pretty well, but it had taken the whole morning. Now I only had the afternoon to deal with my considerable to-do list. I had to work on my conference paper, finish up my Student Retention Office forms, start preparing next week's classes, and get some laundry done. I felt tired just thinking about it.

Then I heard the knock on my door.

I pulled the door open. Officer Medeiros hulked in my doorway, wearing his work uniform: white short-sleeved shirt with stitched-in seams, black slacks, and shiny black shoes.

"Professor Barda." He eased his hand down from knocking position. "Sorry to bother you on a weekend. I need to ask you a couple of questions. This will just take a minute."

Chapter Eleven

I hurried through the drizzle to my classroom, fuming. I had barely managed to get caught up on my grading this weekend. But I hadn't made any progress on my conference paper, my Student Retention Office forms were overdue, and I hadn't had a chance to do laundry, which meant that I was wearing swimsuit bottoms instead of underwear. I had spent my entire Saturday afternoon getting grilled by Officer Medeiros.

It wasn't his fault, of course. He had been nice enough to explain what had earned me the house call. Stephen Park had told him that *I* was the expert on how the prop room was set up. The basis of Stephen's infuriating half-truth was that once upon a time I had *tried* to help him to organize his inventory, but he never put my system into place. If Stephen had listened to me in the first place, none of this would have happened.

I paused at the door of my classroom, retrieved a disinfectant wipe from my bag, and busied myself scrubbing greenish-black mold from the various surfaces. After the latest budget cuts, we no longer have regular janitorial service in our building. As usual, my efforts seemed to make little difference. The room was a monument to years of deferred maintenance. The acoustic ceiling tiles were mildewed and crumbling, and some had fallen away entirely, exposing the moldy ductwork overhead. The cinderblock walls were a discouraging shade of gray that looked like something left over from painting a submarine. A sign printed on pink paper, taped to the wall over the wastebasket, read: No tobacco. No gum. NO BETEL NUTS! Directly below the sign, the wall and floor were encrusted with blood-red betel nut spit stains.

I hoped that today's guest lecture would be better than the time Emma's husband Yoshi came to talk to my students. I suppose it was nice of him to volunteer, but instead of imparting helpful advice about navigating corporate culture, he had spent most of the time talking up his Ivy League credentials and keen business acumen. One of my students had come to see me in my office the next day. He told me that Yoshi's visit had taught him a lot about what kind of person he might become if he remained a commerce major. He then presented me with some forms to sign. He was dropping my class and changing his major to social work.

Donnie Gonsalves, owner and founder of Donnie's Drive-Inn, poked his head into the classroom.

"Oh, great, you're a little early!" I gushed. "Fantastic! Parking was okay? Thanks so much for coming." I hurried over to him and clasped his hand in a businesslike handshake.

"Happy to do it," he smiled, drawing me closer for a hug and a cheek kiss. "Did your security person ever find you?"

"In fact, he did. He came to my house right after I had lunch with you. I guess this thing is pretty serious."

Donnie released me and began to leaf through a deck of index cards. He'd prepared lecture notes.

"Of course it's serious," he said, examining and rearranging the cards. "You want to stay on good terms with your donors."

"Not only that. Officer Medeiros told me that the skull was real. The chair of our theater department apparently had a genuine human skull. And he claims he didn't know. He thought it was plastic, or so he said."

Donnie looked up sharply.

"So why are *you* involved with this?" he asked.

"Oh. I put together a spreadsheet for . . . for the department. To keep track of their inventory. I don't think they ever used it though."

"That must have been a lot of work for you."

"Oh. Well, we're all expected to contribute service hours to the university." I didn't see any need to go into my personal history with Stephen.

"So who's the audience today?" he asked. "You told me these are your advanced students."

"That's right. BP has mostly juniors and seniors enrolled."

"BP?"

"Business Planning. BP."

"Business Planning. That's right."

He checked the index cards again.

"These students are all Commerce majors," I said, "and they're pretty motivated. Between you and me, I really prefer this class to IBM. It's night and day."

"IBM?"

"Intro to Business Management, sorry. Oh, gosh, what can I say about my Intro students? Same classroom, totally different experience. I mean, bless their hearts, on the very first assignment of the semester, a quarter of the class turned in plagiarized papers."

"I think my son told me he's taking one of your other classes."

"Oh! Your son! Really?"

Donnie had a college-age son? Gonsalves is a common name. Now that Donnie mentioned it, though. . . .

"Davison Gonsalves." Donnie smiled a little. "I hope he's not giving you a hard time."

"Well, I don't know all of the students' names yet," I said truthfully. I knew Davison Gonsalves's name, though. I'd seen it on one of the plagiarized papers.

"So how's he doing?" Donnie asked.

I picked up the eraser and began wiping stray marks from the whiteboard. "Well, even if I knew, I wouldn't be allowed to tell you," I said to the whiteboard.

"Why is that?"

"The Family Educational Rights and Privacy Act. FERPA. We're not allowed to give out any information about college students. Even to parents. Especially to parents."

Donnie laughed. "Legal stuff. I understand. You can't blame me for asking, though. I'm trying to encourage Davison to get a little more serious about school. I think he'd do well if he'd just apply himself a little more."

I finished cleaning off the whiteboard and turned around to see Donnie surveying the classroom, looking confused.

"You can stand up here," I said. "This setup can be a little disorienting. Our Student Retention Office remodeled the room over the summer, and we're still getting used to it."

The Student Retention Office had indeed come in to refurbish the room, but they didn't repaint it or replace the rotted ceiling tiles or fix the broken blinds. What they did was transform the classroom into a "learning center" by removing all of the desks and installing round tables in their place. The idea was that there should be no single focal point in the room from which a professor could lecture. We were no longer to play the role of "Sage on the Stage," but instead we were to be "Guides on the Side," moving around the room to facilitate student discussion.

A few weeks after the Student Retention Office remodel was finished, the Associate Vice Chancellor for Student Engagement attended an ed-tech conference. Upon his return, we were directed to record our class sessions and post them online, so that students could watch them at their leisure. The problem was that we were "guides on the side" now, and the Associate Vice Chancellor for Student Engagement didn't want to post hour-long videos of students sitting in circles talking. So we all had to go back to being "sages on the stage," lecturing to the video camera, but this time we were cautioned to act as "facilitators of experience" rather than "providers of knowledge." We're still stuck with the immovable round tables.

The wall clock was off by several hours and a random number of minutes. I took out my phone and watched the time display as students accumulated in the classroom. When the readout hit the right time, I stepped up to introduce Donnie. Students lifted their headsets off, snapped their game consoles shut, switched off their phones, and turned their attention to me.

CHAPTER TWELVE

I stepped up to introduce Donnie to the class.

"Remember the first day of class," I asked, "when I told you that whatever business you choose, whatever you do, don't open a restaurant? Today we're very fortunate to have as our guest speaker Mr. Donald Gonsalves, owner and founder of Donnie's Drive-Inns, who obviously didn't listen to my good advice."

A ruffle of polite laughter mingled with applause. Donnie segued smoothly from my introduction. "Your professor is right," Donnie said. "Restaurants have a high fatality rate. People start restaurants because they love cooking for their friends, but they sometimes ignore important business basics."

Margaret Adams, my straight-A accounting major, raised her hand: "Like cash flow?" she asked.

"That's exactly right." He smiled. She beamed back at him. Donnie went on to discuss vendor contracts, health inspections and worker's compensation insurance. He seemed at ease in front of the classroom, effortlessly holding the students' attention. And mine. He shared his own story. He had started right out of school working for Jimmy Tanaka. He had worked his way up to a management position at Merrie Musubis before opening his own restaurant chain.

"That's really the key," he said. "You don't just jump in to owning your own business. You work for someone else for a while, learn the ropes, and then go out on your own."

One student raised her hand. "Did Jimmy Tanaka get mad

when you started your own restaurant?"

"Business people in an island community can't afford to make enemies," Donnie said. "We don't think short term like that. We have to think of ourselves as partners and work toward our common interests."

"Mr. Gonsalves, Miss Barda—I mean Professor Barda—told us when Jimmy Tanaka rebuilt the Hanohano Hotel, they ran out of money and let it go all bus' up and now it's so junk the university don't put its guests—"

"Micah," I interrupted, "do you have a question for Mr. Gonsalves?"

"Oh, yeah, sorry." Micah sat up in his chair and pushed up the brim of his baseball cap to clear his line of vision. "Mr. Gonsalves. Professor Barda always telling us, act professional, keep your commitments, show up on time."

"That's excellent advice," Donnie said with a glance in my direction.

"I heard the College of Commerce guys jus' had one big party for Jimmy Tanaka and he never come! So this guy. Unprofessional, yah?"

I watched Donnie to see how he would respond. I was pretty unimpressed with Jimmy Tanaka's disappearing act myself, but I couldn't say that in front of my students. Donnie spun out an effortless answer, something about giving people the benefit of the doubt and seeing the good in every situation.

At the end of class, students clustered around Donnie. I gathered my things undisturbed, and then I heard Micah shout, "Eh, Professor. Professor!" He was pointing at the trash can in the corner. I went over and peered in. I'm afraid I let out a rather unprofessorial shriek.

"Want me to call security?" Micah asked.

"Yes. Yes, please do that."

Officer Medeiros arrived within a minute. He strode to the

trash can, plunged his hand in, and pulled out the skull.

"No gloves?" I asked.

"Looks like the glow-in-the-dark kine," someone said.

Officer Medeiros brandished the skull at me.

"This your classroom, Dr. Barda?"

"I teach my classes in here, yes. But so does Dr. Rodge, Roger Cowper. And I think Larry Schneider teaches in here too." I remembered hearing Larry complaining about Rodge not erasing the whiteboard.

Officer Medeiros turned the skull over and examined it.

"This one get the sticker. See?"

He turned the skull to show me the holographic inventory sticker indicating university property.

"You know anything about how it got here?" he asked.

"No."

"*I* found it," Micah said. "Professor Barda, she never come back here."

"I'm gonna have to take this back up with me," Officer Medeiros said.

"By all means. Please. One thing. Can you play back the lecture tapes for the last few days? Maybe the camera caught what happened."

"Hm," said Officer Medeiros. "Not a bad idea. I'll look into that. Lotta footage to go through, though."

Donnie had waited for me. He accompanied me out of the classroom, avoiding any mention of the skull in the wastebasket, his plagiarizing son, or any other unpleasant topic. Instead, he said nice things about my students, and I said nice things about his talk. When the path split off and it was time for him to head toward the parking lot, he thanked me as if I had done him a favor, rather than the other way around.

As Donnie disappeared around the corner, I realized that we had made no plans to meet again. I was the one who had invited him to give the talk in my classroom. If he had wanted things to keep going, *he* should have taken the initiative this time. He certainly had the opportunity. Maybe he didn't want to get involved with his son's teacher. Who could blame him for that, really?

I thought the class had gone well, but for some reason I wasn't feeling that good. I needed to focus and get my mind off this skull business, which, after all, was Stephen's problem, not mine. I had to deal with the plagiarists from Intro to Business Management. If one of them happened to be Donnie's son, well that was just too bad. My awful dean, Bill Vogel, wasn't going to back me up, but Dan Watanabe, my department chair, just might. It was worth a try.

Chapter Thirteen

Dan Watanabe has served as department chair for the past decade or so, and has been part of the College of Commerce for years longer than that. Not quite as long as the mutual loathing society of our two most senior professors, Larry Schneider and Hanson Harrison, but long enough to know where the bodies are buried, so to speak. Dan has been voted back in as department chair for years because he's even-tempered and fair, and also because no one else wants the job. I sat across from him in his tidy office, printouts of the plagiarized assignments stacked on the desk between us.

"I couldn't believe it," I said. "This is the first semester that I've used the plagiarism checker. Now I'm wondering how much cheating has been going on this whole time."

"Sometimes ignorance really is bliss." Dan looked particularly wornout today. Maybe it was the way he was dressed, his hair, skin, glasses, and reverse-print aloha shirt of all grays and beiges.

"Vogel won't let me refer these students to the Office of Student Conduct," I said.

Dan pulled his glasses off and rubbed his eyes.

"Bill's the dean. Those referrals need his signature. If he says no, I can't go against that."

"You know what's almost worse than the cheating? They uploaded plagiarized papers *to a plagiarism detection site.* I mean, *they* can't be that stupid, so they must think *we* are!"

"I get that, Molly."

"And what's the point of us paying for this website to help us catch cheaters, if we won't do anything about it anyway?"

"Listen, even if you could get a referral to the Office of Student Conduct, I'm not sure you'd get the result you want."

"I know," I sighed.

During our most recent reorganization, the Office of Student Conduct was moved into the Student Retention Office in order to cover salaries with the SRO's grant. The most severe penalty that comes out of that office these days is that the offender has to write a one-page reflection paper. Still, it's something.

"I can't do anything, Molly. Bill wants to give them a second chance, doesn't matter what I think. He outranks me. You should know that he wasn't happy that I passed along your complaint to him. He told me that my job was to contain problems like that."

Dan placed his hand on the jar of antacid tablets on his desk.

"Where'd you get that huge jar?" I asked. "Galimba's Bargain Boyz?"

"Special order. Pharmacy." Dan unscrewed the lid, shook out a handful of tablets and stuffed them into his mouth.

"So when Vogel tells you to contain problems, what he means is me, the complaining professor. Not the cheating students."

Dan finished chewing and made an effort to swallow. "Thing is, our budget comes from tuition. If we kick a student out for cheating, that costs us real money."

"Oh, well. If that's all we're worried about, why not just pay us based on how many students get passing grades in our classes?"

"Oh, you mean pay-per-pass. Yeah, it's come up."

"*What?* That's an actual thing?"

"Don't worry. Our accreditation people nipped that one in the bud."

I half rose to leave, and then Dan said, "Hang on. There was something else I wanted to talk to you about."

I sat back down.

"Is it about me getting that interview with Jimmy Tanaka?" I asked. "I'm not getting anywhere with that. Maybe you guys should get someone else to write it."

"No, it's not about that. Listen, this is not for sure. But in the near future, it's possible that Bill Vogel may be unable to fulfill his duties as dean. If that happens, I've been asked to step in."

"Oh! Congratulations! That'd be such an improvement!"

"So if I do that, someone from the Department of Management needs to fill in for me. That would be you."

"Me? But I don't have tenure!"

"You'd be the *interim* department chair." Dan said.

"The *interim* department chair still has to make unpopular decisions. I'd have to choose whose conference travel gets funded and whose doesn't. I'd have to deal with all the grievances that get filed—"

"You seem to have a pretty good understanding of what the job entails." Dan seemed cheerful for the first time. "That's a great start. Look, it's been decided that you're the best choice for the department. You haven't made a lot of enemies."

"I haven't made 'a lot' of enemies?"

Dan shrugged. I gazed longingly at the pastel-colored antacid tablets scattered on the dusty bottom of the jar.

"What about Rodge Cowper?" I said. "He has tenure! And sorry to say this, but maybe it would be a good thing if he had a little less free time on his hands."

"We don't really have a choice . . ." Dan took off his glasses, set them on the desk in front of him, covered his eyes with his hands, and took a deep breath.

"You're the only person in our department who hasn't been the target of some kind of grievance or complaint."

"Oh."

Dan was right. Hanson Harrison and Larry Schneider have been filing grievances against each other since Frederick Winslow Taylor was in short pants. Both of them regularly go after Dan as well, for either taking the wrong side or for not taking sides at all. As for Rodge Cowper, he's in a category by himself. I heard that Human Resources has an entire file drawer dedicated to him, but that might have just been a rumor. "What exactly is going on with Bill Vogel, anyway?" I asked.

"Maybe nothing." Dan produced a chamois square from his desk drawer and polished his glasses. "But be ready to step up. Listen, one thing you can do? Call the plagiarists in for individual meetings. That usually scares them straight. But make sure you keep your door open when you have a student in there."

"Right. The Rodge Cowper rule."

"Forty-five-degree angle or greater," he reminded me.

"Got it."

Chapter Fourteen

I was meeting with the plagiarists one by one. Addressing them together in my office would presumably violate student confidentiality. Fortunately, I only had three of them to deal with. The rest had all dropped the class after I requested the individual meetings. This was promising to be a long, unpleasant afternoon. I made sure I had a full tissue box sitting on my desk.

At least I had something to look forward to afterward. The university's theater department starts each season with Stephen Park's original work, *The Drowning,* and tonight was the dress rehearsal. This would be the first time that Pat, Emma and I would be attending since Stephen and I had broken up. It was a rare opportunity to dress up, something that people don't do much here in Mahina. I hadn't worn my vintage crushed-velvet slacks in at least a year, and I hoped that the dry cleaner hadn't shrunk them too much. If I had to leave the top button open, that gold hapi coat with the embroidered dragons would cover it. Now the hard part was my hair . . . A knock on the door frame interrupted my fashion reverie.

Davison Gonsalves, Donnie's son, loomed in my doorway. I remembered him now from the first session of Intro to Business Management. He had strolled in ten minutes late, seated himself at the front of the room, and folded his hands behind his head at an angle that maximized the bulge of his biceps. For the remainder of the class, I had to look at his wiry black armpit hair. I blinked to clear the image from my mind. He was even taller than his father, and his bulky shoulders strained the seams of his hoodie. He had Donnie's strong features, with a sprinkling of acne on his cheeks.

"Davison," I said. "Terrific. You're right on time. Come in. Either chair is fine."

Davison dropped his backpack on the floor, and then plopped down in the more comfortable of my two chairs: the upholstered one left over from the last remodel of one of the Student Retention Office's auxiliary lounges, not the plastic one with the crack across the seat.

Two secondhand chairs might not sound like the height of luxury, but my visitors are relatively lucky. We have no budget for office furniture, so I've had to be resourceful about scrounging leftovers. Pat, who never misses a chance to make a statement, has furnished his office in the English Department with a pair of attached hot pink vinyl hairdryer chairs that he bought for $25.00 out of his own pocket when Tatsuya's Moderne Beauty went out of business. The pitted chrome hairdryer bonnets are still attached. Emma refuses on principle to spend her own money to buy work furniture. If you visit her in her office, you have to stand and stare at that brain in a jar she has sitting on her file cabinet.

As Davison made himself comfortable, I mentally composed an addendum for next semester's syllabus: *Attention male students: That toxic plume of drugstore body spray you've just wafted into my office will not compel me to accept your late paper or give you extra credit. What are you trying to do, gas me into submission? Why do you do this? Please stop.*

Of course I would never actually put that on my syllabus. Not before I had tenure, anyway. I pulled out a tissue and dabbed my watering eyes.

"Eh, Professor," Davison said, "I thought you might be hungry."

He reached into his backpack, produced a shallow, foil-lined cardboard box, and placed it on my desk, right on top of my stack of unopened mail. The box was filled with chunks of some kind of dried meat. I coughed to cover the sound of my stomach growling.

"Thank you," I said. "It was very thoughtful of you to bring this in. I'll put the dish in the conference room so everyone can enjoy it." We're not supposed to accept gifts from students, but refusing can be awkward. Our solution is to share everything, thus dispersing the bribery. Or the poison, if it comes to that.

"This is wild pig me and my friend Isaiah hunted," he said. "We been hunting together since we was small kids." Then with the condescending air of a tour guide, he launched into a lecture on feral pigs and the life cycle of avian malaria. He made sure to drive home the point that it was hunters (like him) who were the saviors of the native bird population.

I glanced at my watch. Our allotted time was almost over. I noticed a kid in a green baseball cap lurking outside my door. It was my next customer, Isaiah Pung, whose paper was identical to Davison's.

"That was very educational," I said. "Thank you for that. Now. Let's set up a schedule for you to turn in your revised assignment."

"Professor," he said, "I appreciate you letting me rewrite my paper. I enjoy your class a lot."

"Well, that's very nice—"

"Eh, you and Dr. Rodge, you're my two favorite professors."

Rodge Cowper, or "Dr. Rodge," as he tells his students to call him, teaches Human Potential (HP). Dr. Rodge assigns no homework, and requires no midterms or final exams. Instead, students get unfocused discussion sessions, funny videos, and the occasional inappropriate anecdote about Rodge's personal life. His classes fill to capacity every semester, and I've never heard of anyone getting less than an A. The Student Retention Office adores Dr. Rodge.

"Me and Dr. Rodge, huh?" I glanced at the flimsy wall separating my office from Rodge's. "Well, that's great."

"Barda, that a Podagee name?"

"It's not Portuguese," I said. "It's Albanian."

I took advantage of his confused silence to move us back on topic. "Here are the deadlines for your revised assignment. I need to get your literature review and outline first, then the draft, and then the final paper." I wrote out the schedule and handed it to him. He took the paper from me and stuffed it into his backpack.

"Eh, Professor, sorry about the misunderstanding, ah? I do good this time but."

Davison fist-bumped his friend Isaiah on his way out and whispered something to him. Isaiah approached my desk, set his backpack down quietly and sat down on the edge of the plastic chair.

Chapter Fifteen

"We never tried to hide nothing, Miss," Isaiah mumbled into his lap. A soap-green baseball cap shielded his plain, round face. "We thought it was okay to work together."

Of course he had heard the whole conversation through the open doorway. Thanks to the Rodge Cowper no-closed-doors rule, and so much for the Family Educational Rights and Privacy Act.

This is what I wanted to say to Isaiah Pung: You were lucky this time. Local working-class kids like you don't usually get a second chance. If anything like this ever happens again, your entitled pal Davison Gonsalves will be fine. You won't.

But this is what I said: "Isaiah, I'm going to ask you to revise this, and in the future don't let anyone else claim credit for your work. Make sure to proofread your paper for spelling and word usage. I found a few errors."

"Like what, Miss?"

"Let's see. *Integrity* only has two t's. The phrase is 'hammer and tongs,' not 'hammer and thongs.' And *Plutocracy* doesn't really have anything to do with planets. I'll write up the schedule for your revisions."

He glanced up at me quickly and then back down at his lap.

"Okay, Miss." He folded the paper neatly and tucked it into the pocket of his backpack. "Thank you, Miss."

"By the way, Isaiah, are you related to someone named Salvador Pung?"

"Yeah. Was my dad."

"I see. I'm sorry." He sat, waiting for me to dismiss him.

"Thanks for coming by, Isaiah. I see someone else is waiting to talk to me."

He nodded, picked up his backpack and left. Poor kid.

I wasn't going to make it through the next meeting without taking a break first. "I'll be right back," I called back to my final visitor as I hurried out the door and down the hall.

When I returned, she had made herself comfortable in my office, and was occupying my good chair. I sidled back behind my desk and lowered myself carefully onto my yoga ball. When I plop down too fast I bounce right back up and bang my knees under the desk.

Honey Akiona was a substantial young woman, with waves of black-and-gold streaked hair cascading over large gold hoop earrings. Multiple gold bracelets of varying widths and weights, adorned with black gothic script, stacked halfway up her sturdy forearms.

I briefly returned her smile, then set her paper down on the desk, facing her, next to a printout of the Wikipedia entry from which it was derived. The identical passages were highlighted. "Ms. Akiona," I said (I'm not always this formal with students, but her first name was Honey, and I simply couldn't bring myself to call her that), "your paper appears to be copied directly from Wikipedia. As it says on the course syllabus, plagiarism is a very serious—"

"I never copied that from Wikipedia," she interrupted.

I raised my eyebrows, speechless.

"I never!" she insisted. "I got 'em from Dr. Rodge."

"Dr. Rodge. How did that happen, exactly?"

"He handed it out in class. Said we could use it. No charge, he told us. He likes to joke around li' dat. Professor's a reliable source, yah? An look, I cited 'em, right down here in the footnote."

And so she had.

"Yes, Dr. Rodge does like to joke, doesn't he," I said. "I didn't see that. This assignment called for a bibliography, not footnotes." I declaimed for a bit on the rules of citation and quotation, wrapping up with a stern warning about checking the credibility of sources.

"You should know all this already," I said. "Who was your comp instructor? It wasn't Pat Flanagan, was it?"

Pat has a complicated relationship with the English language. His intolerance for sloppy communication is continually at war with his anarchist sympathies. I've seen him correct a student for violating a grammatical rule and immediately go on to denounce the same rule as hegemonic.

"Nah," she said, "I never took intro comp here. I get AP English credit from high school. Eh, Miss, you going on one trip or what?"

"Oh, the suitcase? No. I'm not going anywhere. Look, you need to do this assignment over, and you might as well do it right. Is there anything on the topic of integrity or ethics that interests you?"

"Yeah, there is," she said, which surprised me, in a good way. Usually that conversation goes like this:

Is there any topic that interests you? *Not really.* Why did you choose this major? *I dunno.* Why are you in college? *Shrug.*

"I forget what it's called," she said, "where people do the right thing 'cause they don't want to get punished, and other people do the right thing cause it's the right thing? Like you should want to do the right thing. The other kine, you just like one puppy doesn't wanna get smacked."

"Oh! Kohlberg's stages of moral development. At the highest stages you get into interesting questions about whistleblowers and heretics and . . . protesters. Is that what you're thinking of?"

"Eh Miss, you thought of da kine real quick, but," Honey said. "Smart, you."

"Well. We were just discussing Kohlberg's framework at a department meeting, so it was on my mind."

Hanson Harrison and Larry Schneider had been engaging in a spirited exchange when Harrison accused Schneider of being a "Kohlberg level one." Schneider had responded to Harrison's critique by pointing out that Harrison was a jackass.

"You said protesters," Honey Akiona said. "You mean like what happened with da kine, at your meeting? Jimmy Tanaka?"

"What did you hear about that?" I asked.

"Lotta people don't like Jimmy Tanaka," she said.

"Do *you* know anyone who doesn't like him?" I asked.

"You know anyone who *does*?" she retorted.

"We did appreciate his gift to the college. It'll be nice to have money for things like fixing the air conditioning."

"I'll do my paper on Kohlberg," Honey said. "Stages of moral development. Sounds perfect. Mahalo, Dr. B. You're right about the AC. It's way too hot in here."

She plucked a morsel of smoked pork from the tray, popped it in her mouth, and sauntered out the door.

The cafeteria was closed by now, and the conference room was locked. I did a quick mental inventory of the provisions at my house: vodka in the freezer, pickles in the fridge, a rust-speckled can or two of olives in the pantry. I supposed it wouldn't hurt to try one piece of that smoked pork.

I crumpled up the empty foil tray and stuffed it into the trash can. Davison's peace offering had disappeared with surprising speed, and I was uncomfortably full. I realized that I hadn't yet written his father a thank-you note for coming to speak to my class. An official letter on letterhead would have been ideal, but it was impractical. I'd have to fill out the requisition with Central Supply and wait two weeks, and even then there was no guarantee I'd get that precious single sheet of official college stationery. An email would have to do.

I started to type:

Dear Mr. Gonsalves:

I wasn't sure that struck the right tone. Too formal. *Dear Mr. Gonsalves: I regret to inform you that your son is a cheating suckup. But I did eat all the food he brought in as a bribe, so who am I to judge? Sincerely, Amalia Barda, Ph.D.*

Tinny music played in Rodge Cowper's office next door. I couldn't imagine why anyone would want to listen to Pachelbel's Canon rendered on what sounded like an eight-bit sound chip. But good for him, getting reacquainted with the classics. Different strokes, and so forth.

Dear Donnie,

"I walk with confidence," announced a male voice in an unconvincing monotone. "Women are irresistibly drawn to me."

Rodge was playing self-affirmations, I realized. I squeezed my eyes shut and tried to concentrate.

Dear Donnie, I have come to the conclusion that this Davison creature cannot possibly be your son. You seem perfectly nice, and he is terrible. Love, Molly.

No, Dear Donnie didn't sound right either.

Aloha Donnie,

That would do.

Thanks again for coming to talk to my students.

I finished typing the message in and sent it. I refreshed my inbox to see if Officer Medeiros had sent any news about the plastic skull that my student had found in the wastebasket, but there was nothing.

"I am a self-assured, confident, sexual, and dominant male," intoned the voice from Rodge's office. The cheesy music swelled, even louder than before. It was time to leave. I'd walk the long way to my car, so I wouldn't have to pass Rodge's door and risk embarrassing us both.

I shut down my computer, picked up my bag, and stepped into the hallway. As I eased my door shut, the door to Dean Vogel's office burst open and two police officers strode out. Not our campus security guards, actual police officers. They nodded a curt acknowledgment to me as they clanked by. They were a matched pair: young, stocky, black hair clipped short. Their badges and weapons and other shiny bits flashed in the dim flicker of the inadequate fluorescent tubes. Rodge's office door was closed. I stood alone, still staring down the hallway, when the echoes of their footsteps had faded. I wondered what could have brought Mahina's Finest to Bill Vogel's office. Crimes against education?

Chapter Sixteen

Emma and Pat were waiting by the campus theater's ticket window when I arrived. It was rare to see Emma in anything dressier than her usual t-shirt and jeans, but tonight she looked chic in a simple sleeveless black dress and black platform mules. Pat, as usual, was dressed like a homeless lumberjack.

"I got us awesome seats," Emma fanned out our three tickets like a poker hand as we made our way into the theater.

"Not the front row, right?" I asked.

"And get splashed again? No, we're in row twenty."

We found our seats and edged in. I can never decide whether to face front or back when I'm squeezing into a row of seats; which intimate body part does the average theatergoer want hovering inches from their face? Someone should do a survey.

Emma and I seated ourselves on either side of Pat.

"Nice outfit, Molly!" He picked something out of my hair. "You look like you're about to conduct a séance."

"Thanks?"

"No, seriously, you look fab! I love the velvet. How did you get termites in your hair?"

"They were swarming at my house," I said. "I kept the light off as long as I could, but as soon as I turned it back on they were all over the bathroom. I tried blasting them away with the blow dryer but I guess I missed one."

Emma leaned across Pat to talk to me:

"You came kinda late, yah, Molly? Not looking forward to

seeing Stephen?"

"She had termites at her house," Pat said.

"You try turning the lights out?" Emma asked.

"I still can't believe there's no bug spray or bomb or anything like that that you can use to keep the termites away," I said.

"Just turn the lights out is all," Emma said. "The light is what attracts the swarm."

"I know that. I was just telling Pat, I actually showered in the dark. That's harder than it seems."

"Tell me about it," Emma said. "Especially if you wanna shave anything. Hey, is that true someone was gonna make a movie out of *The Drowning*?"

"Well, that's what Stephen claims. I guess an operetta based on the aftermath of the tsunami, in the style of Bertolt Brecht and Kurt Weill, *could* be a commercial blockbuster."

"I can't believe a major Hollywood studio hasn't snapped it up already," Pat said.

"Hey," I said, "guess what happened when I was leaving work today! Vogel's office door opened, and these two police—"

Someone plumped heavily into the seat next to me. It was Honey Akiona, my Dr. Rodge–quoting student. I'd have to save my dean-related gossip for later. She comfortably filled the seat and both armrests. I placed my hands in my lap.

"Eh, Professor!" she said. "You was married to da kine, ah?" She pointed at the stage.

"No," I answered truthfully. Stephen and I had not married. The coconut wireless doesn't get everything right.

"Oh." She scrunched her brow as if she were calculating a math problem. Then she turned to whisper something to two young women next to her. All three glanced over at me.

"Are we going to the Pair-O-Dice afterward?" Pat asked. I didn't answer. I had no desire to discuss my social plans in front of my students or their friends.

"I have to get home to Yoshi after this," Emma said. "Otherwise he'll get grouchy."

"Invite him along!" Pat said. "It can't be worse than sulking in the house like he always does."

"That big katonk would never go near the Pair-O-Dice," Emma said. "Too low class for him."

I glanced over at Honey and her companions. They were absorbed in their own conversation. I leaned over to Emma.

"Stephen liked going there," I said, "and he was pretty particular. Yoshi might actually enjoy it."

Pat laughed. "Stephen liked the Pair-O-Dice because it was . . . *authentic.*" He mimicked Stephen's delicate hand wave, pressing his forefinger and middle finger together to suggest the presence of Stephen's cigarette holder.

"Pat!" I hissed. "Shh!"

"He's not going to hear me out here," Pat said. "Hey, I have an idea! Let's invite Stephen to come out with us after the show. Cheer him up."

"Absolutely not," I said.

The musicians started up the vertiginous *oom-pa, oom-pa* of the overture as the heavy velvet curtains parted to reveal a bare stage. I knew there was supposed to be an actor standing downstage holding a pail. The Messenger, who muses on the nature of Time and Eternity from the point of view of a wave traveling across the ocean at six hundred miles an hour. The curtains closed again, and the music trailed off. Then we heard muffled yelling, and the curtains parted once more to reveal Stephen Park in profile, screaming at someone offstage.

I watched, stunned, as Stephen railed about self-respect and commitment to the craft. I had never seen this side of Stephen. I was watching a stranger. I glanced over at Honey and her friends. One of the girls had her phone out. I wondered if she was recording Stephen's outburst, or just bored and checking her messages.

It had been a while since I'd seen Stephen last, but I didn't remember him being so skinny. His legs looked like sticks in his pants. Certainly the lighting wasn't doing him any favors. His cheekbones jutted and his eyes were pools of black shadow on his pale skin.

Emma leaned across Pat and whispered to me, drawing out each word: "You dodged a bullet!" I nodded, and then glanced over to make sure Honey wasn't watching. She was. I gave her a weak smile.

"Professor Park get one temper, yah?" she said, as casually as if she were commenting on the surf report.

"We're in his class," her friend added. "We get extra credit for come watch the dress rehearsal."

Stephen finally ran out of steam and stood panting for a few seconds. Then he stalked off, eyes fixed on the floorboards, ignoring the audience. The curtains closed. After a long pause, the music started up and the play began again, from the top

I'd forgotten how long *The Drowning* was. By the time the performance was finished, we were all too tired to go out to the Pair-O-Dice. I no longer had any desire to confront Stephen about sending Officer Medeiros after me. I drove home and hung up the fancy clothes that I hardly ever wear. I brushed termite wings off my bed, switched off the light, and climbed under the comforter. Watching Stephen's meltdown hadn't given me any satisfaction. It just made me feel embarrassed and sad.

The night air was still warm and close. I kicked the comforter off my legs and picked up my phone from my nightstand to check my email one last time. To my intense annoyance, Isaiah Pung had sent a message asking to meet me again, as soon as possible. I had already been forced to give him a penalty-free rewrite thanks to my utterly unethical, I mean "student-centered," dean. What more could this kid possibly want? I dashed off a terse reply suggesting that he come see me on Monday during my scheduled office hours.

My heart thumped when I saw the next email—Donnie Gonsalves had already written a response to my thank-you note:

"my pleasure. hows your schedule look this week or next? let me know anytime but lunch hour."

I winced at the punctuation mistakes, but on the plus side, Donnie Gonsalves wanted to see me again. My mother would have advised me to decline. A lady always turns down the first offer, lest she appear too eager. On the other hand, my mother was three thousand miles away, and what was so bad about being eager to see someone you liked? I typed, "Do you like trivia? How's Thursday night at the Pair-O-Dice?"

Chapter Seventeen

I arrived on campus just in time to get one of the last two spaces in the close parking lot. As I pulled in and parked, I saw Rodge Cowper starting up the walkway to our office building. I decided to wait a few seconds to put some space between us; making small talk with coworkers is stressful for me, even when I haven't overheard their embarrassing self-affirmations.

A gigantic black truck with dark-tinted windows rolled into the spot next to mine. The driver's-side door swung open and Davison Gonsalves climbed down. He did a double-take at my Thunderbird and gave me a grinning thumbs-up, then moved toward me, apparently intending to engage me in conversation. I acknowledged him with a polite smile, and hurried to catch up to Rodge.

"So Molly," Rodge said, "are ya workin' hard, or hardly working?"

"I'm managing. Just fifteen weeks to go."

"How's your little friend? What was her name, Ella?"

Rodge knows very well what Emma's name is. I'm genuinely bad at remembering names, but I am under no illusion that this is in any way charming.

"Emma's good," I said. "She and her *husband* just got back from the mainland."

Rodge also knows that Emma is married. This doesn't dissuade him in the least. He seems to think that trading Yoshi in for him would be a step up for Emma. Emma doesn't think much of Yoshi, but she thinks even less of Rodge.

"They were visiting Yoshi's parents," I added.

We walked in silence for a few moments. That conversation with Honey Akiona had me wondering. When she told me that Rodge Cowper had handed out a Wikipedia entry to the class, I assumed that he was taking credit for someone else's hard work, but what if Rodge himself was the original author? Maybe I had underestimated him. I decided to give him a chance to exonerate himself.

"Hey, Rodge, I wanted to tell you, I've been hearing a lot of positive things about your class."

This was technically true. Every semester I hear students say things like, "I'm so glad Dr. Rodge doesn't have any midterms" and "Dr. Rodge's class saved my GPA," and "Why do you give us so much homework, Miss Barda? Dr. Rodge never assigns homework."

"Good to hear," he said.

"One of my students showed me a handout she got from your class. On integrity?"

"Yeah?"

"I had an assignment in Intro where the students had to write about what integrity means to a future business leader."

"Yup," Rodge said.

"So what you gave the students was very useful. It looked like a lot of work went into it."

"You betcha."

"You know what I thought was interesting?" I said. "The Erhard, Jensen and Zaffron piece. I'd heard of Erhard, but I wasn't familiar with his work in business ethics."

"What was that?" Rodge looked perplexed.

"Erhard, Jensen and Zaffron. 'Integrity: A Positive Model that Incorporates the Normative Phenomena of Morality, Ethics, and Legality.' Two thousand nine. One hundred and twenty-six pages. Remember? You cited it in your handout."

If Rodge had written the original article, he would know the papers he had cited. He didn't say anything until the path split off. Instead of continuing to our office building, he veered off to the right.

"Well," he said over his shoulder as he walked away, "nice talking to you Molly, gotta get going. Have a good one."

"Rodge, aren't you going to your office?" I called after him.

"Gotta pick up my clubs. I'm taking my class golfing." He took his leave with a wink and a finger-gun. "See ya back in the salt mines!"

I picked up speed as rain spattered the concrete walk. My conversation with Rodge had only confirmed my most uncharitable assumptions, and the thought of what the rain was probably doing to my hair blackened my mood even further. It would have been a pleasant surprise to discover that Rodge Cowper had hidden depths: a scholar of ethics, a selfless contributor to public knowledge. Nope, just someone who copied an article from the Internet and handed it out as his own work. Is there a word for that awful realization that your colleagues are as bad as your students? There should be. *Gedämpfteerwartungenenttäuscht* or something like that.

The odor hit me the instant I pushed my office door open. It smelled like coffee mixed with decay.

"How did you get in here before me?" Pat and Emma looked up, surprised to see me.

"This is early for you," Emma said. "Eh, what happened to your hair?"

I edged around the desk and settled onto my yoga ball. "Does it smell funny in here to you?" I brewed myself a fresh cup of coffee, but the aroma couldn't mask the stench.

"You've been brainwashed by the fragrance industry," Pat said. "Everything doesn't have to smell like flowers all the time."

"It smells okay in here to you?" I asked.

"I'm trying to train myself not to be bothered by natural odors. You know there's a whole industry of—"

"Oh, shut up, Pat. You were just complaining about it before she got here. Molly, it's true. Your office is *stink*. Your AC's been broken so long, I bet something crawled in there and . . ."

All three of us looked at the big, black suitcase. Then we all looked at each other.

Emma broke the silence.

"So you ever find out what's in there?"

"No. I never opened it," I said. "It's not my property."

I stuck my nose into my coffee cup and inhaled.

"Nate Parsons brought the suitcase up from the Cloudforest and dropped it off," I said into my cup. "Remember? Pat? You met him when we were down there this weekend. He's one of your devoted fans."

"Oh, yeah. The nervous kid. Yeah, he brought up *a* suitcase from the Cloudforest, and then your dean gave your secretary *a* suitcase to give to you. We can't assume it's the same suitcase."

"Ooh, that's true!" Emma exclaimed. "And even if it is the original suitcase, someone coulda switched what's inside it. Molly, you should open it."

"Look, you guys, my dean entrusted me with the personal property of the biggest donor in the history of the college. I can't just—"

"Don't be paranoid, Molly. We can do it right now. Pat?"

Pat reached back and yanked my door shut.

Emma crouched down by the suitcase. She gingerly took hold of the zipper tab and tugged it gently. The tab moved. The suitcase was unlocked. But instead of opening it, she stood up, rubbed her hands on the back of her jeans, and took a step back.

"You're the reporter, Pat. Go ahead. There's a story in there. Open it."

Pat didn't budge from the plastic chair. "You're the biologist," he said. "You're the one who's equipped to deal with this kind of thing."

"Wait," I said. "*What* kind of thing? Why do we need a biologist?"

"This is Molly's office," Emma said. "Maybe it's *her* kuleana."

My cowardice was overcome by curiosity.

"Oh, for crying out loud, fine. I'll do it. Emma, when did you suddenly get all squeamish?" I bounced decisively up from the yoga ball into a standing position.

"I was kidding!" Emma cried. "I'll do it!"

"No, no, no, too late. I'm not some dainty hothouse flower. Step aside."

I tipped the suitcase over to lay it flat. Emma backed away. The bag was heavier than I'd expected. I couldn't slow its fall, and it smacked hard onto the floor.

My bravado deserted me, but it was too late to back down.

"Nice job, Molly," Pat said. "Now you broke him."

I braced my left hand against the side of the suitcase, pressing hard to still the trembling. With my right hand I grabbed the zipper tab, took a deep breath, and pulled. My hand was so sweaty it flew back empty. The zipper stayed put.

Emma shouldered me out of the way and unzipped the suitcase. I held my breath and squeezed my eyes shut. The foul odor swelled. I clapped my hands over my face.

Emma squealed. Pat started to laugh, and then Emma joined in.

I opened my eyes. The smell was coming from something that used to be a sandwich. On one side the sandwich had liquefied. Black goo oozed through the plastic wrap. I tottered back behind my desk and lowered myself carefully onto the yoga ball, my heart pounding.

The sandwich rested on an unremarkable aloha shirt, a blue-and-gray reverse print of the type favored by local bankers and businessmen. Beside the shirt was a transparent plastic bag containing a toothbrush, toothpaste, and a crumpled tube of Brylcreem. Aside from those two items, the suitcase was full of glossy magazines—hundreds of copies of the latest issue of *Island Business.* The cover featured a photo portrait of Jimmy Tanaka. He was posed at a slight angle against a white background, his arms folded and his chin tilted up, in a flattering shot that promised an equally flattering story inside.

Emma pulled a paper towel from the stack on my desk and plucked the leaky sandwich out of the suitcase. She propped my door open on her way out. Pat and I sat staring at the open suitcase.

"Well, that's a relief," I said, at the same time that Pat said, "That's disappointing."

"I'm relieved too," Emma said as she came back in. "Pat, what's wrong with you?"

Pat pulled out one of the magazines and flipped through it, then set it on my stack of unread mail.

"This interview has a lot of information about Tanaka," he said. "You could probably put together most of your quote–unquote interview from this."

He zipped the suitcase back up and pushed it back to its former standing position. He was just in time.

Dan Watanabe knocked on the open door and then stuck his head into my office. "Molly, can I have a word?"

"Sure," I said. "Come in."

"Is it bad?" Emma asked.

"I'm afraid it is."

Pat and Emma sipped their coffee serenely, clearly expecting to be included in whatever conversation my department chair and I were about to have.

Dan looked from Emma to Pat and back again. "I guess she'll tell you all about it anyway," he sighed. He stepped into my office and pulled the door shut.

"I just came from an emergency department chairs' meeting. It's about that incident at the breakfast for Jimmy Tanaka."

"Is Stephen Park in trouble?" Emma asked eagerly.

"I think we're all in trouble."

Dan pinched his nose and tilted his head back. I handed him a tissue.

"Thanks. Sorry. Nosebleed. You going somewhere?"

"Me? Oh, the suitcase? No, that's actually Jimmy Tanaka's. Bill Vogel had Serena store it in my office."

Pat stood and offered Dan his chair, and then perched on my desk. Dan nodded thanks and lowered himself gingerly, trying to avoid the crack across the seat.

"It's a real skull," Emma said, to help Dan along. "Right? The security people told Molly that. And Stephen didn't have the permits—"

"Worse than that, Emma," Dan said. "They ID'd the skull. It's Jimmy Tanaka."

Chapter Eighteen

"Well, first things first." I picked up the phone. "I'm sure the police will want to take this important evidence off my hands."

The nice lady on the phone didn't seem to share my sense of urgency about Jimmy Tanaka's suitcase. She took my message and assured me that someone would get back to me.

"I need a headline," Pat said. "What do you like better? *It Was Murder!,* or *Grisly Campus Find Identified*?"

"Pat!" Emma gave him a shove. "Dan said don't publish it!"

"I think I prefer the second one," I said, "but when you say 'grisly campus find identified,' it could sound like you're describing the *campus* as grisly."

"I'm not going to publish it right away," Pat said. "I'll wait a couple days."

"This is terrible," I said.

"I know. I hate having to sit on a story."

"I don't mean about your story, Pat. Of course that's important," I added quickly, "but what about Stephen? It was bad enough when he was connected with a—a prank. Now he's involved in a murder."

"Eh, not your problem," Emma said.

"It *might* be her problem. Everyone knows that Molly had a relationship with Stephen. So what about that plastic skull in your classroom?"

"It's not just my classroom," I said. "Rodge and Larry teach in there too. I have to follow up on that, though."

"On the bright side, at least you don't have to write that press release," Emma said.

"I'm calling security right now," I said.

I retrieved Officer Medeiros's card from my wallet and dialed his direct number. The conversation was short and disappointing.

"So?" Emma said. "Did they look at the tapes?"

"Not yet," I said. "They can't find them."

"Can't find them!" Emma exclaimed. "What kine baboozes they got working up there in security?"

"Officer Medeiros has been nothing but professional," I said. "I don't think it's nice to call him a . . . whatever you called him. You know what? I'm going to go talk to Stephen."

"Molly, don't be an idiot," Emma said. "You don't confront a murderer! Don't you ever watch movies?"

Pat took Emma's side at first, but after a perfunctory attempt to talk me out of it, they both insisted on coming with me. It was just Stephen Park, after all, during daylight hours. True, there was his temper tantrum at the dress rehearsal, but yelling at people was different from doing them physical harm. And Stephen Park couldn't overpower a tightly capped pickle jar, let alone all three of us.

The theater department chair's office reeked of Stephen's Indonesian clove cigarettes, exactly the way it used to before the smoking ban. Stephen never thought the rules applied to him.

"Hi, Molly." He sounded defeated. "Pat. Emma."

Facing his desk were two orange plastic classroom chairs with chrome legs, the same style as my one beige one, but in better repair. I sat down in one. Emma and Pat did an Alphonse and Gaston routine over the remaining chair. Finally, Emma sat and Pat slouched against the electric blue cinderblock wall.

"You repainted," I said. "That's some color." I thought it looked like it belonged in a 1970s preschool, not a university.

"The graduating seniors repainted my office as a going-away present," Stephen said, then added, "We're allowed to do that in the theater department."

That was obviously meant to be a dig at the College of Commerce. I decided to let it go. Stephen clearly wasn't in peak fighting condition anyway. He looked cadaverous under the fluorescent lights.

"Stephen," I said. "Your angel? The one who was going to finance your movie? It was Jimmy Tanaka, wasn't it?"

Stephen looked down at the papers on his desk and swallowed. He looked miserable.

"I didn't kill him, Molly."

"You know about the skull?" Emma asked.

Stephen nodded. "They had an emergency meeting for the department chairs. I had no idea. The way everyone looked at me . . ."

"There were terms that you couldn't agree to," I said. "That's why the deal fell apart. Right? Okay, look. This is kind of my problem too. Thanks to *you,* our security people think I have something to do with this. Oh, did you know that one of your props showed up in the trash can in my classroom?"

"Yeah, they asked me about it when they brought it back. It was one of mine, but I don't know how it got into your classroom. Is that why they think you're involved?"

I restrained myself from vaulting across his desk and throttling him.

"Stephen, they think I'm involved because *you* told them that *I* was responsible for organizing the prop room! And now it turns out that Jimmy Tanaka's skull might not even have anything to do with your prop room! So I'm in trouble for nothing!"

"Molly." Emma patted my shoulder. "It's okay. Breathe! Anyway, weren't you the one who brought up the idea of the skull being from the prop room in the first place?"

"Okay, look," I said. "Forget what you said to campus security. As long as you don't say anything to the police. If they ask to talk to you, just lawyer up, okay?"

Stephen stared at his desk.

"What is it?" I asked.

Stephen flinched, but said nothing.

After a long pause, I said quietly, "You did not already talk to the police. Did you?"

Silence.

"Stephen, what did you tell them?"

"Nothing," he said.

"Oh." I slumped with relief. "Well, that's good."

"I mean, I told them the truth."

"You *what*?"

Emma placed her hands on my shoulders and eased me back down into the chair.

"All I told them was, I had had some business with Jimmy Tanaka years ago, but I didn't know anything about this, you know, the murder. And they ordered me . . . they said don't leave town."

I felt protective and infuriated at the same time. It was a familiar sensation.

"Anyway," Stephen said, "I don't think I have anything to worry about. I mean, what's my motive? Why would I hide Jimmy Tanaka's decapitated head in a food tray?"

"It's not a decapitated head!" I said, very calmly. Pat and Emma stared at me. I lowered my voice.

"There's no such thing as a decapitated head," I continued, in a soft and reasonable tone. "Decapitate means to remove the head. You can't remove the head from a head. That doesn't make any sense. What you want to say is *disembodied* head."

"No, I *don't* want to say disembodied head," Stephen

snapped. "That makes it sound like the head is floating in the sky like a balloon. Decapitated head is common usage. Everyone says decapitated head."

"Just because *everyone* does something doesn't mean it's right. *Everyone* is not an authority." I paused. "*Everyone* thinks Andrew Lloyd Weber is a musical genius."

Stephen blew air out, as if someone had punched him in the stomach. It took him a moment to regain his breath.

"Fine, Molly. Fine. *Disembodied* head." He raised his hands and twiddled his fingers as he said it.

"Is there someone who has a grudge against you?" Pat asked. "Someone who knows about your history with Jimmy Tanaka?"

Stephen shook his head.

"We were at the dress rehearsal," Emma said.

"You were there? Were all three of you there?"

"Wouldn't miss it," I said.

Stephen rested his forehead in his hand.

"What did the students do to make you so upset?" Pat asked.

"Oh, they had been moving things around in the prop room. It was impossible to find anything . . ." He trailed off, avoiding eye contact with me.

On the way back to my office, Emma was the first to speak.

"So. Who thinks Stephen is guilty?"

"I feel sorry for him," Pat said.

"I know, right? Especially after Molly got through with him."

"No one has to feel sorry for him," I said. "He brings it on himself."

"You don't think he did it, though?" Emma asked.

"No. I don't. Stephen doesn't have the stomach to decapitate someone. He couldn't even stay in the kitchen when I cooked chicken liver."

"I thought Stephen was a vegetarian," Pat said.

"I think he is now. Can we walk faster? It's starting to rain."

"Oh, no," Emma said. "I know what that does to your hair."

"My hair? What are you talking about?"

"What? Nothing."

We proceeded single-file under the huge monstera leaves that sheltered the footpath. With most of our groundskeepers furloughed, the endemic foliage has taken over our campus. My office building has been swallowed up by maile pilau, which is fine, as long as you don't have to smell it.

"What if he did do it?" Emma asked. "If we didn't know Stephen already, and all we saw was how he acted on the night of the dress rehearsal, I mean think about it!"

"How would he kill someone, though?" I asked. "I mean, *Stephen*?"

"I dunno," Emma said. "By boring the victim to death with his plays?"

"How about your boyfriend Donnie Gonsalves?" Pat said. "Maybe he was the one who killed Tanaka."

"Oooh, yeah, Donnie's pretty fit," Emma cooed. "He has that great body, and those *arms*."

"Why are we talking about Donnie now?" I said. "Just because Donnie's Drive-Inn and Merrie Musubis are competitors?"

"That's a motive," Pat said.

"No, it isn't. You know, when I tell my students that the restaurant business is cutthroat, I don't mean it literally."

"What about the police officer?" Emma asked. "The one who found Tanaka, you know. And got pushed out of his job afterward."

"After all these years, though?" Pat said.

"Yeah," Emma sighed. "Stephen doesn't seem like a likely suspect, but everyone else seems even less likely."

And then I heard these words come out of my mouth: "I have to help Stephen."

Chapter Nineteen

"Molly, you have to help me."

Stephen Park stood in my doorway, his skinny frame silhouetted against the darkening sky.

"Stephen! What are you—"

"I'm sorry. I should've called first. I'm sure you have better things to do than . . . I'm sure you're busy."

He turned to leave.

"It's okay. You're here. You might as well come in."

A birdlike whistle pierced the air.

"You have coqui frogs?" he asked.

"It's recent," I said. I stood to the side and motioned him into my living room.

When I first bought my house, there were only a few of the tiny frogs in the neighborhood, and their distinctive "peep PEEP" was tolerable. Now, the population had swelled exponentially, and coqui frog racket ruled the night.

"You have to disclose coquis to any potential buyers," Stephen said.

"I know that, Stephen. Fortunately, I don't plan to sell my 'bourgeois little suburban house' anytime soon."

I closed the door behind him. Stephen looked even worse than he had earlier this afternoon in his office, if that were possible. He tottered over to the couch and hovered next to it. I poured two glasses of wine and brought them over. He waved his away.

"Fine," I said. "More for me." I sat down on the couch and gestured to him to do the same.

He sank down next to me and rested his bony elbows on his bony knees, radiating a kind of negative energy that sucked all of the life out of my living room. He reached into the pocket of his leather jacket, pausing only when I caught his eye.

"Okay if I smoke?"

"No! It's not okay to smoke inside my house. You know that."

I don't care what he says, clove cigarettes are still cigarettes. He withdrew his hand from his pocket and clasped his hands in front of him. I noticed a tremble in the slender fingers. For a moment I thought he was going to be sick, and hoped my leather couch was as easy to wipe clean as the saleswoman at Balusteros World of Furniture had claimed.

"Sorry, Molly," he said. "I'm so sorry. I'm pathetic."

"That's not helpful."

I wasn't going to let myself get sucked into pitying him.

"Have you thought of any reason why someone would want to involve you in this?" I asked. "I mean, *you* obviously didn't decapitate Jimmy Tanaka and plant his skull in the breakfast buffet."

Stephen glanced at me and then back down at his lap.

"That's sweet. You have faith in me."

"Not really," I said.

"The thing is, I don't know . . . I don't *know* if I killed Jimmy Tanaka."

"What do you mean *you don't know if you killed Jimmy Tanaka*?"

"I can't remember," he said.

I stared at him. "You can't remember whether or not you *murdered* someone? How does something like that slip your mind?"

I scooted away from him, into the arm of the couch, as if that would keep me safe. I realized that letting Stephen into my house was a stupid thing to do. I imagined the story in the *County Courier* the following day: *There were no signs of forced entry. It is believed that the victim let the killer into her home voluntarily.*

Stephen stared into the middle distance. "You're right," he said. "My prop room is a mess. My life is a mess. All my department chair duties, my theater classes, the performances, my work with KidsPlay, it's impossible to keep up with it all."

"Well, no one forced you to agree to all that," I said. "You can't be everyone's hero."

"Just say no." He stared at the floor. "I can't do that. Turn people away. Just look after number one. That's not me."

"Stephen, why did you come here? What do you want?"

He leaned back and closed his eyes.

"Have you ever tried to function on no sleep, Molly? I mean, literally no sleep. Rehearsal ends, you get something to eat, then it's time to get ready for a morning meeting."

"No," I said. "I don't know how you can do that."

"So one night one of my students told me she had a prescription—"

"Oh, no! Stephen, tell me you didn't—"

"It was magic," he said. "Suddenly, I had all the energy I needed. I could go for days if I had to."

"But things started to get out of control," I said.

"It's such a cliché, isn't it?" Stephen sighed.

"You know, I've heard this story before, Stephen. Many, many times. From my students. But *you*?"

"Why not me?" Stephen said.

"I mean, that kind of thing happens to people with—"

I realized that there was no way to finish that sentence that I wouldn't regret.

"When did you start?" I asked.

He laughed weakly and looked down at the floor.

"I don't remember. That's the thing. It's like someone just ran a big eraser over parts of my life."

"Were you using the whole time I knew you?" I asked.

He stared at his jittering knees.

"What about your teeth?" I asked. "Let me see."

"Stop it. My teeth are fine."

"You know, your skin looks—"

"I know. You don't have to tell me. I have a mirror. Listen to me, Molly, did you ever notice any of this? Me having memory problems? Could you tell?"

"Memory problems. Yeah, funny you should bring that up. Do you remember what happened on my birthday?"

"Your birthday." Stephen drew his eyebrows together, and his eyes lit on the second glass of wine on the table. "Is that for me?"

"I thought you didn't want it. Help yourself."

"Why wouldn't I want it? Wait, what were you saying now?"

"My birthday, Stephen. Remember? You told me you'd made a reservation at Sprezzatura. I got all dolled up and waited for you, and you never showed up. Remember Tatsuya's Moderne Beauty, before it closed? I had Tatsuya do my hair that night. It looked magnificent."

Stephen was staring at me, his hand paused halfway to the wine glass.

"You were supposed to pick me up at six," I said.

"But I—"

"You finally called at four in the morning. After I'd gone to bed."

"I called you at four in the morning? What was I doing at four in the morning?"

"You're asking *me*? You said you were busy and lost track of time. I was too tired to fight with you at that point. I think I just said something like, sorry it didn't work out."

I had probably said some rather less ladylike things as well, but if Stephen didn't remember, I certainly didn't have to remind him.

"So is that how it ended? You and me?" he asked.

"Stephen, you never even knew why we broke up? So you just, what, said oh well, and went on with your life?"

"I . . . I guess I knew something had gone wrong, and I was afraid to ask. I didn't want to stir things up."

"You didn't want to stir *me* up, you mean."

We sat silently side by side, Stephen glum, me freshly indignant over the birthday incident.

"Molly, what if I did it? Killed Jimmy Tanaka? I mean, if I was, you know, impaired, would I still be legally accountable for what I did? What about extenuating circumstances?"

I stared at him. Those cheekbones, the ones I had admired and envied, looked like they were about to cut through his waxy skin.

"Look, Stephen, I'm not a lawyer. But I suspect 'sorry I committed a murder, but it's okay, 'cause I was totally tweaking' wouldn't be a very compelling defense. Anyway, I don't believe you did it."

"Oh." He took a sip of wine, made a face, and set the glass back down.

"Yes, it's that fruity red blend I like. The one that you say is half a step above pink Jacuzzi wine. You don't have to drink it. Look. You need an actual lawyer. *And* you know what else? You need to get into rehab. Stay right there. I'm going to call your parents."

I stood up and went to the phone.

"No, Molly, I can't go now! It's the beginning of the school year!"

"You're not indispensable," I said. "You can get someone else to take over as chair and—"

"No! If I leave, I might come back and find my department gone."

I came back out of my little office nook.

"They're not going to get rid of the whole theater department," I said.

"You have no idea how bad it is, Molly. Everything is 'on the table.' Everything except for the Student Retention Office, of course."

"Yeah, the SRO seems pretty bulletproof," I said.

"Not just bulletproof, Molly. It's metastasizing."

I walked back over to the couch and sat down.

"I thought you liked the SRO, all student-centered and everything."

"Have you really taken a look at them, Molly?" Stephen had a wild glint in his eyes. "Their ever-expanding offices and lounges, their catered workshops and custom websites and award ceremonies and four-color glossy booklets designed to spend down their lavish budget to precisely zero dollars and zero cents by the last day of the fiscal year? Have you seen it? Have you really looked? It's a monster. We're feeding a monster."

"They do have some nice furniture up there," I mused.

"Meanwhile, we have to beg for the things we need. Beg! You, a professor, you don't even have a proper office chair. You sacrifice your dignity every day by sitting on a yoga ball."

"My dignity is very well toned from sitting on that ball, I'll have you know."

"Do you know that the cost for just one print run of *Learning Styles in the Classroom* would have covered Janey's salary for a year?" Stephen said.

"Ouch. Really? I didn't know that."

"It's bad enough for me, losing my department secretary. But it's worse for her. Her husband is disabled. He can't work. They were both depending on her health insurance."

I watched him for a few moments. Then I got up to call his parents while he sobbed quietly on my leather couch. I still knew their phone number by heart.

Chapter Twenty

Despite the name, there is (officially) no gambling at the Pair-O-Dice Bar and Grill. Trivia games, on the other hand, are perfectly legal. I don't like to brag, but I'm rather good at trivia, and I was looking forward to tonight's tournament. The Pair-O-Dice is generally pretty empty and therefore ideal for quiet conversation, but trivia night is the exception. Pat, Emma and I had secured the last free table.

"What?" I asked as I surfaced to rejoin the conversation. I had just finished stuffing a folded paper napkin under one leg of the wooden table to stop it from wobbling.

"Pat was wondering if Donnie had any friends of his own," Emma said.

"I think he might be a psychopath," Pat said. "Psychopaths can't form close friendships."

"Who cares? Molly and me can be his fake friends. Hey, did you guys hear about Stephen? I heard he disappeared."

"Stephen?" I repeated, trying to sound nonchalant. I hadn't told them that Stephen had come to my house, or that I'd driven him out to the airport and put him on the redeye direct to Los Angeles with no baggage except for the boarding pass from my home printer. He wasn't exactly thrilled about getting shipped off-island, but I explained to him that if he were really a murderer, then getting him into some kind of lockdown rehab would make everyone safer. If he were innocent, then at least he'd be getting the help he needed. He couldn't really argue with that logic. His sister was going to meet him at LAX, and his family would take care of him from there.

"I heard he just went out on sick leave," Pat said.

"That's kinda suspicious either way," Emma said. "Maybe he really is guilty. Molly, did you hear anything about it?"

"I'll tell you later," I said. I wasn't eager to have everyone know what happened. Stephen certainly needed help, and his mother had seemed appreciative on the phone, but in retrospect I could see how people in law enforcement might start throwing around ugly words like "aiding" and "abetting" and "fugitive."

Donnie stood in the doorway of the Pair-O-Dice. I waved and he nodded and made his way toward us. He made slow progress through the noisy crowd, turning sideways to edge between the closely packed tables. When he finally reached our table he embraced me, kissed me on the cheek, and then turned to Pat and Emma.

Pat was barely polite. Emma was more than friendly enough to make up for Pat.

"Hey, Donnie," Emma shouted over the din as he sat down. "When someone is murdered, you want to know who would benefit from their death, right?"

Donnie leaned in to hear her. "I suppose so," he shouted back. "Why?"

I tried to shoot Emma a disapproving look, but she wouldn't return my eye contact. What was she up to? She leaned closer to talk directly into his ear. I leaned in too, to hear what she was saying.

"I bet you know a lot of people in the business community," she said. "Could you find out if Jimmy Tanaka had a will? Or if he was about to make one?"

"Jimmy Tanaka?" Donnie said.

"Molly wants to know," Emma said.

"I do?"

Pat put his phone away and joined our conversation.

"Donnie," Pat said, "you heard about Jimmy Tanaka's murder?"

"Pat!" I exclaimed.

"I'm on the College of Commerce Community Council," Donnie said. "They had an emergency briefing for us. They asked us to keep it confidential. But it sounds like all of you already know about it."

"Good," Emma interrupted. "We're all caught up. What about the will?"

"I believe wills are public record," Donnie said.

"Molly thinks her dean did it," Emma said.

"What? I never said that."

"You told us you saw the police coming out of his office after hours," Emma said. "You did, right? You weren't making that up?"

"I'm sure Donnie doesn't want to talk about this," I said.

"And you said that Dan told you that Vogel might be leaving, so you'd have to step up and become department chair. Eh, I can put two and two together."

"What do you think the trivia topics are tonight?" I said.

"You might become department chair?" Donnie asked me, in a tone implying that would be a good thing. Clearly, he knew nothing about my workplace.

"Well, that's what I was told," I said. "If Bill Vogel leaves for any reason, my department chair, Dan Watanabe, is going to become the new dean. And if *that* happens, he says I have to step up and serve as chair of my department."

"So it would be to your benefit if Bill Vogel were guilty?" Donnie asked.

"What? No! Not at all."

"But it would mean a promotion," he persisted.

"I don't want a promotion."

Emma nodded agreement. Both she and I knew that being "promoted" to department chair meant that for an insultingly small bump in pay, I'd double my workload. There were all of the grievances that needed to be processed, and then there was having to answer to the Student Retention Office with all of their Student Satisfaction Reports and Disruptive Innovation Reports and Classroom Engagement Reports that I'd be responsible for filling out. I'd have no real authority, but if anything went wrong, I'd get all the blame. On top of all of that, I'd still have to teach, and I'd still be responsible for publishing enough research to get tenure.

But for Donnie's benefit, I said: "It's ghoulish to worry about my own career at a time like this."

Donnie nodded sympathetically. Emma rolled her eyes.

"That was beautiful," Pat said. "Very convincing."

Donnie glanced over at Pat, and back at me.

"How did the three of you meet?" he asked.

"It was that committee," I said. "I forget the name."

"Oh, yeah!" Emma said. "The Assessment of Faculty Development Committee. I remember."

"No," Pat said, "I wasn't on AFDC. I don't remember which one it was."

"Anyway," Emma said, "we all thought Pat was taking notes on his laptop, but it turned out he was updating his newsblog, and in between he was writing fake reviews for all of us online."

"On that professor rating site that shall not be named," I added.

"Those are fake?" Donnie looked genuinely surprised, which surprised me.

"Most of them," I said. "The well-written ones, anyway. I thought everyone knew that."

"That explains quite a bit," Donnie said.

"Donnie," Emma giggled, "did you search for Molly online?"

"Of course. I had to do my due diligence."

"I'm very easy to find, unfortunately. Not a lot of Molly Bardas out there."

"You could get yourself a more common last name," Pat said. "Like Gonsal—ow!"

Emma pushed back her chair and stood up. "Come help me order drinks," she said. She grasped Pat's elbow and dragged him away from the table.

"So I suppose you really don't know where Jimmy Hoffa is buried," Donnie said, leaning close to be heard above the clamor of the increasingly boisterous crowd.

"No. And I don't have X-ray vision, I am one hundred percent human, and I never shot a man in Reno."

Emma and Pat returned with their hands full of food and drink. "Fried mozzarella," Emma announced as she set down a red plastic basket lined with grease-stained paper. "Fried calamari. And for the health conscious, fried zucchini. And, a pitcher of Mehana Volcano Red Ale."

"Watch out, Donnie," Pat said, as they sat down. "Last time we were here, it was a bloodbath."

"Oh, yah! Molly knows every useless fact you can think of! She's gonna wipe the floor with us."

"Watch this," Pat said. "Molly, the band New Or—"

"Joy Division," I said.

"Okay, but—"

"After Ian Curtis committed suicide in nineteen eighty."

Pat turned to Donnie and raised his hands in a "see, I told you" gesture.

"Ask me something about Steve Soto!" I said.

"We're doomed," Emma announced cheerfully.

Unfortunately, Emma turned out to be wrong. The first topic was Hawaiian royalty. Donnie was apparently on a first-name basis with every last one of King Kamehameha's wives, and his exhaustive knowledge of the details of King David Kalakaua's life and death seemed to me to border on the obsessive. I could practically hear my mother's voice: "Men have fragile egos, Molly. You have to let them win once in a while." Well, Donnie was winning. I hoped he was enjoying it. For some reason the game didn't seem very interesting tonight.

Donnie won the category, to no one's surprise. Emma high-fived him.

"Emma," I asked, "where's Yoshi?"

She gave me a blank look.

"Your husband?" I prompted her. "I thought you were going to invite him along tonight."

She shrugged.

The next topic, "Science," was even worse. One obscure, irrelevant question followed another. Somehow Emma was guessing all the right answers now. I watched the local news flickering silently on the overhead television.

"I had absolutely no idea what that question was about," I heard Pat say. "I thought a radius was the distance from the center of a circle to the edge."

This gave Emma a perfect opening to flaunt her arcane knowledge: "The radius and the ulna are two bones in the forearm. Humans don't have to walk on our arms, so those bones don't bear weight. They're slender, like two sticks. In quadrupeds those bones are thicker, and fused to bear the weight of the animal's body."

I stopped listening and read the captions on the television. I learned that I could make cash money selling my gold jewelry, remodel my kitchen with an E-Z loan, and start my future tomorrow at an online college. So many possibilities, all of which sounded much more appealing than sitting through this boring trivia game.

Pat nudged me and shouted into my ear. "Sorry they don't

have any questions about Rodney Bingenheimer this time."

I shrugged and shouted back. "It's okay. I don't really care about winning or losing. I'm just here to have fun."

"Obviously. Anyone can tell you're having a blast."

Pat went back to the trivia game, and I went back to reading the captions for the evening news. A honeymooning couple from Oregon had been enjoying a long hike miles from the nearest road. They'd spied a gap in the forest floor and shone a flashlight down into what turned out to be a system of lava tubes. About twenty feet below them the beam of the flashlight caught something that looked at first like a heap of dirty clothes. They were able to read their GPS coordinates to the nine-one-one dispatcher. The clothes turned out to contain a body. The remains were still unidentified.

I was so engrossed in the story that I barely noticed when the trivia master announced the top scorer for the evening: Emma Nakamura. Her grand prize: a gift certificate for fifty percent off a weekend for two at the Hanohano Hotel.

It was a pleasure to offer her my sincere congratulations.

CHAPTER TWENTY-ONE

It was finally Friday. I was happy to be on my way to the Maritime Club and done with the workweek. Well, maybe not done, exactly. I had a stack of papers in my bag that I planned to grade over the weekend. And I still hadn't completed my weekly reports for the Student Retention Office. But I had a juicy tidbit of outrage to share, and I was looking forward to commiserating with Pat and Emma.

They were already seated at a small table out on the lanai when I arrived. The morning's rain clouds had dispersed, and the ocean glittered behind them in the afternoon sun.

"You won't believe what I just heard about Rodge Cowper," I announced as I sat down with them. I still couldn't believe it myself.

"Oh, no," Emma said. "What'd he do now?"

I paused for effect.

"He's been nominated for the all-campus *teaching award.*"

Pat laughed and shook his head. "That must be a joke," he said.

"No joke. I ran into Larry Schneider today when I was walking out to the parking lot. He knows people on the awards committee. Oh! He said I wasn't supposed to tell anyone. So don't tell anyone."

"Seriously? *Rodge Cowper* might actually get the teaching award? That's like—" Emma looked from Pat to me and back again. "I don't know what it's like. It's like something bad!"

"Why do you two care?" Pat asked.

Emma and I looked at each other.

"*I* don't care," Emma said.

"Me neither."

"If you really want to be popular," Pat said, "you know what to do. Give everyone A's, tell a lot of jokes, don't assign too much homework, don't question their worldview, tell them how smart and wonderful they are."

"*You* don't do any of those things," Emma said.

"I know. That's why I can sleep at night. You know, this is actually pretty nice." Pat gestured toward the ocean. "Emma, your husband is missing out."

Out on the shore, small children splashed in the shallows. A man balanced on a black lava rock outcropping, pulling up a fishing net.

Emma had joined the Maritime Club hoping that Yoshi would enjoy spending time here with her. Unfortunately, the weather-beaten little clubhouse with its archaic menu was not up to his standards. In fact, nothing on this island is up to Yoshi's standards. Emma met Yoshi when she was finishing her doctoral work. When they married, they agreed that wherever she could find a job, he would follow. With his MBA, Yoshi had a lot more options than someone with a specialized PhD.

Now that Emma has a job here, just a few miles from the house where she grew up, Yoshi wants to back out of the deal. He simply can't live in a town without VIP rooms, where no one can tell he's wearing a two-thousand-dollar suit (nor would anyone care), where no one is impressed by his trendy brand of vodka. (Sure, he can order it from Hagiwara's Specialty Liquors whenever he wants, but that's not the point.)

Emma decided to keep the membership anyway. The Maritime Club has a nice oceanfront location and decent food, even if the menu hasn't changed since the fifties.

"What does Rodge do in his classes, exactly, that's so award-worthy?" Emma asked.

"I don't know," I said. "I heard he shows funny videos and tells jokes."

"I have a joke you could tell," Pat said.

"Not the canoe joke," I said. "I mean, it's funny, but it's totally inappropriate."

"The canoe joke is not funny," Emma said. "It's gross."

"Besides, why do I have to do that?" I said. "I'm not an entertainer. What happened to holding our students to high standards and expecting them to actually learn something?"

"Well, there's your big mistake, Professor Pious," Pat said. "High standards and learning? Nobody likes that."

"What about the refrigerator joke?" Emma said.

"I'm not telling the refrigerator joke. That would get me fired for sure."

"How about bringing in home-baked muffins?" Pat suggested. "Like what's her name, in my department."

"Ew," Emma said. "The one who gives the students backrubs?"

"Yeah, that's the one. Her students love her. If part-timers were eligible, she'd get the teaching award every year."

"I don't even *touch* my students," I said. "I'm certainly not going to start giving them *backrubs.* I guess I could try baking muffins."

"Molly, don't you use your oven to store your extra shoes?" Emma asked.

"I could move them somewhere else. Hey, what about that 'classroom innovations' website that the Student Retention Office set up?"

"Ohhh, no. I tried one of the ideas off that website once," Emma said. "The in-class poetry slam."

"Really?" I asked. "How did that go?"

"All my students thought it sounded fun at first. But when it came time for the performances, no one wanted to do it. They all had stage fright."

"Well, no teaching award for me, I guess. Listen, Pat, before I forget. I just got a paper from one of my students. I think you'll be interested in this." I handed him Honey Akiona's latest revision.

"Isn't this a FERPA violation?" Pat said as he took the paper from me and started reading.

"I'm sharing the paper with you because of your expertise in composition," I said.

"Sounds plausible to me," he said. "This is interesting. She has a pretty clear-cut sense of right and wrong."

"I noticed that."

"As long as she doesn't wake up one day and decide that rolling a grenade into your classroom is the Right Thing to Do, you'll probably be fine."

"Is she the one who was sitting next to us at the dress rehearsal?" Emma asked.

"Exactly," I said. "Anyway, Pat, look at the bibliography. The first entry. That website looked like the real thing to me, but I wanted to get your opinion."

"Sure. Let's take a look." Pat pulled out his phone and typed in the address.

The website that Honey Akiona had cited did not look particularly impressive. It wasn't optimized for a small screen, which made it awkward to navigate on Pat's phone. On a black background was a list of electric blue links to downloadable files: Planning_Dept, Mayor's_Office, County_Council, Police.

"Try click something," Emma said.

"This is fantastic," Pat said. "How did they get all this?"

He pressed the screen and waited.

"Look at this! It's a video of a police interrogation!"

"It's amazing what they have up there," I said. "I just hope they don't plan to post everyone's driver's license information."

"Molly, I told you, you have no reason to be embarrassed about your weight."

"I wasn't talking about my *weight,* Emma. But thanks for assuming that."

Emma's dinner of rare prime rib arrived looking like a crime scene. The two mounds of rice shaded from white at the top to pink and then red at the base.

"It's not blood," Emma said to me, her mouth full of meat. I don't know how she knew what I was thinking. "They pretty much drain the blood. The red liquid that you see on the plate is called sarcoplasm. It's fluid from the muscle that's released during cooking."

"That's very informative, Emma. Thanks." I angled my chair so I didn't have to look at her plate, and started on my fish and chips. "Now I'm going to forget all about plagiarists and cowardly deans and everything else stressful that happened this week, and enjoy my meal."

"You know, Molly,"—Pat gestured at me with his veggie wrap—"I know why your dean wouldn't let you punish your cheaters."

"Eh, genius! You miss the part where she said she doesn't want to talk about that right now?"

"That's okay," I said. "What's your theory? Besides the fact that my dean is terrible?"

"I think he wants to shake down your entrepreneur friend for a donation to your college."

"You mean Donnie?" I asked.

"Yeah!" Emma exclaimed. "Pat's right. You're not gonna get a big donation from Donnie if you bust his kid for cheating." Emma swallowed her mouthful and continued, "Hey Pat, you should do a story about that!"

"Please, Pat, do not do a story about that. Do you think Vogel knows that Davison is Donnie's son? I mean, Gonsalves is a pretty common name."

"Of course he knows," Pat said. "That's his job. He can't let you—"

"Pat!" I saw Donnie Gonsalves and another man get up from a table a few feet away. How long had they been here? I hoped the sound of the ocean had drowned out our conversation. This is what happens when you gossip about people using their real names. I have to stop doing that. Using real names, I mean.

Donnie caught my eye and started toward our table. He greeted Pat and Emma, and the three of them traded some chit-chat about our evening at the Pair-O-Dice. I was surprised that everyone else seemed to have such pleasant recollections of last night's trivia tournament. I thought the evening had been a disaster. Then Donnie lowered his voice and leaned toward me.

"I tried to call you this morning at your office," he said. "I wanted to invite you to lunch at my place next week."

"What time should we be there?" Emma said.

"Sorry," I said. "This invitation's just for me."

We agreed on a time, and Donnie went out to meet his dinner companion, now waiting at the door. Both were dressed in the standard business uniform: reverse-print aloha shirt, tucked into black dress slacks.

As they walked out, Emma said, "He's handsome, yah? Donnie."

"He smells like a hamster cage," Pat said.

"That's cedar, babooz," Emma snorted.

"I like it," I said. "It's better than that stinky sweet stuff some of the boys wear. Why do they do that? Do they think it smells good?"

"Nah," Emma said. "No one thinks that stuff smells good. They only use it 'cause it covers up the smell of pakololo. So when a boy comes into your office reeking of that stuff? You know he's probably high as a kite."

"Good to know," I said.

"If Donnie's so great," Pat said, "why is he single?"

"*You're* single," Emma said.

"I'm not that great."

"So Molly," Emma asked, "you think it's gonna go anywhere?"

"You know, I don't know. He started working right out of high school. He never went to college. I mean, not that that should make a difference."

"No college?" Pat exclaimed. "Ooh, rough trade!"

"He really seems to like you. He couldn't take his eyes off you."

"I can't imagine that I'm really his type," I said.

"Why not?" Emma said. "You're pretty and smart. Why wouldn't he like you? Don't be so modest."

Pat chimed in: "She's not being modest. She's thinking, how could some untraveled, uneducated, small-town petit-bourgeois who doesn't even listen to NPR possibly appreciate *me*, with my cosmopolitan glamour and sophistication?"

"Oooohhh, Molly, is that true?"

"Of course it's not true! I just made a date to have lunch with him!"

Sometimes Pat really gets under my skin. I ordered another glass of wine.

Chapter Twenty-Two

My lunch with Donnie was scheduled for midafternoon, after the lunch rush at Donnie's Drive-Inn. The late time worked well for my schedule, and also ensured that my appetite was sharp. Actually, I was starving. As I approached Donnie's address, the houses thinned out and the lots became larger. By the time I reached his immediate neighborhood, each house sat on a three-acre lot. The expansive yards featured well-kept avocado, papaya, and mountain apple trees. Anthuriums and orchids bloomed in the shade. The houses themselves were unexpectedly modest, considering how pricey this neighborhood was. (I knew the prices and acreage because I'd looked up the recent sales online that morning.)

I drove past Donnie's house and stopped the car on the street a few houses down. I didn't want my distinctive turquoise and white T-Bird sitting right in Donnie's driveway, in case someone I knew happened to drive by.

The subdivision had no sidewalk. Front lawns shaded into the ragged asphalt of the narrow street. The ground was muddy from recent rain, so I walked in the road and kept an eye out for traffic. There was none. The homeowners' association apparently allowed chain-link fences. Most of the houses in the neighborhood had them. I didn't like the idea of living in a house with a chain-link fence.

Not that anyone had asked me to. After all, Donnie and I were only having lunch. My mother would never have approved of my accepting a date on such casual terms, or such short notice. She would take a dim view of my visiting a man's house unchaperoned, in any case. I reflected that my mother was thousands of miles away and didn't need to know everything.

As I approached Donnie's house I saw that the backyard was bounded by a chain-link fence. Keep an open mind, I told myself, noting that the front yard was a lovely manicured arrangement of green ground cover around black lava rock formations. I recognized Donnie's spotless charcoal gray Lexus in the carport. A blue and white Kamehameha Schools window decal provided the only dash of color. The space next to Donnie's car was thankfully empty. No sign of his son Davison's gigantic black pickup truck with the boar-hunting sticker on the back window.

The sound of a metallic crash froze me in midstep. I flashed back to the sound of the dropped tray in the campus cafeteria. Snarling shapes hurled themselves against the fence, bulging it outward with each body blow. They gnashed at the rattling metal mesh, but the chain-link fence stood firm against their fury. It seemed like forever, but it was probably only a few seconds before Donnie came out to order the dogs back to whatever smoking hellhole had disgorged them.

This wasn't exactly how I'd envisioned our lunch date starting off.

Donnie closed the front door behind us softly, as if he were trying to avoid jangling me any further. Thoughtful.

"Sorry about that," he said. "Those are Davison's hunting dogs. They're wary of strangers."

"Just doing their job, I guess." I tried to sound humorous and breezy, and hoped Donnie didn't notice the quaver in my voice. I slipped off my shoes and padded into the living room still wearing my expensive opaque hose. I knew I was supposed to remove my shoes before entering someone's house, but what about stockings? I couldn't exactly wiggle out of my Wolfords and leave them in a crumpled wad by the front door. I hoped I wouldn't get a run.

The living room was so clean that I felt like I was viewing it in high definition, and so beautifully arranged that I wondered if it had been staged by a professional designer. Framed posters hung on the pale yellow walls: Commedia Del'Arte, Django Reinhardt Paris Swing, a past season of the Honolulu Symphony. A low-slung sofa in gunmetal leather with black seat cushions sat on a squat frame of chrome tubing.

"This is lovely," I exclaimed. "I like the sofa. It has that midcentury Memphis thing going on."

Why did I say that? I had to name-drop furniture designers now? What was I trying to do, show off my big-city sophistication? I felt like a jerk. Why couldn't I just say, "nice couch"?

"Good eye," he said. "It is an Ettore Sottsass. Nineteen eighty-six, though. A little past midcentury."

He headed to the kitchen, comfortably barefoot. I took another look around the room. On a quarter-sawn oak side table stood a slender celadon bud vase holding a spray of red cymbidium orchids. It was hard to imagine Davison Gonsalves, with his tough-guy tattoos and pirate earrings, in this setting.

I followed Donnie into the kitchen and perched at the counter, watching him pour and stir.

"Does Davison live here with you?" I asked.

"M-hm. His room is right down the hall. I hope you like risotto."

If I lived someplace this nice, I would keep Davison locked outside with the Rottweilers.

"Just you two?" I asked.

"M-hm."

I waited for him to say something more, but he didn't.

"Well, sounds great!" I said. "The risotto, I mean."

I actually didn't care for risotto. Every time I'd tried it, I thought it tasted chewy and undercooked. I glanced around the kitchen. The copper pans hanging from the ceiling had the rainbow patina that comes from repeated heating. The stainless steel range was gas, which meant that Donnie had gone to the trouble of installing his own propane tank somewhere on the property. On this volcanic island, there are no gas lines. This was a functional kitchen, not a decorative one.

"I'm just sitting here," I said. "Can I help?"

It smelled like someone had forgotten to take out the garbage.

"No, just relax," Donnie said.

In front of me there was a glass bottle of what looked like olive oil. Tartufo nero. Product of Italy. Black truffle (infused) oil. I unscrewed the top and sniffed, and realized where the smell was coming from. I quickly put the cap back on and screwed it tight.

"Actually, Molly," he said, "could you get the salad ready? It's over there by the sink."

I slipped off the stool and went to the sink, glad to have something to do. I popped the top off the plastic shell that held two small heads of delicate hydroponic lettuce and turned on the water.

"You don't need to rinse those off," Donnie said over his shoulder. "They're already washed."

"I always wash 'prewashed' lettuce. Someone had to touch it to get it into the container, right?" I rinsed both heads thoroughly, and then started tearing little pieces into the salad spinner.

"You probably don't want to know what goes on in the average restaurant kitchen," he said.

"I'm *sure* your kitchens are spotless."

"They are." He smiled. "I said the *average* restaurant kitchen."

"Where did you get the truffle oil?" I asked.

"I bought it the last time I was in Honolulu. They didn't have the hundred-milliliter bottle, so I bought the two hundred milliliter. I had to check my bag to bring it back. I hope it was worth the humbug."

"When were you in Honolulu?" I asked.

"Right before the breakfast. When you sat next to me. Remember?"

"I sat next to Mercedes Yamashiro," I said. "*You* happened to be there too."

"Well, I'm glad I was. I came right over from the airport, so the oil was sitting in my car out in the parking lot the whole time. You're supposed to keep it away from heat and light."

"It seems to have retained its potency," I said.

By the time the risotto was ready I was hungry enough to tear into the chunk of Parmesan sitting next to the stove. Donnie ladled the risotto onto two large white porcelain plates and carried them out to the small round dining table. Two places were set with white cloth napkins, precisely folded. I followed him with the salad bowl. He pulled out one chair for me, and then seated himself and poured some Sangiovese into my glass. I took a bite of the risotto.

"Donnie, this is incredible!"

I wasn't even saying that to be nice. It was delicious.

He smiled. "Glad it's acceptable."

"Have you ever thought about extending your brand?" I asked. "I mean, you know, opening a more formal restaurant and serving food like this?"

"I looked into it. But our research showed that that's not what the local market wants. No 'foodie' restaurant has ever survived here."

"What about Sprezzatura?" I asked. "I really liked their food."

"Sprezzatura went out of business after eight months."

"They didn't even last a year? I never realized that."

"People here like their food a certain way," Donnie said. "Lunch means mac salad, two big scoops of rice, and a thirty-two-ounce soft drink."

"Too bad. It would be nice to have some variety."

"Not if no one's going to buy it. You know what they say, Molly. The customer is always right."

"Yeah," I said. "I've heard."

CHAPTER TWENTY-THREE

"So what's Donnie's house like?" Emma asked. "Does he have an air-conditioned dog house and solid-gold toilets and stuff?"

I had come back to my office right after lunch. I could have worked from home for the rest of the afternoon, but it's always good to put in face time. Plus, I'm not entirely comfortable having Emma and Pat in my office when I'm not there, and they always seem to turn up whether I'm there or not.

"No solid-gold anything," I said. "There are dogs, though."

"Are they cute? I really want to get a dog."

"The dogs are *not* cute," I said. "They're the opposite of cute. Donnie's house is nice, though." I said. "He has good taste."

"Ha, of course you'd say that," Emma said.

"No, really. Plus, he really knows how to cook. I tried truffle oil for the first time."

"So?" Emma leaned forward expectantly. "Are you two a thing now? Is he worth missing office hours for?"

"Well, he's very different from Stephen—wait, did you say missing office hours?" I glanced at my watch. A bad word slipped out before I could stop it.

"Sister Ignatius would rap your knuckles for that," Pat said.

"Isn't Sister Ignatius a fictional character?" I asked.

"I had a real Sister Ignatius in sixth grade. That was her name. And boy did she have an itchy ruler finger."

"I can't believe I missed office hours. Were you guys here?

No students came by to see me, did they?"

"Someone knocked," Emma said. "Your door was closed, so we just waited for them to go away."

"Don't worry," Pat added. "We won't rat you out to your dean."

"Thank you." I got up and propped the door open. "Geez. What's wrong with me? I can't believe I lost track of the time. Maybe whoever it was will come back."

"So looks like things are moving pretty fast with you and Donnie," Emma said. "Bradda ono for you, girl."

"You think?"

"Yeah, even I can see it," Pat said. "He's probably an Italophile."

"Oh yeah, Molly! He thinks you're a . . . wait, not a hot tamale."

"A spicy calzone," Pat said.

"Really?" Emma asked.

"Emma, don't listen to him. No one calls anyone a 'spicy calzone.' Anyway, I'm not—"

"I know, I know," Emma said. "You don't have to keep reminding everyone. You're Armenian."

"Albanian."

"That's what I said."

A knock on the door frame interrupted our conversation. Davison Gonsalves loomed in my doorway, wearing a deep v-necked shirt covered with a garish snake design. I didn't feel up to dealing with him right now. *Dude, I had lunch at your house today! I was like this close to your bedroom!* Gah, no.

"Oh, Davison, listen." I braced my hands on my desk and tried not to wobble on my yoga ball. "I'm in a meeting right now, but—"

"It's okay," Emma interrupted, "we were just leaving." And just like that, Pat and Emma pushed through the door and then they were gone, with me staring helplessly after them.

"Come in," I sighed.

Davison had come to ask me for an extension on an assignment he'd missed. His timing couldn't have been worse. Or better, if you looked at it from his point of view.

"Davison," I said, "I can't grant an extension unless there's a real—"

A disembodied voice interrupted me.

"I exude confidence, sex, power and self-esteem," said the voice.

Rodge had to do that *now*?

Davison glanced around and then looked at his lap. Even he seemed embarrassed, something I hadn't thought possible.

"Dr. Cowper is, uh, anyway," I stammered. "What was I saying now? Right, I don't accept late work unless there's a genuine emergency."

"Attractive women are drawn to me," declared the voice.

"Okay if I close the door?" Davison asked.

"I'm sorry," I said. "We have a department rule about keeping the door open when we're in conference with a student."

Davison folded his hands on my desk and leaned toward me.

"Okay, Professor," he said. "Gonna be honest."

"Okay," I replied, wondering if he was going to confess the real reason he was wearing all that stinky cologne.

"Here it is. Had one fight with Isaiah, now he won't talk to me."

"I'm sorry to hear that," I said, "but I'm not sure that this rises to the level of—"

"He was mad at me 'cause I got 'im into trouble," Davison said.

"I have my pick of hot babes," said the recorded voice, and at that moment I realized to my horror that we were hearing Rodge's actual voice. These were not prepackaged motivation tapes. Rodge had recorded himself speaking.

"I take full responsibility for my situation," Davison said. When a student says this to me, it usually means "I take no responsibility for my situation and I now expect you to fix it."

"Taking responsibility is good," I said. What was I supposed to do about Rodge's obnoxious recordings? Get up, go next door, and tell Rodge to turn it down? Emma could do something like that. But Emma's much braver than me, plus I think she'd actually enjoy humiliating Rodge.

"Isaiah's not talking to me no more," Davison said.

"What? Oh. Isaiah. I'm very sorry to hear that. Interpersonal conflict can be very stressful."

"It's hard for me, Professor, 'cause I cannot talk to Dad about it. And I tried come for your office hours, knocked on the door and everything, but no answer."

He had me there.

"I think your friends was here, but—" I met his gaze, keeping my face as still and expressionless as I could. I suppressed my urge to bounce on my yoga ball, something I do when I'm nervous. Pat claims it makes him seasick when I start oscillating.

"My previous appointment ran late," I said.

"Usually I can talk to Dad about everything, no problem. My dad and me, we always been real close, 'cause it's just us two, yeah? But lately he's kinda, I dunno. Kinda too busy for me. Got other things on his mind."

I nodded to show polite interest.

"I think he get one new girlfriend is why."

Davison lifted his baseball cap and ran his hand through his buzz-cut hair. " 'Cause a that, no time for me an my problems. My dad an Isaiah, the two a them is all I got, pretty much."

"I see."

"I am a self-assured, confident, sexual and dominant male,"

added Rodge's voice.

Davison's expression was flat. Neither of us broke eye contact.

"So what, exactly, are you requesting?" I asked.

"I am able to pick up and attract any woman I desire."

Oh, for crying out loud. That, I knew, was demonstrably false. Just ask Emma.

"I'm requesting an additional two weeks to make up my assignment, Professor."

"Two *weeks*? That's a long—"

"I tried calling Dad at his lunch break time today, after I saw you wasn't in your office, yah? But his phone went to voice mail. He always picks up when I call."

"I see." My face felt hot. I hoped that I wasn't visibly blushing. Davison pressed his advantage.

"So could not get a-hold of you, 'cause you wasn't in office hours. And could not get a-hold of Dad neither."

"Yes. You explained that already, but thank you for clarifying."

"I'm glad you're so understanding, Professor. About my personal hardship. It means a lot to me."

Davison and I sat and looked at each other. After what seemed like a lengthy poker-face staring contest, but was probably only a few seconds, I let out a breath.

"Personal hardship," I said. "Fine. I guess that's a good enough reason to let you make up the work."

It wasn't, of course, but I didn't have any choice. Davison didn't even need to resort to blackmail to get his extended deadline. All he had to do was complain to Bill Vogel, who would just get on my case again about "customer satisfaction" and "meeting the students where they are," and I'd have to give Davison whatever he wanted anyway.

"Professor?"

"What? Oh. Right. Here, let's work out a schedule for your

makeup assignment."

He snatched up the paper as soon as I had finished writing out the revised deadlines. Maybe he was afraid I'd change my mind.

"Eh, nice talking to you, Professor. Thanks for being so understanding. I gotta go see Dr. Rodge now."

"You might want to tell him to turn down the volume," I called after him.

Chapter Twenty-Four

A moment later, Margaret Adams knocked on the door frame.

"Hi, Dr. Barda," she said. "I'm so sorry to bother you."

"No bother at all," I said. "I always have time for my students."

Students like Margaret—by which I mean the good, conscientious ones—need to be reassured that they're not imposing. The not-so-good students—well, you've seen what they're like.

"So what are you going to do with Mr. Tanaka's suitcase?" she asked.

"I'm still trying to get the police to come pick it up. Oh! I mean—"

"It's okay, Professor. I already heard the bad news. Mercedes told us. They had a special meeting for the College of Commerce Community Council."

Mercedes has many sterling qualities, but stoic tight-lippedness isn't one of them.

"That must be so freaky having that in your office, after what happened," she said. "Have you opened it?"

"Me? Open it?"

I thought of Emma shoving me aside and unzipping the suitcase while I clapped my hands over my face and tried not to faint.

"No," I said. "*I* didn't open the suitcase. I think it's better to leave that kind of thing to the police, don't you? Anyway, you wanted to see me about something?" I gestured toward the good chair, inviting her to sit.

Margaret lowered herself carefully onto the chair. "I-I'm so sorry to bring this up. But I thought you should know."

"I appreciate that," I said. "Whatever it is."

She took a deep breath and pursed her lips. Thankfully, Rodge had paused his self-affirmations when Davison had knocked on his door. The bass murmurs of their conversation came through my wall, but I couldn't hear the individual words.

"There are rumors going around," Margaret said. "I want you to know that I don't believe them."

"Rumors?" I asked. "What rumors?"

Margaret tucked her mousy hair behind her ear. Her hair must be naturally straight, I thought. There's no flatiron on earth that stands a chance against this humidity. I should know. When I first moved here I tried them all, and the result was always the same: within minutes, my hair would curl up and frizz out. It looked like I hadn't done anything to it at all. I finally gave up, weary of feeling like the Sisyphus of hairdos.

". . . so that's why some people say that you're playing favorites," Margaret concluded.

"I'm sorry," I said, "Could you just summarize that for me? I'm not sure I understand."

She sighed, as though the discussion were causing her pain.

"People are saying that *certain students* are getting preferential treatment. Not to name any names, but he just left your office and went over to Dr. Rodge's."

Margaret glared at the wall that separated Rodge Cowper's office from mine.

"Preferential treatment? Why would anyone say that?"

"Well, the rumor is that you let *some people* get away with cheating because you're, you know, *friends* with certain families."

Oh, great.

"What have you heard, specifically? Can you give me some

more detail?"

No, she couldn't. But she did express concern for my reputation, and skepticism about the rumors. At the same time, I could tell she thought there might be something behind the whispers, and wanted to find out more.

This was infuriating. If it had been up to me, Davison Gonsalves would have been unceremoniously booted out of the College of Commerce, along with his sad little friend Isaiah. It was only because of Bill Vogel's interference that this was even an issue.

"Margaret, we don't tolerate cheating in the College of Commerce." As I spoke the words I realized sadly that this was as much of a fiction as "people are our most important asset" or "we respect your privacy."

"In fact," I continued, "according to the Student Honor Code, if you are aware of academic dishonesty, it's *your* duty to report it. You know what you should do? You should bring these concerns straight to our dean, Bill Vogel."

"Really? The dean? Gosh, I don't know . . ."

"No, this is important," I said. "No one should be playing favorites. It would be a huge breach of trust and, without trust, we're nothing. I'm sure Bill Vogel doesn't want to be Dean of Nothing."

"Oh. I guess that makes sense, when you put it that way. Of course the dean would want to do the right thing, wouldn't he?"

"Oh, yes," I agreed. "Of *course* he would."

In some parallel universe that I would very much like to visit someday.

"Are you going down to class?" she asked.

"I have to finish making some copies. I'll be right down. I'll see you there."

I plodded though gray drizzle, feeling like I'd swallowed an anvil, and barely registering the fact that my stack of handouts was getting wet. A pinkish gecko skittered across the walkway in front of me, startling me. I blinked and looked around. I had been so deep in thought I had walked right past my classroom.

Intro to Business Management is a broad survey class that touches on every discipline in business. We cover a different topic every week, bouncing from financial ratios to theories of employee motivation to the basic accounting equation. The class reminds me of those five cities in one week package tours. If it's Tuesday, it must be market segmentation.

I rechecked my syllabus and confirmed that I had the correct lesson plan with me. I'd have to catch Honey Akiona after class and talk to her about her revised paper. At least that would be the pretext. I hoped I wasn't forgetting anything. I wasn't exactly thinking clearly after my conversation with Margaret Adams.

Did everyone know about Donnie and me? And what was there to know, anyway? A couple of lunch dates. But Donnie just happened to be the father of my most obnoxious and unrepentant cheater. And now the coconut wireless was humming with nasty rumors, and even one of my best students doubted me. I hoped Donnie was worth all this trouble. I realized I rather thought he was.

Chapter Twenty-Five

"How many of you drive?" I asked the class. Most hands went up.

"How many of you like paying for gas?"

A lone student in the back, who hadn't been paying attention, kept his hand raised, looked around, and quickly pulled it back down.

"Say I'm a car dealer," I said. "Gas costs a fortune. I'm stuck with all of these big trucks and SUVs in my inventory, and I want to move them out. What can I do?"

A young woman with dangling dream-catcher earrings raised her hand. "Explain the features of the product," she said.

"Okay," I said. "That's something you could do. Margaret?"

Margaret Adams put her hand down. "Audit your dealer network to optimize your distribution," she said.

"Yes, okay," I agreed. "You've been reading ahead. Great. What about this week's chapter? Marketing?"

Silence.

"Remember? How our buying behavior is driven by a need to preserve our sense of ourselves as competent, honorable, and so forth?"

Margaret Adams nodded confidently in the front row. I scanned the blank faces behind her.

"Okay," I said. "Let's look at it another way—"

Dream-Catcher Earrings raised her hand again. "Is this about our self of steam?"

"About your . . . sorry, what?"

"About having positive self of steam," she said.

"Ah. Well, let's see. As a marketer, one way to create a perceived need for your product is to make the customer think something is wrong and needs to be fixed, and that your product will fix it. You can do this by threatening the customer's self-image. Self-image, according to the reading, is what? What was the word they used?"

Margaret Adams looked around. No one else had a hand up, so she raised hers.

"Self-image is sacrosanct," she said.

"Exactly," I said. "Thank you, Margaret. Now let's talk about how you use this idea to sell cars."

I handed the stack of papers to Margaret, and she started to pass them out.

"For this study," I said, "the researchers had men and women take a personality test, and then randomly informed them that the test had revealed that they had a masculine or feminine personality. Now, the test didn't actually reveal anything. The researchers were just giving random feedback."

A young man in the back raised his hand and flipped a curtain of brown hair out of his eyes. "Isn't that lying?" he asked.

"Social science research usually requires some deception," I agreed. "If you tell people what you're looking for, they'll tell you the answers they think you want to hear. Anyway, the men who had had their masculinity threatened—the ones who were told that their tests had come back 'feminine'—what do you think happened?"

Margaret read from the handout without bothering to raise her hand this time: "According to the article, they expressed a greater desire to buy a sport utility vehicle, compared to the men whose masculinity was affirmed."

"What about the women?" Honey Akiona asked.

"Women weren't affected either way," I said. "Not in this study. So this isn't going to help me sell cars to women. But the men whose masculinity was threatened were willing to pay, on average, over seven thousand dollars more for the SUV."

Floppy Hair raised his hand again.

"So okay, sorry I keep bringing it up, but isn't it morally wrong to mess with people's self-image like that, just to sell cars?"

"Well, that is something you'll need to think about when you're out there in the workplace," I said. "Doing what's right versus keeping your job. Your boss might order you to do something that you think is morally wrong." I glanced at Davison Gonsalves. He was slouched in his chair, fists tucked behind his biceps.

"It's a hard thing to have to make that choice," I said. "I wouldn't wish it on anyone. Anyway. What was my point? I'm not telling you to use these techniques. I'm telling you how they work, so that you can recognize and understand them. So back to the question. I'm an auto dealer. How can I use this result to move my inventory?"

Honey Akiona raised her hand this time before she spoke. "You get one ad say, 'Eh, you! Girly man! You need one big shiny kine truck, and we get 'em! Come on down! Zero percent financing!' "

When the laughter died down I said, "That's actually right. This isn't the kind of purchase that's decided with logic. It goes beyond features and benefits. I'm sure everyone in that study knew that the wise and responsible thing would be to buy a vehicle that gets good gas mileage. But emotionally—"

Dream-Catcher Earrings raised her hand again.

"Dr. Barda," she asked, "what kind of car do *you* drive?"

"Well, I drive an older car—"

"Professor Barda gotta T-Bird." Davison unfolded his arms

and leaned forward, grinning. "A *fifty-nine.*"

"Um, that's correct," I said. "Davison, you're very observant."

"Three hundred horsepower V-8," Davison continued. "Cherry, that thing."

"Yes, thank you. Let's not get too far off topic. The point is that consumers are driven by the need to preserve and enhance their self-image. Now go ahead and turn to the next paper in the handout. Same principle, but the participants are from Taiwan, and the researchers are looking at consumption of energy drinks as a means of masculine self-completion."

As I was packing up to leave, I saw Honey Akiona take a pair of sunglasses out of her bag, ready to put them on when she stepped out of the classroom. The rain had cleared and the sun glared from the wet metal rooftops. The sunglasses were the black, bug-eyed kind that a lot of the girls were wearing. But that wasn't the only reason they looked familiar to me.

Chapter Twenty-Six

I intercepted Honey Akiona as she was about to exit the classroom.

"Eh, Miss," she said. "Good class."

"Thanks. Listen, I read your revised paper."

We moved to a corner of the room, out of the way of the stampede of exiting students.

"Looks good?" she said.

"Yes. It was very good. You covered the topic thoroughly, and I think you gave the reader a real insight into your own moral reasoning."

She folded her arms and looked down.

"I could understand why, for example, a student, or a group of students, would protest someone like Jimmy Tanaka being on campus."

She jerked her head up to look at me. "I don't know nothing about that."

"Listen," I said. "I'm sure that the demonstrators, whoever they were, intended to make their point without hurting anyone. The problem is that—" I stopped myself. Jimmy Tanaka's murder wasn't public knowledge yet. "The problem is that the . . . prop, the skull, might turn out to be important for another investigation."

"What other investigation?" she asked.

"Well, I don't know all the details," I said, "but it's very serious. And right now the police seem to believe that the skull came from Dr. Park's prop room."

"But it did! I mean," she added quickly, "where else could it of come from? Eh, how come you're asking me all this?"

"Well, I'm concerned about Stephen Park, of course."

"Oh yah, he's your ex!"

"Stephen—is a friend. And there's something else. Another skull, a plastic one, turned up in the rubbish can in *this classroom.* Do you know anything about that?"

Honey tossed her highlighted hair out of her face. "Nah. No worries, but. If someone was trying to scare you, they woulda hung it from the ceiling or something. If they put it in the rubbish, it's cause they was trying to get rid of it probably."

"You're in Stephen Park's class, right?" I asked. "Have you ever seen anything strange in the prop room?"

"Dunno about strange. It's all kapakahi, that's for sure. Thousands a dollars' worth of stuffs in there, all jumbled up. An' he never remembers to lock up. I told him he should have some kinda system, like a spreadsheet . . . eh Miss, you okay? Your face getting all pink."

"Fine," I said. "I'm fine. Yes, some kind of spreadsheet to keep track of the inventory would have been a marvelous idea. So, it sounds like it's common knowledge that the prop room doesn't get locked up?"

"Anyone looking for one human skull or any kine prop coulda just gone in whenever. Just guessing what coulda happened," she smiled. " 'Cause I don't know nothing about it."

"Of course you don't," I said. "But thanks for the useful . . . speculation."

She hoisted up her bag, a pricey designer number covered with a monogram pattern.

"Okay, Miss. Eh, I hear anything, I'll let you know."

So the demonstrators supposedly got their skull from Stephen's prop room. Unless they were guilty of more than a harmless prank, a possibility I didn't even want to consider. One thing I couldn't understand was how Jimmy Tanaka managed to go out to dinner with Bill Vogel on Thursday night, and then turn up as a bleached skull on Friday morning.

Margaret Adams had been waiting patiently by the classroom door. I invited her to walk back up to my office with me.

"That was so interesting, that study!" Margaret said. "Now I'm thinking about what everyone drives. I think Dr. Rodge has a motorcycle. What do you think that means?"

"I really couldn't say."

She clasped her white hands in an apologetic gesture. "Sorry to be bugging you so much, Professor Barda. I wanted to ask you about something else, but I was afraid you'd think it was kind of weird. I mean, I wasn't going to say anything about it, but then you started talking about SUVs in class, so it was like the universe wanted me to ask you."

We started up the concrete stairs to the second floor.

"You should always feel free to ask," I said. "Regardless of what the universe says."

"Do you believe in a spiritual world?" she asked.

"Sure. I'm Catholic."

"Oh, that's right. Barda must be Italian."

"No, not Italian. My ancestry is Albanian."

"One of my high school friends had a bunch of Albanian guinea pigs! I mean they started with two, you know. They thought they had two boys, but one was a girl. They just kept having babies. They were so cute, with that tufted fur."

"I've never heard of Albanian guinea pigs," I said. "There are *Abyssinian* guinea pigs. Is that what you're thinking of?"

"Wait. Oh, no, you're right. Oh, sorry, Dr. Barda! I didn't mean to compare you to a guinea pig."

"It's okay," I said. "What did you want to ask me about?"

"So that night? That Jimmy Tanaka checked in? Nate told me

something really weird. You remember Nate Parsons?"

"Sure. We saw him when we were down at the Cloudforest."

"Nate was working that night, cleaning up in the kitchen. He told me that around ten o'clock he heard a voice. Not Mercedes. A man's voice."

"Did the voice sound angry?" I asked. "Could there have been a fight?"

I imagined Bill Vogel engaged in hand-to-hand combat with Jimmy Tanaka. Vogel would have the size advantage, but Tanaka wouldn't be afraid to fight dirty. I pictured Vogel's slender fingers grasping Tanaka's throat as Tanaka snatched Vogel's gleaming pompadour and waved it aloft like a scalp. But why? What could they have been fighting about? And none of this explained how Jimmy Tanaka's head ended up in Stephen's prop room.

"Nate said it sounded like the voice was summoning Jimmy Tanaka," Margaret said. "He thought it was calling his name. Mr. Tanaka. *Mr. Tanaka.*"

Despite the sun glaring from the wet concrete and a temperature in the high eighties, I shivered. Would I hear that voice when it was my time and Death came to claim me? How would it summon me?

"Dr. Barda? Dr. Barda! Oh, sorry, did I startle you?"

"No! No, I was just thinking. So how can I help?" I asked.

"I just wanted to get your opinion. You usually have a rational explanation for everything."

She wanted a level-headed adult to reassure her.

"I don't know what to say about that," I said. "Maybe Nate should call the police?"

Down the hallway I saw Dan Watanabe, lurking outside my office door. I stopped walking.

"Nate doesn't want to call the police," Margaret said. "He thinks they won't believe him. Also, there's something else."

"Something else?"

Hanohano, Schmanohano. If you're looking for a haunted hotel, apparently the Cloudforest Bed and Breakfast is where it's at.

"This is the part with the SUV," Margaret said. "Nate says he remembers earlier that night, he saw an SUV. But after he heard that voice, he went to get a flashlight and then walked back to the cabins to take a look, and where it was parked before, there wasn't anything there. It had disappeared."

"Margaret, I'd say the same thing. If Nate is really sure that he saw something, then he should call the police and tell them. Anyway . . ." I gestured down the hall toward my department chair. Dan spotted me and started walking toward us.

"But what would cause all of that?" she asked. "The voice and the disappearing car and everything?"

"I don't know. But I'm sure there's some nonsupernatural explanation that makes sense. Listen, I have to go."

"Oh, I almost forgot," she said. "I went to talk to the dean, like you told me to."

"You what?"

"Right before class. Oh, hi, Dr. Watanabe! Anyway, thanks, Dr. Barda. See you guys later!"

And she left.

"Dan, you wanted to see me? I was just on my way back to my office. Uh-oh. This seems serious."

"Uh-oh is right," Dan said.

Chapter Twenty-Seven

I turned the key and pushed open my office door.

"So Dan, what is this about?" I asked. "Did you change your mind about me being the next department chair?"

"Oh, no. That hasn't changed."

"Do you want to come in?" I held the door open.

"No, that's okay. This will be short. Look. Bill doesn't want you sending your students to him."

"What do you mean?"

"A student of yours approached Bill Vogel earlier today, to file a complaint about cheating among her classmates."

"Ah," I said. Margaret Adams. I stepped back into the hallway and let my office door close.

"Look, Dan, Bill Vogel—"

I stopped talking as Vogel's secretary Serena walked by. The three of us nodded greeting. I continued when she was out of sight, around the corner.

"Bill Vogel told me not to report the cheaters," I continued. "Remember? He said if I did report them to the Office of Student Conduct, he wouldn't support me."

"True."

"Dan, they all talk. It's not like there are any secrets around here. The honest students don't like it when the cheaters get away with it."

"I know."

"So if I catch people plagiarizing, Vogel doesn't want to be bothered with that. He wants me to let the cheaters redo their assignments."

"Right," Dan said.

"But when I do what Vogel tells me to, and I let the plagiarists get away with it, then the honest students want to complain, but Vogel doesn't want to be bothered with that either."

Dan nodded. "I knew you'd understand. You're going to make a great department chair!"

He clapped me on the shoulder, turned, and went back down the hallway. I let myself into my office and yanked the door shut behind me. I pushed past the suitcase, balanced myself on the yoga ball, and turned on my computer. I set up a cup of coffee and logged into *Island Confidential.*

What I saw didn't help me calm down. Far from it. I grabbed the receiver and furiously punched in Pat's phone number.

"Flanagan."

"Pat, tell me this is a joke."

"Oh, hi, Molly. No, it's true. The *County Courier* finally ran the story about Jimmy Tanaka's murder, so no more embargo. I was able to—"

"Embargo? Oh, yeah. No, that's not what I'm calling about."

"It isn't?"

"No," I said. "And I think you know what this *is* about."

"What do you mean? Oh, yeah." He laughed. "Yeah, I thought you'd like that."

I was bouncing on my ball, but it wasn't sufficient to dissipate my nervous energy. I looked around for something to doodle on. The latest copy of the Student Retention Office 'zine sat atop my stack of unread mail. It's not really a 'zine. It's actually a glossy, four-color magazine, with the letters SRO on the cover in a ransom note font, Sex Pistols style. It would do. It's not like I was planning to read it.

"Pat," I said, "I'm looking at the *Island Confidential* website.

It says a 'source' in the College of Commerce advised the guardian spirit of Mauna Kea to *incorporate*." I paused. "A source. Like no one could possibly guess who that might be."

"The judge initially ruled that Mo'oinanea lacks standing because she's not a person as defined by law," Pat said. "Your solution was ingenious. Corporate personhood."

I pulled a pen out of my desk drawer and paged through the 'zine. I stopped at a full-page photo of Bill Vogel. It was from a few years ago, but his insincere smile and dead, soulless eyes were the same.

"That was not *my* solution!" I took a ballpoint pen and outlined two small, curved horns on Vogel's head.

"Molly," Pat said, "I heard you say it! Your exact words were—"

"That was supposed to be a *joke*! Pat, someone's going to figure out that *I* was the one who said it! Have you thought about that?"

"Well, some people were kind of offended at the idea. I guess it could seem a little flippant."

I examined Vogel's photo and decided that the light was coming from the upper right. I started shading in the horns accordingly.

"Some people were offended? Great. Which people? People who are going to be voting on my tenure application?"

I drew flames rising behind Vogel, which added another light source. I sketched in some shadow in the front of the horns and on Vogel's face, to make it look more realistic.

"Oh, come on, Molly. You should be proud. It was a stroke of genius."

"Yeah? I'm having a stroke right now. Oh, hey Emma. Pat, Emma's here. I'm done yelling at you now." I slammed the receiver down without saying goodbye.

Emma sat down in the upholstered chair

"Did you see *Island Confidential*?" she asked. "Hey, nice picture of Bill Vogel!"

"Oh, I better not leave this lying around," I closed the magazine, rolled it up, and stuffed it into my laptop bag. "Want some coffee?"

"Well, if you're offering." She pulled a mug out of her backpack and handed it to me. "Are you the one who said that thing about the guardian spirit?"

"What? Why would you think *I* said it?"

"It sounds exactly like something you'd say. Anyone who knows you would guess right away. Is that why you were yelling at Pat just now?"

"Why doesn't Pat write about some real news? Like Rodge Cowper handing out printouts from Wikipedia in class and trying to pass it off to students as his original work."

"Why would Rodge need to use Wikipedia when he possesses all of the knowledge in the universe?" Emma asked.

"All the knowledge in the universe. Why does that sound so familiar?"

"Oh, that's called Baader-Meinhof syndrome," Emma said. "That's when—"

"I know what Baader-Meinhof syndrome is," I said. "What I meant was, why does that all the knowledge in the universe thing sound familiar?"

"It's from those pickup-artist recordings Rodge plays for himself in his office. What do they call them, self-aggrandizing?"

"I think it's called self-affirmation, not self-aggrandizing."

"Nope. Self-aggrandizing is the right word. Believe me, I've heard them enough times. Hey, I have an idea! Let's pin it on Rodge!"

"Let's do what?"

"Let's make people think *he's* the one who had the idea about Mo'oinanea incorporating."

"Shh! You can hear everything through this wall!"

"Oh, right," she whispered, glancing at the wall that separated my office from Rodge's. "Do you think he's in his office?"

"I don't know," I whispered back. "Rodge isn't my favorite person, believe me, but that's going a little far. You don't want to cause an incident."

"Yeah, I guess I'd feel kinda bad if someone blew up his car or something," she said.

"Motorcycle," I said.

"What?"

"Rodge has a motorcycle. Not a car." I filled Emma's mug with coffee and handed it back to her.

"Whoa, wait! That tiny little beat-up thing that always parks across two spaces?"

I nodded.

"I shoulda known that was him. You get some cream?"

Emma wasn't looking at me. She was focused on the wall that separated Rodge Cowper's office from mine, eyes narrowed, as if she were aiming a gun at a distant target.

"Here you go," I said. I set the carton of cream down in front of her. "Emma. Please don't do anything I'll regret."

Chapter Twenty-Eight

I was already halfway home when I remembered that I had nothing to eat at my house. Going out of my way to buy groceries, bring them home and cook them would take much too long. Donnie's Drive-Inn, however, was almost right on my way. I figured I could stop there for dinner without looking like I was stalking Donnie. He might not even be there.

I parked in the small lot, walked up to the window, and ordered a loco moco to go. A mountain of sticky white rice topped with a hamburger patty, a fried egg, and lots of brown gravy sounded just right. As I thought about it, my stomach made a joyful sound that was halfway between a *zip* and a *boing*. I hoped the young woman who took my order couldn't hear it.

A smiling Donnie appeared at the takeout window and handed me the white paper bag. I'm not sure why seeing him took me by surprise, but it did. I couldn't think of anything to say, so I blurted out that I lived a couple of blocks up the street and why didn't he stop by for a cup of coffee when he was done here? To my surprise, he agreed. I grabbed a handful of napkins to protect my upholstery from the gravy-stained bag and hurried home.

As soon as I had finished the loco moco, I cranked open all my windows and turned my ceiling fans up to maximum. I wanted to blow out any lingering Gudang Garam smoke that Stephen might have trailed in with him the last time he came over. Donnie's first visit to my house didn't need to be marred by the smell of clove cigarettes. I swept the floor at double speed, emptied the trash cans, and then searched the refrigerator for something I could set out as a snack. I found a carton of heavy whipping cream, a jar of olives, and a ragged tangle that I recognized as the vegetables I had bought from the Farmers' Market. My freezer contained only vodka and pantyhose. (The cold is supposed to make the pantyhose last longer. I don't know if that's true, but I can tell you that putting on a new pair is a bracing experience.)

I was about to check the pantry when I spotted a large cockroach sitting next to the kitchen sink. I retrieved my hand vac from its charging station, crept up slowly, and then with one swift action I sucked the cockroach in with a decisive "thwack." After I'd shaken the angry insect into the toilet and flushed six or seven times, I got out the rubbing alcohol and wiped down every surface in the kitchen. My kitchen smelled like an infirmary, but at least it was clean.

I was still washing my hands when I heard a knock on the door.

"I thought it might be a little late for coffee," Donnie said. "So I took the liberty of bringing some wine." He strode in, gave me a strong one-arm hug and cheek kiss, and headed into the kitchen. "Do you have a corkscrew?" He sniffed the air.

"Everything okay?" I asked.

"Fine. It smells really . . . clean in here. Do you have wineglasses?"

"Wineglasses. Not exactly. I've been using furikake jars. It's sustainable. Reduce, reuse, recycle, right?"

I retrieved two of the small cylindrical glasses and set them on the counter.

"By the way," I said, "the loco moco was really good. Thanks."

The rice had been pebbly, and the meat patty was full of gristly bits, but Donnie hadn't let me pay for it. I watched

Donnie take the corkscrew down from the wall hook and open the wine.

"You seem to know your way around," I said.

He smiled as he glanced around at the compact space. "I grew up in a house a lot like this. Listen, Molly, I want to thank you for what you did for Davison."

"What I did?"

"You helped him out with his deadlines. He told me you were very understanding."

"Is that what he told you?"

"I can see why you're one of his favorite teachers."

"Oh, it's nothing. There's really no need to mention it."

Donnie poured wine into the two small glasses, filling them to the top.

"It feels comfortable here," he said. "I like it. You have good taste." Donnie brought the glasses over to the couch, sat down, and moved to make space for me right next to him.

"I suppose I do have good taste," I smiled as I sat down.

We clicked glasses and sipped.

"So," I said.

Now what? The last time Donnie and I were together, we were occupied with preparing lunch, and we talked about food. If Emma and Pat were here, there would be no lack of conversation. We could discuss Emma's solvent-sniffing lab tech, my corrupt dean, Pat's survivalist neighbors, or even Jimmy Tanaka's murder. That's the problem with the still-trying-to-impress-someone stage of a relationship. Negative topics are off the table, which leaves you very little to talk about.

"So," I repeated, "what's new at the Drive-Inn?"

That worked better than I'd expected. We were deep into a discussion about the breakdown rate of frying oil when my cell phone began to buzz on my desk. The metal surface resonated like a drum, but I ignored it. I didn't want to be one of those people who interrupts a conversation to answer the phone. The humming paused, and then started up again. A moment later, someone started banging on the door. A series of odd clicking sounds followed, and then the door swung open. Emma and Pat crowded in.

"Molly!" Emma shouted, "where—oh! You have company!"

Emma came over and grabbed Donnie's wine bottle from the coffee table. Pat followed her into the kitchen.

"Why don't you come in?" I said. I got up and closed the door behind them.

"You weren't answering your phone," Emma called back over her shoulder. "Did you forget we were coming over?"

"No, of course not. Kind of. Yes."

Pat returned to the couch holding a cup of coffee. He gripped Donnie's hand briefly and then plopped down on the couch between Donnie and me.

"I have it," he announced. "The smoking gun."

"What's the smoking gun?" I asked.

He put his cup down on my coffee table. I picked it up and slid a coaster under it.

"The permits on record for the rebuild of the Hanohano are completely fabricated," Pat said. "They're in the county files, but they don't have the stamps."

Emma came over holding my treasured Chicken Boy coffee cup.

"Emma, you don't have to use that. I have glasses for wine."

"No you don't. You have furikake jars. They're way too small."

"That's a sixteen-ounce mug," I said.

"Yeah, so?"

Emma squeezed onto the couch between Pat and me, so that Donnie and I were on opposite sides.

"Fine," I said. "Use the mug. Hey, how did you get my door unlocked?"

"I think it was already unlocked," Emma said.

"I'm *sure* my door was not unlocked. I always lock my door."

Emma looked over at Pat. Pat pretended he didn't notice her. "It's more than just the sketchy permits," he continued. "There's bribery, and nepotism, and even negligent homicide."

"Is anyone else covering this story?" I asked. "It seems kind of important."

"No. The Honolulu paper isn't interested in some old news from the outer islands."

"What about the *County Courier*?" Donnie asked.

Pat winced at the mention of his former employer. "They don't really have investigative reporters anymore. They're down to one or two guys cutting and pasting the AP news feed in between the car dealer ads. Not to blow my own horn or anything, but *Island Confidential* is pretty much it for real news reporting on this island anymore."

"Not to blow your own horn or anything," Emma said. "Hey, guess what though. Pat thinks Nehemiah Silva might of killed Jimmy Tanaka."

"That's brilliant, Pat," I said. "Who is Nehemiah Silva?"

"That's the police officer I told you guys about," Emma said. "The one who went looking for Jimmy Tanaka when his wife reported him missing, and then found him, and then lost his job, remember? It's the same guy."

"Emma," Pat said, "You're not supposed to—"

"Did you know that story about Nehemiah Silva and Jimmy Tanaka?" Emma asked Donnie.

"I believe I did hear something about it."

"Silva still had friends in county administration, though," Emma said. "That's how he ended up working at the county building. Um."

And then, dispelling any possible doubt over the identity of Pat's confidential source, she added, "Oops. Sorry, Pat."

Pat sighed deeply.

"Could Silva get in trouble for giving you that information?" I asked Pat.

"He didn't give me anything," Pat said. "He just told me what to look for. I could find it myself from those links your student gave you."

"Your student?" Donnie leaned forward to make eye contact with me. "Molly, *your* students are involved in this?"

"Oh, no," I said, "nothing like that. One of my students did a paper on stages of moral development, and her bibliography had a link to this website full of government documents, that's all."

"So that's one possible motive for Tanaka's murder," Emma said. "Payback for ruining Silva's career. Although it still doesn't explain why it would happen now."

"Opportunity, maybe?" said Pat. "Tanaka doesn't come to this island that much anymore."

"All of that was years ago, though," I said.

Pat shrugged, "Never underestimate the power of a grudge."

"So why would Tanaka try to bypass the permitting?" Emma asked. "Why take that kind of risk? I mean, he was already really well connected. I'm sure he could get things done more or less by the book if he wanted to."

"He had to speed it up," Pat said. "A few days' delay, and the Hanohano would've gone on the Registry of Historic Places. Once the building was registered, Tanaka wouldn't be able to do anything with the property.

Emma drained her mug of wine.

"Silva was too cooperative," she said. "I don't think he was the killer. I think it was Isaiah Pung."

"Isaiah Pung!" Donnie exclaimed.

"Sure," she said. "Both his parents lost their jobs when Jimmy Tanaka bought the Hanohano, and then his father was killed during the rebuilding. Isaiah Pung has a pretty good motive."

"No," Donnie said. "I've known Isaiah since he was a kid. You're right. He's gone through some real hard times. But he's not a murderer."

"Isaiah is a good friend of Donnie's son, Davison," I said, directing a warning glare at Emma. "Anyway, I agree with Donnie."

"Of course you do," Pat snorted.

"No, really. Isaiah is my student. I've spoken with him. I can't picture it."

I couldn't imagine the diffident Isaiah masterminding a cold-blooded revenge killing. Or masterminding much of anything, really.

We spent the rest of the evening discussing murder and corruption and local politics. Eventually Pat stood up and said something about his long drive home, and we all looked at our watches and our little party drew to a close.

Donnie was last out the door. "This was fun," he said "Next time, let's have a proper dinner at my place. How does that sound?"

"Sounds great!" I said.

"I really should get going though. It's late. Davison's probably home by now, and he's going to wonder where I am."

"Of course," I said. Let's not forget about Davison.

Chapter Twenty-Nine

The next morning saw Emma, Pat and me sharing an unusually low-key coffee break in my office. I had the blinds closed to keep the sun out. The only sounds were the hum of the desk fan and the quiet coffee-slurping of three slightly hungover college professors.

I had barely finished my second cup when Dan Watanabe knocked on my door frame, and then stuck his head into my office. We all mumbled, "Hey, Dan." He nodded in response and came in. He sucked his lips in as if he had bad news that he was unwilling to give.

"Molly," he said. "It was—that fan's kind of loud, isn't it?"

I reached over and turned the dial to the lowest setting. Immediately the humid air closed around me and beads of sweat popped out on my upper lip. Emma snatched a magazine from my bookshelf and fanned herself with it.

Dan cleared his throat. "Molly, it was decided that you should host the academic year's first College of Commerce Community Council get-together this Saturday."

"It was decided? In the passive voice?"

"Well, we"—Dan peered at Emma's makeshift fan—"*Search and Destroy*?" Emma stopped, looked at the cover, rolled her eyes, and resumed fanning.

"Oh, yeah." I shrugged. "That's one of the old punk 'zines I used for my dissertation. Anyway, Saturday is the day after tomorrow. I'm guessing I wasn't the first-choice hostess?"

"It is a little last minute," he said, "but it shouldn't be too much work. It's potluck. Friendly and casual."

"Wow Dan, that's . . . that's quite an honor. I've never even been invited to the CCCC. I don't even know who all the members are. I mean, I know Mercedes and Donnie."

"Make sure to have plates, cups, utensils, and drinks. Don't worry about invitations. Everything's set. People will start arriving at three."

As soon as Dan left, I turned the fan back to the highest setting.

"Can I see that *Search and Destroy*?" Pat asked.

Emma handed the 'zine to Pat.

"You can borrow it if you want," I said. "You guys are coming on Saturday, by the way."

"We're not invited," said Emma.

"Of course you're invited. It's my house."

"This means you're still on the administrative fast track, doesn't it?" Pat said.

"I don't know," I said. "Maybe. I hope not."

"Meaning your dean is probably still under suspicion for Jimmy Tanaka's murder, right?" he said.

"Yeah, speaking of suspicion. I didn't really want to bring this up in front of Donnie." I summarized Margaret Adams's strange story about Nate Parsons.

"I wonder how Vogel fits in to what Nate Parsons heard," Pat said. "That would be around the time that Vogel and Tanaka would have come back from dinner."

"I tried to imagine how the voice could've been Bill Vogel's," I said. "I couldn't really come up with anything plausible."

"What do the police think?" Emma asked.

"Not much progress after they ID'd the skull," Pat said. "I think they'd really like to find the rest of Jimmy Tanaka. You should know, Molly, it doesn't look good for Stephen Park that he left town."

"I'm sure he had a good reason," I said, feeling a little defensive.

"Why would the dean of the College of Commerce want to kill Jimmy Tanaka?" Emma asked. "That doesn't make any sense at all. Tanaka just gave you guys a bunch of money."

"Maybe Tanaka was thinking of backing out?" I said. "Still, that doesn't seem like a motive for murder. Unless Vogel is a complete psycho. Which, believe me, I wouldn't necessarily rule out."

"It's too bad Emma had to blab to your friend about Isaiah Pung," Pat said.

"Oh, shut up," Emma snapped. "I didn't say anything I wasn't supposed to."

"You brought up the idea of Isaiah as a suspect," Pat said. "Now Donnie can warn him."

"Warn him about what?" I asked.

"The police want to talk to him," Pat said.

"So why don't they?" Emma asked.

"They can't find him."

"Come to think of it," I said, "I haven't seen him in class recently."

"He must not make much of an impression," Pat said, "if you're just realizing that now."

"He's kind of quiet," I agreed.

Pat leafed through the *Search and Destroy.* "Bringing the head onto campus to make some kind of statement is consistent with a revenge motive. Look at this. Patti Smith, the Ramones, this is probably worth something."

"I do want it back at some point," I said. "Don't go selling it on eBay."

"Wait a minute," Emma interrupted. "Was it Jimmy Tanaka's head, or his skull? Pat just said 'head.' Which one is it?"

"It was a skull," I said. "I saw it. In fact, I thought it was fake. Ew, a head? That would've been horrible."

"A skull's not horrible enough for you?" Pat said, without looking up from the photocopied pages. "I wonder whatever happened to the Weirdoes."

"Something's wrong with the timeline, though," Emma said. "Jimmy Tanaka goes out to dinner with your dean. The very next morning his skull shows up at breakfast, all polished and clean. How does that happen so fast?"

"I was wondering the same thing," I said. "What if there's an impostor Jimmy Tanaka, and the real Jimmy Tanaka was murdered like a year ago? And the head of the real Jimmy Tanaka has been festering in Stephen's prop room unnoticed, which believe me, could totally happen. Oh! And the whole thing was orchestrated by Bill Vogel so he could get impostor Jimmy Tanaka to give us a big donation out of the real Jimmy Tanaka's money."

"So where's fake Jimmy Tanaka now?" Pat asked.

"I don't know."

"I got it," Emma said. "Fake Jimmy Tanaka double-crossed Bill Vogel."

"I like that," I said.

"He played along until he realized he'd have to be at this breakfast with a bunch of people who had known the real Jimmy Tanaka for years. So he grabbed a bunch of the real Jimmy Tanaka's money and skipped town."

"How did he fool Mercedes, though?" Pat asked. "She saw him when he checked in to the Cloudforest, remember?"

"Maybe Mercedes doesn't know him that well," Emma said. "I still think Isaiah Pung has something to do with it. It's kinda coincidental that he disappeared when he did, isn't it?"

"Where would Isaiah go?" I asked. "We're on an island. He can't get on a plane without ID."

"Maybe one of those little commuter flights to Oahu," Pat said.

"Then he's stuck on Oahu," I said.

"There's a million people there," Emma said. "Easy to blend in and get lost."

"Maybe he snuck onto a cruise ship," Pat said.

"Sneaked," I said. "You know, Isaiah emailed me."

"Recently?" Pat asked.

"No. When we were at Stephen's dress rehearsal. I saw his email when I got home. I had just met with him and told him to revise his paper, but he wanted to meet with me again. Why would he be worried about his grade if he was planning to disappear?"

"Maybe he sent that to throw everyone off," Emma said. "He mighta been already gone by the time he emailed you."

"Time! I almost forgot!" I glanced at my watch. It was later than I'd thought. "I'm going to be late for Business Boosters if I don't leave right now."

I stood up to signal that it was time for all of us to leave, and picked up my bag.

"We'll be fine here," said Emma. "Pat and I will think of ideas for your party."

"Have fun kowtowing to the plutocrats," Pat said.

"Pat, Business Boosters is hardly some cabal of robber barons. They're insurance agents and pet store owners."

He held up the copy of *Search and Destroy* and cast a meaningful look at me.

"You're seriously going to Business Boosters," he said.

"Yeah, I know. So much for my street cred. Well, we all have to grow up sometime."

And before he could return fire, I slipped out the door.

Chapter Thirty

The Lehua Inn, one of the Hanohano's competitor establishments on Hotel Drive, used to boast magnificent mountain and ocean views. Now the floor-to-ceiling dining room window overlooks the service entrance of Jimmy Tanaka's New Hanohano Hotel. The mildew-streaked monolith blocks the ocean view and the sunlight, so that no matter what time of day it is, the Lehua's formerly cheery dining room sits in perpetual twilight. I spotted an unoccupied table in the rear and took a seat with my back to the window.

I generally occupy myself by catching up on my journal reading until the formal program begins. I like either *Administrative Science Quarterly* or *Academy* of *Management Review.* They're both great at scaring off small-talkers. Unfortunately, I had forgotten to bring either one with me today. All I had was the copy of *Island Business* that Pat had taken from Jimmy Tanaka's suitcase.

I turned to the cover story and skimmed over the slice-of-life opening paragraph. Next was a flashback to Tanaka's childhood, an anecdote illustrating Tanaka's incipient entrepreneurial talent. After that came a description of his early career and a mention of the brief marriage that buckled under the stress of starting up a business. The writer was clearly doing his utmost to present Jimmy Tanaka as a sympathetic character.

The tables around me were filling up, which caused me a twinge of anxiety. There was a real possibility that someone was going to sit with me before the formal program started. I directed my gaze back to my magazine, to avoid eye contact with any potential tablemates.

You might wonder why I joined an organization like Business Boosters when interacting with strangers causes me so much stress. The simple answer is that I didn't really have a choice. Every faculty member in the College of Commerce is expected to join at least one local civic organization. I'd settled on Business Boosters because the meetings are highly regimented, leaving little time for unstructured socializing. First, we stand and sing the official Business Boosters anthem. Then, we eat lunch while we watch a presentation related to some project in the community. Finally, we stand again and recite the Business Boosters creed. Then we all go back to work. As these things go, it's relatively painless.

A waitress came by and filled my coffee mug. I thanked her and turned my attention back to the magazine, where I read this:

Jimmy and his former wife, Mercedes Yamashiro, remain good friends to this day. Mercedes is an entrepreneur in her own right. She runs the renowned Cloudforest Bed and Breakfast, where Jimmy is a frequent guest.

Someone sat down next to me. From the jangle of jewelry and perfume I knew it was Mercedes, even before I turned to look.

"Wow, hey. Mercedes!" I exclaimed. "Wow!"

That wasn't the best way to open a conversation, but in all fairness, she had startled me. Also, the blond hair was kind of a surprise.

"They had to process three times to get the brassiness out," she said, holding up three be-ringed fingers for emphasis. "I thought I wasn't going to make it here on time!"

"Mercedes, I'm so sorry. About Mr. Tanaka."

"Well. Poor Jimmy had a way of finding trouble. But let's count our blessings, Molly. He had a full life."

"Oh, that's putting it—I mean, I suppose you're right." I gestured to the open magazine on the table. "You're in *Island Business* magazine!" I said.

"Can you believe it, Molly? They interviewed me for two hours, and all I get is three sentences. Well, that's show biz!" She laughed.

"That's amazing that you stayed friends," I said. "It must be hard to do that. Stay friends with an ex."

"Oh, it's not that unusual. Like you and your Stephen, yah?"

"Stephen and I have sort of an arms-length relationship these days."

"I think Donnie is a better match for you anyway," she said. "If you don't mind my saying so. Anyway, it was easier after the divorce, to tell you the truth. Jimmy's bad habits were not my problem anymore. Also, better to have a friendly business contact than an unfriendly ex-husband. We all have to get along, you know. No point in having enemies."

"No point in having enemies," I repeated. "I guess that makes sense. Who needs enemies, right?"

Why did she say no point in *having* enemies instead of no point in *making* enemies? I wondered if the magazine interview had opened old wounds for her.

"Molly," she said, "I wanted to tell you, I'm so happy with my interns this year. Your college is doing a great job."

"That's nice to hear!" I was grateful for the change of topic. "Business is good?"

"Yes, you'd be surprised! It's not our usual high season, but we have a big group in this week from New Zealand. They're lovely people. Very interested in sustainability. They told me I should install composting toilets. I don't think all of my guests are quite ready for that, but it was nice to see that people are thinking about that kind of thing. Oh, and they love the little goats."

"You still have the goats? I didn't see them when we came down."

"I let them out once a week to mow the grass. Mostly I keep them away from the guests. After what happened to you. Remember? When you were staying with me?"

I certainly did remember. As I was making my way from the main building to my cabin, hands full of luggage, a little goat came skipping toward me. I thought it was adorable until he playfully head-butted me in the stomach. I went to my campus interview the next morning with bruised ribs.

"Oh, it was fine," I said. "I got the job, so no complaints."

"Well, you were very nice about it. Molly, that girl Margaret has been so good, helping me out with everything. Even the slaughter and butchering!"

"Slaughter? Margaret Adams?"

"The little goats. For the Cloudforest's famous goat stew. They don't cook themselves, Molly!"

"You do that on site?"

"Margaret really surprised me, you know. I was afraid she was going to be one of those fussy haole ladies. No offense, Molly, you know what I mean."

"Sure."

"But she turned out to be so good! Much better than Nate! That poor boy just turns green and has to go lie down."

By this time a few more people had joined Mercedes and me at our table, and it was time to stand up and sing. I tried to concentrate on the words to the Business Boosters anthem, but I was thinking about Mercedes's delicious goat stew. I couldn't shake the image of Jimmy Tanaka as a spry little satyr.

Chapter Thirty-One

I walked in to my office to find my phone ringing. It was Donnie.

"It was nice to see you last night," Donnie said. "I had a good time. I'm glad you stopped by the Drive-Inn."

"Me too. Sorry about Pat and Emma barging in. Hey, I'll see you this Saturday too, right? The CCCC meeting?"

"You'll get sick of me," he laughed.

"Impossible," I said. "In fact, didn't you say you're in Business Boosters? I didn't see you at the meeting today."

"I'm in the Tuesday group. Listen, you asked me about Jimmy Tanaka's will that other time at the Pair-O-Dice."

"I did?"

"I found out some things for you."

"Really! Well, don't keep me in suspense!" Emma was actually the one who had asked, but I was dying to hear what Donnie had to say. I looked in my bag for something to write on. I had misplaced my yellow pad, but I had a Student Retention Office publication in there, and it looked like it had a lot of white space. I wrote while Donnie spoke. My hand muscles cramped as I tried to get down the names of all the organizations that were about to benefit from Jimmy Tanaka's posthumous largesse.

"Animal shelter, art museum, cultural center . . . you think he was trying to buy himself some karma?" I asked.

"There's quite a bit more here." Donnie continued reading and I scribbled madly, trying to keep up. Then he read:

"Two hundred thousand dollars to Mercedes Yamashiro."

"Sorry, what was that? Did you say Mercedes?"

"He left two hundred thousand to Mercedes."

"Did you know that Mercedes used to be married to Jimmy Tanaka?"

"Sure."

"I just found that out. I read it in *Island Business*. Why doesn't anyone tell me anything?"

Donnie laughed. "I'm telling you things right now."

"So you are. How did you find all this out?"

"My attorney was doing some research, and he happened to come across this. I think you'll be interested in the next item."

Emma slipped in and sat down. "Hey, Moll—" She clapped her hand over her mouth when she saw I was on the phone, and then sat and fidgeted while I listened and wrote.

"You won't believe this," I said when I'd hung up. "Jimmy Tanaka left a pile of money to the College of Commerce."

"More than what he already donated?"

"Much more." I told her the amount.

"What? No way. What's the catch?"

"We'll be known as the . . ." I glanced at my notes. "The James Hisashi Tanaka College of Commerce."

"You'll have to spend some of that money to hire security," she said. "Anything with Jimmy Tanaka's name on it is gonna get vandalized. You know, it's ironic. Hisashi means 'long life.' Hey, there's your motive for Bill Vogel."

"What, his name? I don't understand."

"No, not his name, dummy. If Vogel knew about the will, maybe he wanted to get the money now instead of waiting for Tanaka to die on his own. He killed the golden goose!"

I opened my mouth to say something, but Emma steamrollered on.

"Look," she declared, "if your college gets thirty million dollars while Bill Vogel is in charge, think how good that would look for him! He'd be able to get a job anywhere!"

"Sure," I said, "as long as no one found out about the murder."

"Well it's not like Vogel would put that on his resumé."

"Anyway," I said, "it's the goose that laid the golden eggs, not the golden goose."

"No, it was a golden goose. That's *why* it had golden eggs."

"It was *not* a golden goose," I said. "That was the whole point of the story. It was a *regular* goose that happened to lay golden *eggs.*"

"That's crazy," Emma said. "Why would a regular goose have golden eggs?"

"Because that's the whole point of the story. Once the goose's owners got greedy and killed it, it was just a worthless, dead, *ordinary* goose. If it was a *golden* goose then it still would have been worth something when it was dead."

"Molly, that's the saying. Killing the golden goose. Not killing the ordinary goose that for some unexplained reason laid golden eggs."

"Well, a solid-gold goose wouldn't be able to lay eggs at all, right? It would just be a chunk of metal."

Emma opened her mouth to interrupt, but I wasn't about to let her derail me any more than she already had. "Anyway, if Vogel is this brilliant mastermind, why would he make it so obvious that Tanaka didn't die of natural causes? If he was really smart he'd have made it look like a heart attack or something."

"Yeah, maybe," she said.

"There was something else Donnie told me," I added reluctantly, "Tanaka left money for Mercedes. A couple hundred thousand dollars."

"Mercedes!" Emma exclaimed. "You think *she* killed Jimmy Tanaka for the money?"

"No, I don't think that at all. I'm just telling you what Donnie told me. Here's the list of all of his beneficiaries."

I handed Emma the magazine.

"Mercedes is so nice!" she exclaimed as she scanned the list of Jimmy Tanaka's bequests. "Remember that time you brought us down to the Cloudforest for brunch? She wouldn't even let us pay!"

"I thought you didn't like the goat stew. You said it was like eating meat with body odor."

"Yah, but it was still nice of her to invite all of us."

"She just told me she slaughters the goats right there at the Cloudforest," I said.

"Didn't you know that?"

"No! I always thought of the Cloudforest as a charming bed and breakfast, not some kind of blood-soaked goat abattoir."

"So you think Mercedes needs the money?" Emma asked.

"I know she likes to 'go Vegas' a few times a year. I wonder how the Cloudforest's cash flow is these days." I felt traitorous even saying that out loud.

"Maybe you should look into it," Emma said. "Just to rule Mercedes out. Hey, can I keep this magazine? I already threw mine away. I didn't realize they had an article about the biology department."

"Be my guest," I said. "I was just using it for scratch paper."

Margaret Adams made one of her frequent visits to my office later that day. After we went over her draft assignment several times and she was satisfied that she was on track to get an A, I decided to work the Mercedes question into the conversation.

"Margaret," I said, "I have to tell you how much I appreciate your contributions to the classroom discussion. You come prepared, and it definitely shows."

"Thanks, Dr. Barda! I really enjoy the class."

"This must be a busy semester for you. The drive down to

the Cloudforest takes, what is it, forty minutes? Each way?"

"When there isn't traffic. It can be an hour and a half if I start out at the wrong time."

"Mercedes tells me you're doing very well," I said. "It sounds like you're learning *all* aspects of the business."

"Oh, Mercedes is great! I'm learning so much more with this internship than I could in any classroom. No offense to the professors, of course."

"No, I understand," I said. "So how is business? Lots of guests? Good cash flow?"

"The Cloudforest is doing so well!" she said. Her straight hair popped out from behind her ear; she tucked it back into place. "We have purification ceremonies booked every week through February, and the sweat lodge isn't even built yet!"

"Who's your internship advisor?" I asked.

"Professor Legazpi. I was so lucky to get him!"

Iker Legazpi is probably the sweetest man I've ever met. The only bad thing about Iker is that his sunshiny personality makes me feel like a black-hearted misanthrope by comparison.

"Well, I'll make sure to tell him not to work you too hard," I said. "I want you to concentrate on my management classes."

"Oh, he's a teddy bear!" She laughed. "But thanks, Dr. Barda."

Not two minutes after Margaret left, I was in Iker Legazpi's office.

Chapter Thirty-Two

A putty-colored topcase sat on Iker Legazpi's desk next to the exposed guts of his computer. Iker was pulling black fluff out of the fan vent with plump pink fingers.

"Hello, Molly!" He paused long enough to beam at me. "To what do I owe this honor?"

I could see why Margaret might describe Iker as a "teddy bear." He had a smooth round face, a sunny demeanor, and side-parted brown hair so fastidiously groomed it looked injection-molded.

"I tried taping a coffee filter over mine," I said, gesturing at the dismantled computer on the desk. "It didn't help. The dust still gets in."

"I find I do this often," Iker said. "I have become quite skilled. Perhaps I should hire out my services."

He gestured for me to sit on one of the two matching visitor chairs.

"Very nice," I said. "Black and chrome. Looks like real office furniture!"

"Free super-saver shipping," he twinkled and resumed working on the computer.

"So I was just talking to Margaret Adams," I said.

"Oh yes! Margaret!"

"She's doing well this semester? I know the internship must take a lot of her time."

"She is doing splendidly. Her grades speak by themselves."

"That's good to know," I said. "I really wanted to find out a little more about the Cloudforest's business model, if you wouldn't mind. I was hoping to get an idea of how a real local business is surviving in this economy."

Iker placed his elbows on the table and rested his pink cheeks in his hands. Wet stains spread under the arms of his dress shirt. This humid indignity did not seem to affect his cheer.

"The Cloudforest is very beloved," he said. "It has many raving reviews. Margaret tells me that in the recent months it has plummeted to the top of the travel sites."

Iker gestured expansively, which sent the screwdriver rolling off his desk. I caught it before it hit the ground and handed it back to him.

"Listen, Iker, I know how important cash flow is, especially for a small business. Can you tell me how they're doing with that?"

I worried that I had pushed my inquiry too far, but Iker obliged me with a thorough description of the Cloudforest's financial position. Occupancy rates were high, and their added services (sessions in the crystal bed, half-hour blocks in the meditation chapel, sweat lodge ceremonies) provided extra revenue for very little variable cost. Their social media presence was solid. The Cloudforest's organic garden was tended by unpaid lodgers, which helped contain costs.

"Mercedes gets people to work for nothing?" I asked.

"Young people work in exchange for room and board," Iker said. "The Cloudforest is only one of the available destinations, and it is a very popular one."

"Does she actually get people to sign up?"

"Oh, yes indeed. One can stay in the most beautiful places in the world, for very little money. Hardly more than the cost of their airfare, in many cases. They meet other like-minded young people."

"Okay, I can see that. And Mercedes pays herself a regular salary?"

"Oh yes. A very good salary. But considering the performance of the Cloudforest, she has certainly earned it."

I involuntarily rolled my chair back when Iker told me the number, as if I were making room for a dump truck load of cash.

"So Mercedes doesn't need—the Cloudforest is doing really well, is what I mean."

"Yes. Margaret is having a wonderful experience there. Molly, if you don't mind, please hold this up just like this?"

I helped Iker move the topcase back into position over his computer. I felt immensely relieved. Mercedes didn't need Jimmy Tanaka's money.

"I will see you later at the meeting?" Iker asked.

"Sorry, what? Meeting?"

"The Student Retention Office retreat. Do you remember? They are doing one especially for the College of Commerce."

"Marvelous." I sighed. I had had kind of a lurking feeling that something unpleasant was awaiting me today, and Iker had just reminded me what it was.

"When was that again?" I asked.

Iker glanced at his watch. "It begins thirty minutes from now."

"Oh, great. Thanks, Iker. I need to get back to my office. I'll see you up there."

In the short time that I was visiting Iker Legazpi over in the accounting department, Emma and Pat had materialized in my office. Had I forgotten to lock the door? I decided that it wasn't even worth bringing it up. I would say that I had locked my door and they would just insist that I hadn't.

"I can't believe this thing is still here!" I rubbed my ankle and glowered at Jimmy Tanaka's suitcase. "Why aren't the police sending anyone over to get it? It's evidence!"

"Evidence of what?" asked Pat, "Besides Jimmy Tanaka's massive ego?"

"Pat," Emma said, "why don't you take it the next time you go down to the station?"

"Yeah, I keep calling them," I said. "They keep saying they'll get back to me."

"They probably don't have space in the evidence room," he said.

"Come on, Pat," Emma said, "it's your civic duty. Besides, aren't you tired of having to step over that thing when you get your coffee?"

"Oh, all right. So much for the chain of custody. So Molly, Emma caught me up. What did you find out about Mercedes?"

"It turns out that Mercedes is doing just fine," I said. "Jimmy Tanaka's bequest is chump change for her."

"Okay," Pat said, "so Mercedes doesn't have a financial motive anyway. By the way, they've tracked down Stephen Park."

Chapter Thirty-Three

I felt a rush of panic. "Who found Stephen Park?" I asked. "What are you talking about?"

"He's at a rehab facility in Malibu," Pat said. "I think the police had to get a court order to get the information from our human resources department. Stephen's out on medical leave."

"Are they going to do anything to him?" I asked. "He didn't do anything wrong. What's going to happen?"

"I don't think they have enough to charge him with anything yet," Pat said. "But he doesn't have an alibi."

"Stephen can't be the only suspect," I said. "Is he?"

"He's not even officially a suspect," Pat said. "Just a person of interest. They don't have an actual suspect yet."

"What about Molly's dean?" Emma asked.

"Oh yeah, Bill Vogel. Yeah, they're keeping an eye on him too. Vogel says he dropped Tanaka off at the Cloudforest after dinner. Tanaka got out of the car, and that was the end of it. The thing that makes Vogel interesting is that he was the last one to see Tanaka alive, as far as we know."

"I wonder how that fits in with Nate hearing the voice," I said. "The one calling Jimmy Tanaka's name."

"Oh yeah, we've got a kid hearing voices too," Pat said. "At least, according to your student."

"Maybe Margaret's trying to make Nate seem crazy for some reason," Emma said.

"Good point," Pat said. "Maybe he really saw something and

Margaret Adams is trying to discredit him."

"Maybe she's the one who did it," Emma said, "and he's the only witness!"

"What possible motive would Margaret Adams have?" I asked. I remembered what Mercedes had told me about Margaret's goat-slaughtering prowess.

"Or maybe Nate did it," Pat said, "because his voices told him to."

"Wow, Pat," I said, "I can see why Nate didn't want to report anything."

"If Bill Vogel was still the last one to see Jimmy Tanaka," Emma said, "maybe he's lying about bringing him back to the Cloudforest. Maybe Tanaka never got back to his room."

"Right!" I said. "Maybe the voice that Nate heard was someone who was trying to warn him about Bill Vogel, but by then it was too late. Maybe Jimmy Tanaka was planning to meet someone back at the Cloudforest. That person waited for him, then knocked on his door and called his name. And that's what Nate heard."

"Oh!" Emma interrupted. "But Tanaka wasn't there. Because instead of driving him back to the Cloudforest after dinner, Vogel drove him somewhere else."

"Like where?" Pat asked.

"Over to the lava flow!" I said.

"And then what?"

Emma and I started speaking at the same time.

"You go ahead," I said.

"No, you go."

"Okay, how about this?" I said. "They're at the lava flow, and then Bill Vogel casually asks Jimmy Tanaka to get something from the trunk, and when Tanaka leans into the trunk, Vogel slams it down and decapitates him."

Pat started laughing.

"What?" I said. "Vogel is tall and he has long arms. That gives him a lot of leverage. And Jimmy Tanaka was kind of tiny and brittle, right? So now the head is in the trunk, all Vogel has to do is dump the body into the lava flow. It would vaporize instantly."

"No it wouldn't," Emma said. "That's a myth."

"Fine," I said. "One of you come up with something then. I can't do all the heavy lifting around here."

"Okay," Emma said. "They'd probably had a few drinks at dinner! So Vogel took Tanaka for a walk in the jungle. And Tanaka got disoriented and fell into a lava tube. Have they ID'd that lava tube body yet?"

"Not yet," Pat said. "I have someone who's gonna let me know when they do."

"What about Tanaka's head?" I asked. "How did his head come off his body and then travel up to campus?"

"I don't know," Emma said. "Maybe Vogel decapitated him with a samurai sword."

"You think Bill Vogel carries around a samurai sword? My idea is better."

"Your idea sucks," she said.

An email alert popped up on my computer screen. I had a message from Bill Vogel.

"Oh, look," I said, "we shouldn't have spoken Bill Vogel's name. Now we've summoned him."

"Read his message!" Emma said. "Maybe it's about the murder!"

"I doubt that. The title is Syllabus Policy."

I clicked it open and read aloud:

Dear Molly,

I received the attached email from a student of yours. I think he has a point, and I would encourage you to reconsider your policy on late work, which appears to be overly strict. Please provide an alternate assignment for Joshua so that he can make up the points for the quizzes that he has missed. I suggest that you check the website of the Student Retention Office for ideas for Joshua's makeup assignment. They have some excellent suggestions on increasing classroom engagement.

Bill Vogel, Ed.D.

"Joshua," I said. "Why does that sound familiar?" I read the next message in the email chain.

Dear Dr. Vogel,
I am a student in Miss Barda's class.

"He's *Dr.* Vogel and you're *Miss* Barda?" Emma said.

I shook my head and continued reading.

For reasons which are not my fault, I missed some assignments she says late work is not excepted unless I have a doctors not. I am a good student and believe this is to harsh. Thank you for your help.

Sincerely Joshua Benson.

"Vogel never even talked to me about this," I said. "And look at this. He copied the student on his reply to me. Wow, thanks for the support, *sir.*"

Emma shook her head. "I'm so sorry, Molly. You have the worst dean ever. And that little brat needs a kick in the okole."

"I guess you have to let him do a makeup assignment," Pat said.

"I guess I do," I said.

I pulled up the Student Retention Office website and searched until I found what I thought was a suitable alternate assignment. Then I hit "reply-all" on the email and outlined in detail the makeup assignment that Joshua would have to complete in order to replace the points for his missed work. I pressed "send" just as Dan knocked on my office door.

"Hey, Molly, are you going up to the Student Retention Office meeting?"

"Do I have a choice?" I asked.

"Not really."

Chapter Thirty-Four

It took a while for Dan and me to find Auxiliary Lounge B. The Student Retention Office has expanded so quickly that their room numbers don't follow any discernible pattern. We found the double door propped open, wantonly spilling chilled air into the humid afternoon.

Dan and I each picked up a copy of the Playbill-style program from the stack on the front table. "Look at this, Dan. Four-color printing on glossy paper, for a one-time event. What do you think it cost to print this?"

ADVANCE, shouted yellow block letters on the cover, vibrating against a teal background.

Dan shrugged. "I know what you're thinking, Molly. Probably enough to fix our building's air conditioning and keep the library open for the whole semester. But the SRO's grant can't pay for operating costs."

"I know," I said. "Still. It seems like a waste."

"Either we spend the money on things like this, or we lose it. The money."

I saw Iker Legazpi sitting in the front row, near the other accounting professors.

"Up there?" I said to Dan.

We took our seats next to Iker. Iker smiled at us as we sat down, and then went back to reading his program. The front of the room was so cold that I wished I had brought a jacket. Breathing the chilled air was making my head hurt. The chemically smell of new chairs and fresh drywall didn't help.

"Your conference is coming up soon, isn't it?" Dan asked. "What are you presenting? I'm sorry, I should remember that."

"That's okay. I'm working with Betty Jackson, from psychology. We're doing a paper on rapport and relationship building in the classroom."

"Sure. I know Betty. I've been on some committees with her. She's sharp. That's right. I remember thinking that rapport building sounded like something you'd do in a police interrogation."

"Don't laugh," I said. "We have a whole section on that in our lit review. Students and suspects have a lot in common, apparently."

Dan's phone pinged. "Sorry, Molly, I have to deal with this."

I turned to Iker. "So what are we in for this afternoon? Anything good?"

"The program says we are going to meet someone new today!" He turned the page and his face fell. I leaned over to see what he was looking at.

"STASI?" Iker read, incredulous.

"Iker, I'm sure it's just one of their silly acronyms."

"It would be a very poor joke," he said quietly.

I glanced over at Dan, who was busy on his phone.

"Iker," I said. "Our friends at the Student Retention Office have been accused of a lot of things, but historical literacy isn't one of them. I'm sure if you asked Linda over there what the Berlin Airlift was, she'd tell you it was some kind of foundation garment."

My last sentence rang out in the suddenly quiet room. The program was about to begin. Today's presenter wore her copper hair about an inch long and spiked. Her tunic had a generically ethnic print in an indigo shade that set off her blue eyes. The moving parts on her dangling bronze earrings twisted and flashed as she scanned the room. The effect was hypnotic. Between that and the fumes from the new construction, I struggled to keep my eyes open.

I jolted awake to hear the presenter say, ". . . but today we won't call it a *retreat.* We're calling it an *advance* (here she held up the program with ADVANCE in screaming yellow) because we're moving forward! So I'd like to welcome the Business College . . ."

"Are we the Business College now?" I whispered to Dan. "When did we change our name from College of Commerce?"

Dan shook his head despairingly.

As the slides transitioned, a sound effect that sounded like squealing brakes yanked everyone's attention up to the screen.

Students and Teachers Analyze Strategize and Implement (STASI)

"Today we're proud to introduce . . . Stacy!" enthused the presenter.

I couldn't tell you exactly what she said next. It sounded like someone had fed business jargon and edu-speak into a salad shooter, and we were being served the unpalatable result.

I glanced over at Iker, busy on his laptop. Probably taking notes, like the good student he was. He usually participated in these events with such eagerness that he made me feel guilty about my unreceptive attitude. Today, though, the glum expression on his round face made him look like a sad baby. I wanted to hug him.

Finally, the retreat—sorry, ADVANCE—drew to a close. Dan stood up and went straight to the refreshment table. I stayed seated. I didn't want to leave Iker sitting there by himself, breathing in the fumes from the new furniture and carpeting. I imagined the brain cells of each person in the room bursting like popcorn with each fresh lungful of volatile organic compounds. I wished Emma hadn't explained to me in such detail why she refuses to teach in the new science classroom.

Finally, I asked, “Iker, are you okay?”

Iker’s eyebrows angled up in the middle as he clutched the sides of his laptop. “Molly, it is a very bad news.”

“Bad news? What, the part where if a student is failing the class, it’s really our fault? Don’t worry, Iker, they always say things like that.”

He shook his head.

“I did not understand the young lady. I try very much to listen. I know that the Student Retention Office makes these kind events for us.” He gestured toward the refreshment table, where our College of Commerce colleagues were stuffing themselves with fresh baked oatmeal raisin cookies and Kona coffee. “But for me it is so difficult. They speak a dialect of English that I do not understand.”

“Oh. I thought this whole time you were taking notes.”

“He was only a boy,” Iker whispered. “I told him I was very busy. I would have time for his questions later.”

“Iker, what are you talking about? What happened?”

Iker showed me his laptop screen. It was *Island Confidential*’s home page. Pat had been busy in the last hour. I felt my insides turn cold.

REMAINS FOUND IN LAVA TUBE IDENTIFIED

Isaiah Pung, 20, missing since September 3.

Chapter Thirty-Five

I hurried back to my office. It was a relief to find Emma and Pat still there. I didn't want to be alone.

"Molly," Emma asked, "Were you crying?"

I ignored her and yanked open my desk drawer. The ibuprofen was a few months past its expiration date, so I gulped down four at once.

"Molly, you're not going to believe this," Pat said as I sank down onto my yoga ball and placed my hands over my eyes.

"She already knows, babooz. Look at her. How did you find out?"

"Iker had his laptop with him," I said. "Coffee smells good."

I removed my hands from my eyes and opened my coffee drawer. "At the risk of burning a hole in my stomach, maybe I'll—hey!"

"That poor boy," Emma said. "Oh, Molly, you're out of coffee."

"I see that," I said. "How did it happen?"

"We drank it all," Pat said.

"I mean with *Isaiah,*" I said. "What happened with Isaiah Pung?"

"At this point it's hard to say," Pat said. "They don't know much. No obvious signs of foul play. No one knows what he was doing up there."

"I thought Isaiah had finally stood up for himself," I said. "When Davison told me that Isaiah wasn't returning his calls, I was kind of proud of him. I was rooting for him. For Isaiah, I mean, not for Davison."

I looked up at the ceiling and blinked. Pat came to my rescue.

"Hey, how was Student Retention Office reeducation camp?" he asked. "Can you give us a summary?"

"Let's see if I can remember anything." I shifted on the yoga ball to get less uncomfortable. "Oh, one thing was, there's no such thing as a wrong answer, just a different perspective."

"No such thing as a wrong answer!"

"Careful, Emma," Pat said. "You roll your eyes any harder, you're gonna give yourself conjunctivitis."

"You guys remember my genius lab tech? The one who couldn't read labels? We were celebrating his *unique perspective* on mixing different cleaning solutions all the way to the emergency room. What are they smoking up there in the Student Retention Office, anyway?"

"Grant money," Pat said.

Emma pulled a tissue from the box I keep on my desk, and handed it to me. "Here, Molly. Maybe you should go home and rest. It's almost time to go home anyways."

"Thanks." I tipped my head back and dabbed around my eyes. "That's a good idea. Before I go, though, I told my BP class I was going to post some information on CNCs, and I haven't done it yet. Either of you ever log on to the Lexis-Nexis database?"

"BP class?" Emma asked. "Which one was that?"

"Sorry, Business Planning."

"I use Lexis-Nexis," Pat said. "It's kind of fiddly. What are CNCs?"

"Covenants not to Compete. Sometimes they're called non-compete clauses."

"That sounds fascinating." Pat stood up and pushed his chair back.

There wasn't room for both of us behind my desk, so I squeezed out and Pat sidled in. He tapped away at my keyboard for several minutes, pausing occasionally to ask me to spell CNC. Finally, he said, "Molly, you might want to have a look at this."

He turned the monitor so Emma and I could see it.

"June first," Emma read. "Merrie Musubis files hundred million dollar lawsuit against—oh! Donnie's Drive-Inn over Noncompete Agreement."

"Well, that sounds unpleasant," I said. I was perched at the front of the plastic chair, leaning to one side to avoid getting pinched by the crack.

"So Molly, are you gonna talk to him about it? Or do you think it's too dangerous?"

"Talk to Donnie?" I said. "About this lawsuit? Why?"

"Donnie has a motive now," Pat said.

"To kill Jimmy Tanaka," Emma added. "Are you going to ask him if he did it?"

"Okay, look. If I really thought Donnie was a murderer, I would not ask him, 'Are you a murderer?' But this doesn't really mean anything. Businesses sue each other all the time."

"How come Donnie never told you? He should've," Emma said. "I think you're just intimidated. You weren't afraid to confront Stephen because he's a skinny little twerp and you know you can totally take him. Donnie is a whoooooole 'nother story."

I didn't know what irritated me more—the obvious admiration in Emma's voice, or the word " 'nother." Also, calling Stephen a twerp seemed kind of mean.

"This is the only motive we've seen so far that makes sense," Pat said. "It's the only one that's urgent. Remember we were asking, why now? How about a giant lawsuit? Isn't that a good enough reason?"

"That's right," Emma said. "Losing that amount of money would probably destroy Donnie's Drive-Inn."

"It's the company, Merrie Musubis, that's suing Donnie's Drive-Inn," I said, "not Jimmy Tanaka as an individual. A company is its own legal entity. Tanaka's death wouldn't change anything."

"Speaking of urgent," Emma said, "Donnie's Drive-Inn has been around for years. If Donnie signed the noncompete thing way back when he quit Merrie Musubis, why is Tanaka suing him now?"

"Companies do that kind of thing to each other constantly," I said. "Remind me to give you my patent troll lecture sometime."

"Oh, corporations abuse the legal system to fatten their bottom line?" Pat said. "Color me shocked."

"Here's what's scary," said Emma. "Donnie's on the College of Commerce Community Council. He's going to be at your house for that Four-C party."

"It is not scary, Emma. Don't be ridiculous. Pat, can you email me that article? My students might as well see it. It'll be interesting for them because they've already had Donnie come in as a guest lecturer."

"Isn't that invading Donnie's privacy?" Emma asked.

"It's a published article from June," Pat said. "The information's already out there."

"Okay," I said, "I'll go buy plates and stuff for the potluck, and then I'm going home. To bed."

"Don't forget to buy more coffee," Emma said.

Chapter Thirty-Six

I had purchased all of the plates, cups, and utensils I needed for the potluck, along with a giant bag of frozen peas. My plan was to go home and lie in bed with the bag of peas on my head to calm the throbbing behind my eyeballs.

Unfortunately, I was sitting in the middle of our version of rush-hour traffic. We don't have any freeways on the island, but with single-lane roads and few turn lanes, one left turn can back traffic up for a mile. I tried to ignore the wet burbling from my idling engine, a symptom of a potentially expensive valve problem about which I preferred to remain in denial. I read the tattered bumper stickers on the sun-beaten green hatchback in front of me.

Free Tibet

Coexist

If we live green, we don't have to die for oil

So maybe my 352 Special V-8 Cruise-O-Matic gets eleven miles to the gallon, but on the other hand I live close to campus and my commute is only a few minutes, so that's easy on the environment, right?

Until we stop harming all other living beings, we are still savages.—Thomas Edison

We learn about Edison in Intro to Business Management. To demonstrate the "danger" of alternating current (and of course the relative safety of direct current, from which he was collecting patent royalties), Edison publicly electrocuted animals using alternating current. Stray dogs and cats, horses, cattle, even an elephant named Topsy, whose filmed execution you can find online. If my end-of-semester evaluations are to be believed, the one thing my Intro to Business Management students will always remember about my class is poor Topsy the elephant.

A few hundred feet up a red pickup truck made its left turn into the parking lot of Galimba's Bargain Boyz, and the traffic started moving again. At that moment my laptop bag started humming. I waited until the next stop sign to take my phone out. I didn't recognize the number. The area code was 424, wherever that was. Probably a misdial, or someone trying to sell me identity theft protection. Or maybe it was my alma mater calling to ask for money. They had some nerve. If they called again, I'd make sure to ask them if they had any ideas about how I might pay off my student loans within my lifetime.

My landline phone was ringing when I walked into my house.

"Oh, hey Molly! I tried calling your cell phone but you didn't answer."

The voice was familiar, but it took me a few seconds to register the caller's identity.

"Stephen? Where on earth are you?"

"I'm in Malibu."

"What's the four-two-four area code? I thought Malibu was three-one-zero."

"Yeah, they have both area codes here now. It's been that way for the last few years."

"I can't imagine anyone in Malibu would stand for being assigned some no-name area code. So are you still at the, uh, facility?"

"Yes. I'm making good progress. That's why they're letting me use the phone."

"Stephen, that's great!"

"The whole place is nonsmoking, though."

"Ah. That must be a challenge."

"Indeed. Anyway, Moira told me what you did. I wanted to thank you."

"Thank me? What did I do?"

"She said you arranged to get me into treatment."

I sank down onto my leather couch and flung my head back with exasperation.

"Stephen, you were there."

"I was where?"

"You were there when I called your parents. I drove you to the airport. You didn't have any luggage. Moira met you at LAX. Don't you remember?"

"Oh. Sure. Yeah, I remember."

"Were there any problems with you traveling out of state? I remember you said the police told you to stick around."

"No, our lawyer said that I'm only a person of interest, not a suspect, so they couldn't prevent me from leaving."

I got up and went into the kitchen.

"I'm putting you on speaker now."

I poured myself a glass of wine.

"Are you in the bathroom?"

I ignored that. "Listen, Stephen, do you remember the conversation we had when you came over to my house that day? Any of it?"

"I don't know. What were we talking about?"

I lowered my voice and glanced around, which was silly. I was alone at home.

"Did you kill Jimmy Tanaka?"

"What?"

"You told me that you couldn't remember whether you killed him. Remember? Jimmy Tanaka? Murdered? Skull from your prop room?"

I took my wine over to the couch.

"Oh, that! Yes, I remember. No. I didn't kill him. I didn't even know he'd been in town. Why would I want to kill Jimmy Tanaka?"

"Because he was going to make your movie—sorry, film—and then he changed his mind?"

"Oh. That wasn't completely his fault."

"It wasn't Jimmy's fault?"

"He was just trying to put the deal together," Stephen said. "He was the middleman."

"Well then, whose fault was it?"

I had assumed Stephen was the innocent victim. I should have known better.

Stephen mentioned a famous name, an actor more notorious in recent years for his tumultuous personal life and his obvious plastic surgery than for his movies.

"He was going to finance it," Stephen explained, "but he insisted on playing the part of Pythias, the Sun Guide. Try to imagine that, if you will."

I had seen Stephen's musical more than once, and I had even read through the script at one point, but I still couldn't keep all the characters straight.

"That's the one with the opening monologue?" I asked. "The guy holding the bucket?"

"No, you're talking about Malakbel, the Messenger. And he carries a pail, not a bucket."

"Oh. A pail. Sorry."

"Pythias embodies radiant youth. His physical presence literally illuminates the narrative. Otherwise, the story makes no sense."

"Right."

"I told Jimmy I'd rather not make the movie at all than be responsible for unleashing some nonsensical farce whose sole purpose was to gratify the ego of some pretentious idiot."

"Of course."

"Jimmy couldn't understand. He told me *I* was being difficult, if you can imagine that. Talk about projection. I wasn't angry at him, though. I felt pity more than anything else. His perspective was completely poisoned by money."

Stephen certainly wasn't in danger of contracting money poisoning anytime soon. I wasn't surprised that he'd walked away from a promising deal like this. Stephen's Uncompromising Artistic Vision was a fragile flower that could bloom only in the rich and forgiving soil of his parents' income. The money for his high-end rehab sure wasn't coming out of his theater professor's salary. I fought back the urge to lecture him about passing up what sounded like a good opportunity, to tell him that someday he was going to have to learn to make a few compromises in order to survive in the real world.

"Why didn't you ever tell me this before?" I asked.

He sighed. "I don't know. I thought you would give me some lecture about how you have to make compromises to survive in the real world."

"Stephen, you should know me better than that."

"I'm sorry. I should have told you. So what's new? You know, they try to keep us away from the news here. They say we heal better without the stress."

"Well, let's see. I didn't tell anyone about you going back to the mainland. I assume you worked things out with whomever you needed to. The theater department is still there. Everything will probably be just like you left it when you come back."

"I'm in no hurry to get back to teaching the intro class. Teaching nonmajors is soul-sucking. And no offense, Molly, but your commerce majors are the absolute worst."

"Really? I know Honey Akiona was in your class. I think she's pretty good."

"Honey's one of yours? That's a surprise. She has a lot of

promise. No, there was another one that was making me crazy. It was as if he'd had his personality surgically removed. I couldn't get a thing out of him."

"It wasn't a kid named Joshua, was it? I have a Joshua who went to my dean to complain because I wouldn't move the class deadlines for his convenience."

"No. Let's see. Isaac. No, not Isaac. Isaiah. Isaiah Pung."

"Isaiah Pung?"

"Do you know him?"

"I . . . yeah. I do."

"Trying to work with him was *so* frustrating. There were times I wanted to strangle him."

"You *what*? That's just a figure of speech, right?"

"Listen Molly, they're telling me I have to go. I just wanted to check in with you. And say thank you."

I didn't say anything about Isaiah's body being found in the lava tube. I told myself that Stephen didn't need to deal with that right now. He needed to rest and go to his counseling sessions and eat his spa cuisine and heal the holes in his memory and dream of the authentic cinematic adaptation of his chef d'oeuvre. And maybe I just wanted to change the subject.

"It was nice to talk to you, Stephen. I'm glad you're doing well. Call back when you can."

I set the phone down and leaned back against the cool leather of the couch. I wondered if Stephen's memory would recover. And what might happen if it did.

Chapter Thirty-Seven

Emma and Pat came over Saturday morning to help me set up for the College of Commerce Community Council potluck. We readied my house fairly quickly, which left plenty of time for me to fret about everything that could go wrong. Emma and Pat sat at my kitchen counter while I paced.

"You know," I said, "just attending this event would've been enough to give me a panic attack. But having to play hostess makes it so much worse."

"There's nothing to worry about," Emma said. "It's potluck. Your guests will be bringing the food. And you know most of them from Business Boosters anyway, don't you?"

I looked around for something else to clean. "What if someone cooks something without washing their hands? Or cuts raw chicken and then uses the knife on something else?"

"That could happen at a restaurant," Pat said.

"Well, thank you for that comforting reminder," I said. "But the difference is that when it happens at a restaurant nobody blames it on *me*."

"We'll be here for you, Molly," Emma said. "Jeez, you need to relax."

"Stephen called me," I said. "Pat's source was right. He's in rehab."

"Rehab!" Emma exclaimed. "It's about time. He's been looking pretty bad."

"Moira emailed me," I said. "She said she didn't recognize

him when she met him at the airport, he'd lost so much weight."

"Who's Moira?" Emma asked.

"His sister," I said.

"What kind of Korean name is Moira?" Pat asked.

"Moira's not a Korean name," I said. "Why would it be a Korean name?"

"Yeah, Pat," Emma said. "Stephen's not a Korean name either."

"Why would Stephen be a Korean name?" I asked.

"I didn't say that Stephen is a Korean name. I said it's *not* a Korean name."

"All right," I said, "why would you say it's *not* a Korean name?"

Emma made an impatient, palms-up gesture.

"Because it's not?"

"Why do you keep talking about Korean names?"

"Um, because Stephen Park is Korean?" Pat said.

"No, Mr. know-it-all, Stephen is not Korean."

"Park?" Emma asked. "Is not Korean?"

"Half Korean," Pat said.

"No," I said. "Not Korean at all."

"Really?" Emma said. "I always thought he was half Korean. You know, one of those beautiful, useless hapa boys?"

"His father's from Scotland," I said. "And his mother's maiden name was Schwartz. I'm sure he'd love it if people thought he was hapa, but he's not."

"Molly," Emma said, "you seem even more stressed out than usual. Is it 'cause Donnie's coming over today?"

"Now that we know he probably killed Jimmy Tanaka," Pat added.

"Don't be ridiculous." I said. "A lawsuit isn't a motive for murder. Besides, you know Donnie. Have you ever met anyone *less* impulsive?

"Exactly!" Emma said. "He's a planner. Careful. Methodical. And deadly!"

"That's absurd," I said. "Why focus on Donnie at all? Jimmy Tanaka had lots of enemies."

"Like your crackhead ex-boyfriend Stephen," Pat said.

"My *meth-head* ex-boyfriend," I corrected him. "I don't think he's guilty either." I didn't mention what Stephen had said about wanting to strangle Isaiah Pung.

A knock on the door made me jump.

"The guests aren't supposed to be here yet. Why are people showing up early?" I noticed a cabinet door ajar and ran into the kitchen to shut it. "What am I supposed to do now? I'm so glad both of you—"

"Aaand, that's my cue to leave," said Pat. "These business types give me hives. No offense, Molly."

Pat opened the door, nodded a greeting to whoever was outside, and was gone. Donnie Gonsalves walked in.

I smiled brightly. "Hi, Donnie!"

"Hi, Donnie," I heard Emma echo. Her voice had an edge to it. She came and stood beside me, blocking Donnie from going farther than the middle of my living room. She was probably trying to smile, but to me it looked more like a grimace.

Donnie stood facing us, holding a salad bowl covered with plastic wrap in one hand and balancing a large foil tray on the other. He looked from me to Emma and back again, and then said, "Hi! Where can I put these down?"

"Right over there on the countertop." I stepped out of his way. "I'm glad you came early! I'll get everyone a glass of wine."

"I don't know," Donnie said. "It's a little early."

"I'll have red," Emma said.

"All right. I'll have a glass too," Donnie said. "Thanks. Hey, I have some pork here from one of Davison's pig hunts. I smoked it over kiawe wood."

Donnie watched me tear open the package of disposable wine cups I had purchased for the event.

"No furikake glasses this time?" Donnie said.

"No, I don't have enough for everyone. I don't really like the idea of disposables, but I found these biodegradable cups. They're made out of corn or something."

"Corn isn't that environmentally friendly," Emma said. "It needs a lot of water and fertilizer."

"Yeah, but at least it's not as bad as those petroleum-based foam containers that all the fast f—anyway, how about that meat? It looks delicious!"

"Yeah, look at that." Emma's tone was curiously icy. "Have you ever seen anything like that, Molly?"

"Yes, I have," I said, smiling at Donnie. "Davison brought some in to share with our department. I tried a little bit. It was very good."

"Here, let's get you some. Before everyone else comes and eats it up." Donnie started loading up a plate.

Emma made wide eyes at me.

"What?" I said. "You should try some."

"You shouldn't be eating before the guests get here," she said. "The hostess is supposed to go last."

"I'll have some too then," Donnie said, and helped himself to a few pieces.

Donnie and I ate. I ignored Emma's scowl.

"It's delicious," I said to Donnie. Then to Emma, "You're missing out."

"Eh Donnie," Emma said, "You heard about Isaiah Pung?"

"Oh, that's right!" I said. "That was so sad."

"Terrible," he said. "This has been really tough on Davison."

"At least the bad news hasn't spoiled anyone's appetite," Emma said pointedly.

"Time for a refill," I said. "Who needs more wine?"

More guests started to arrive. Dan Watanabe and his wife were among the first, with a beautiful antipasto salad. Rodge Cowper showed up with a bag of potato chips and asked where the dancing girls were, guffawing at his own wit. Mercedes Yamashiro brought a key lime pie, which happened to coordinate perfectly with her chartreuse and white muumuu.

I made sure everyone had a drink, and set out the various plates on the table. I was decanting Rodge's potato chips into a serving bowl when Emma grabbed my elbow. She yanked me into the tiny nook adjacent to the living room that I use as my home office.

"Molly," she hissed, "did you hear how calm Donnie was when we brought up Isaiah?"

"What was he supposed to do? Have you ever seen him be anything *but* calm?"

"He was *unnaturally* calm! Death doesn't faze him!"

"That's ridiculous," I said.

"*You're* being ridiculous! Ridiculously blinded by lust!"

"Now wait a—"

"What were you thinking, eating that meat?"

"That wasn't *lust,*" I said. "That was *gluttony.* Besides, there's plenty left."

She raised her eyebrows at me.

"What? Oh, come on, Emma! You think Donnie's trying to, what, poison us or something? What possible motivation would he have to do that?"

"Oh! Poison! I hadn't thought of that. No, Molly." Now Emma was overenunciating as if she were talking to a child. "The meat. The muscle fibers in it are very fine."

"Ew! Why are you telling me this?"

"Because listen. Either that meat came from a very young, very small pig, or . . ."

"Or what?"

"Where do you keep your plastic bags? I'm going to take a sample."

"A sample of what? What are you talking about?"

She let go of my arm and stuck her hand in front of my face to count on her fingers.

"I'm going to spell it out for you. One: Jimmy Tanaka was going to ruin Donnie Gonsalves. Two—"

"That's counting, not spelling."

"Two: Jimmy Tanaka was murdered. Three: Jimmy's head was found."

"So?"

"So no one knows what happened to the rest of him. *Where is the rest of Jimmy Tanaka?*"

"I don't know, where?"

Emma stared at me. I glared back at her.

"No way," I said. "That's ridiculous. It sounds like the plot of one of your schlocky slasher movies."

"What did you say?"

Saying "schlocky slasher" is hard, I realized, especially after a glass or two of wine.

"You think Donnie brought a plate of Jimmy Tanaka to my potluck?" I asked.

"It's a perfect way to dispose of the evidence."

"Okay, I know Jimmy Tanaka wasn't very big, but how could he fit into that little tray?"

"That's not all of him, you dummy! Donnie Gonsalves probably made a bunch of it, and he's giving it away to neighbors and stuff, and letting his kid bring some in to school to bribe the teacher."

"Why would Davison tell me that whole story about how he hunted the pig, then?"

" 'Cause that kid's a lying suckup, is why."

"I think I need to sit down."

Emma and I emerged into the living room, where Dan Watanabe was trying to get everyone's attention by tapping a plastic knife against his plastic cup. That trick works a lot better with metal and glass, but eventually most of the guests turned to listen.

"I have some great news," Dan said, in a tone of voice that sounded like he was about to announce the discovery of a smallpox outbreak. "I just found out today that our own Roger Cowper has advanced to the position of finalist for the campus-wide teaching award."

Larry Schneider shot me an "I told you so" look from across the room. The awards committee, Dan went on to say, was especially impressed by Rodge's community involvement, particularly his idea for Mo'oinanea, a guardian spirit of Mauna Kea, to incorporate so that she might have standing in the telescope hearings. Rodge's idea, Dan explained, would provide the basis of the preservationists' legal strategy going forward, and wasn't this terrific publicity for the College of Commerce?

Rodge placed his hands in a Namaste prayer position and bowed his head in what was apparently intended to be a display of humility. I saw that Larry Schneider was helping himself to a refill from the box of Cabernet on the kitchen counter. Hanson Harrison, in a rare show of cooperation, was helping Larry tip the box to get at the last of the wine. I glared at Emma, but she was deliberately looking elsewhere.

I made my way over to the kitchen counter and hiked myself up onto a barstool. I was exhausted from greeting guests and arguing with Emma, and I wanted to sit and recharge for a few minutes. Hanson Harrison had found an unopened wine box in my pantry, and Larry Schneider was helping him set it up. A good hostess would have anticipated this and brought out the second box already, rather than letting her guests fend for themselves.

Hanson filled his cup and lifted it. "To justice," he intoned and touched his cup to Larry's. Larry said something I didn't hear, and quaffed his wine in a single gulp. Hanson and Larry looked like they were actually getting along. Maybe this party was a success after all. Out of the corner of my eye I even saw Emma chatting amiably with Rodge. Then I heard her voice: "Rodge, have you tried this *smoked meat*? You should have some. Molly says it's delicious!"

Chapter Thirty-Eight

"Hey," Donnie said. Then, "Molly, are you okay?"

"Oh! Sorry. You kind of startled me." How long had Donnie been standing next to me? I rebalanced myself on the barstool and smoothed my hair back out of my face.

"You look lost in thought," he said, taking the seat next to mine.

"That's a good way to put it," I said. My head felt like a kicked beehive. Emma's theory about the potluck dish was ridiculous, of course. But I couldn't stop thinking about it.

"You must feel bad about Isaiah," Donnie said.

"I do, actually. That poor kid. Donnie, have you ever thought about starting a new life?"

"A new life? What do you mean?"

"Before they found Isaiah, we all, I mean, I wondered if he'd taken a new identity and left town. Maybe bought a fake ID, hitchhiked across the island, and got onto one of the cruise ships. Think about it. You could leave behind all of your responsibilities, all of your mistakes. You could transcend whatever had been holding you back." I swallowed the last of my wine. "Haven't you ever wondered how it would feel to slip out of your skin and step into another life?"

"Not really." Donnie leaned toward me. "I have a good life, and I've worked hard for it." He touched my hand briefly. "I wouldn't want to walk away from everything I have. What about you? You've invested a lot in your business degree."

"Ha! I don't have a business degree."

"You don't?"

"Nope. My Ph.D. is in Literature and Creative Writing. Although when it comes to creative, I think *Emma* takes the cake."

"Uh-huh. So how did you end up at the College of Commerce with a literature degree?"

"They needed someone to teach business communication, and I needed a job. Turns out shooting for a tenure-track job in English is an even worse bet than trying to become a famous celebrity restaurateur like you."

"Not quite a celebrity." He laughed. "Are you glad you came here? To Mahina?"

"Oh, yeah! It's so much better than where I went to grad school. I mean, we have our differences, but at least the faculty in the College of Commerce don't actually go around trying to poison each other."

"What?"

"Don't ask. There's a reason they say hell has two English departments. Oh!"

It dawned on me that when Donnie asked me that, he wasn't trying to find out about my working conditions. He was wondering if I planned to stay in Mahina, or if I was going to move on after a couple of years as do so many people from the mainland.

"I'm very happy here," I declared. "I'm not planning on going anywhere. I mean, I bought this house!"

"Her grad school friends think she sold out for the money."

"Emma!" I turned to see her standing next to me. "Where did you come from?"

"I've been saying goodbye to your guests while you've been sitting here on your okole," she said.

The crowd had thinned out a bit. Hanson and Larry were sitting on my couch, arguing about something. Larry was furiously sketching out some kind of diagram for Hanson, no doubt leaving pen dents on my coffee table.

"Emma," I asked, "could you put a magazine under whatever Larry is doing? Would you mind?"

Emma rolled her eyes, but complied.

"Did you?" Donnie said.

"Sorry, did I what?"

"Did you sell out for the money?"

"Of course I did! Why else would you sell out? It's called 'selling out' because you do it for the money."

My transition from an English department to a business school hadn't been quite as effortless as I'd made it sound, but I didn't think Donnie would be interested in hearing about the year I'd spent after grad school looking for employment, or about all the hours I'd had to pore over the undergraduate business textbooks before I felt competent to stand in front of a class of commerce majors. Also, anyone who complains about business jargon should spend some time in my former department. Sure, I'm not crazy about tired metaphors like "touching bases" and "heavy hitters," and if I never hear "outside the box" again, it'll be too soon, but at least I don't have to listen to Melanie Polewski blathering on about Phallic Discourse.

"What?" Donnie exclaimed.

"What?" I repeated. Had I been saying all that out loud?

Donnie rubbed my back in a way that was both friendly and a little possessive.

"Good thing you're not driving," he said.

"That's right! I'm not driving, am I?"

I pushed my plastic wine cup toward him.

"Would you mind getting me a refill?"

When the party wound down, Emma made sure to stay behind. She didn't want me to be left alone in the house with Donnie. After we'd said our goodbyes to Donnie (who confirmed Emma's suspicions by being the last guest to leave), she made one last sweep of my house to make sure I was free of leftover guests. Then she reached into her purse and drew out a clear plastic bag containing four pieces of meat.

"It'll take a couple of days to get results," she said as she dangled the bag. "We'll have something by Monday. Come on, get up. You need to get ready for bed."

She offered her arm for support.

"You're not planning to test it for human . . . humanity or something? Test if it's human, I mean?"

"Better than that. When Pat brought Jimmy Tanaka's suitcase down to the police station? He kept the toothbrush. Just in case."

"The toothbrush?"

"Toothbrushes have enough DNA on them to ID someone. There was a case where they caught a guy who tried to skip out on his hotel bill. From the DNA on his toothbrush."

I leaned on the wall for support.

"The meat was so delicious!" I slid down to the floor and landed cross-legged with my back still against the wall. It was surprisingly comfortable there.

"Molly, get up! If you pass out in the hallway I'm not gonna be able to move you." She grabbed my wrists and pulled upward.

"Emma! You're so strong!"

"Come on, you're not even helping."

"Emma! I see now that what we have here is a paradox. A very deep, philosophical paradox."

She let go and I landed back on the floor with a bump.

"What are you talking about, Molly?"

I repeated "philosophical paradox" several times. I thought Emma was being deliberately obtuse, but I realize now that I may not have formed the syllables precisely, nor deployed them in exactly the right order.

Finally, I said, "We're allowed to eat animals, right?"

"Right."

"But! We're not allowed to marry them. We're allowed to marry people. But! We're not allowed to eat them."

Emma squatted down, wrapped her arms under mine, and hoisted me to my feet.

"That's right, Molly, we're not allowed to eat people."

"That's what I just said."

"You need some water." She disappeared around the corner into the kitchen as I braced myself against the wall.

"Emma," I called out, "how you can do that with the meat? Don't you need to send it to a special lab or something?"

"We have the equipment on campus. Even students are doing this stuff now. Don't you remember that disaster with the Balusteros brothers?"

"Ohhh. I do remember that."

Emma had used a grant from the Student Retention Office to order DNA fingerprinting kits for one of her classes. Great idea, right? "I guess the SRO is good for something," Emma had remarked at the time. "This is going to be a terrific experience for my students."

Thanks to Emma's test kits, Boyboy and Baron Balusteros, brothers enrolled in the same section of Emma's class, discovered that there was a 99.9 percent probability that they did not share the same father. This revelation apparently caused some strain in the Balusteros household. Emma has her students run their tests on yeast now.

She returned with a full glass of water and made me drink the whole thing.

"Deadbolt your door," she said when she had steered me into my bedroom. "Sleep with your cell phone next to you."

"I always do that."

"Well, call me if there's any trouble."

"Not nine-one-one?"

"Fine, nine-one-one. Keep drinking that water. And let me know if anything unusual happens."

Chapter Thirty-Nine

Donnie woke me up by phoning close to noon, too late for me to make even the last Mass at St. Damien's. I had been asleep on top of the still-made bed, wearing my clothes from last night. Donnie asked how I was doing, and mentioned I'd looked a little green around the gills at the party. I told him I wasn't feeling well (true) and was in no condition to leave the house (also true). I added that I didn't want him to catch anything (technically true though not strictly relevant).

I spent the rest of my Sunday doing research online. I hoped to debunk Emma's theory and reassure myself that I had not actually consumed morsels of Jimmy Tanaka the previous night. I wanted to confirm that no one could get away with trying to sneak in human flesh as a substitute for pork. Not that I believed Emma's far-fetched theory, but I wanted to be sure.

What I found was far from comforting. Cannibals the world over seem to agree that if you want to pass off human flesh as something else, pork is just the thing. I read about Karl Denke, who sold jars of pickled human at the local market, claiming it was pork. Fritz Haarmann augmented his income in postwar Germany by selling the canned remains of murdered transients labeled as pork. In the Marquesas, human flesh was euphemistically referred to as *pua oa,* or long pig. Armin Meiwes, the "Hannibal of Hesse," described his victim as tasting like pork ("It tastes quite good," he said). When my searching brought up instructions for butchering a human carcass, I decided that I (and my browser history) had seen enough.

I spent the rest of the day reformatting my computer and reinstalling all of my software. When that was done, I washed my hands thoroughly, and then I had a strictly vegetarian dinner of potato chips and Mercedes's leftover key lime pie. Then I went back to bed.

Emma had told me she'd have a result by around ten o clock Monday morning. I arrived at her building half an hour before that. Her lab had the same cinderblock walls as my classroom building, but the paint was a pallid yellow instead of the College of Commerce's steel gray.

Emma sat at a computer monitor examining a wall of G's, A's, C's, and T's on a white background.

"Hey, Molly," she said, without looking up. "Almost done."

I glanced around her lab, which was stocked with gleaming stainless steel and white enameled appliances that looked like space-age refrigerators and bread makers and dishwashers. The general impression was of a commercial kitchen with microscopes.

"So this is your lab," I said. "It's not what I pictured."

"Your idea of what a lab is supposed to look like comes from movies and stock photos that are staged by people who don't know what one looks like either," Emma said without looking up from her screen.

"I'll try that again," I said, "Good morning, your lab looks very nice."

"Sorry, Molly. I go through this every time the Marketing Office sends a photographer over. They expect us to have bubbling colored liquid in open containers with smoke pouring out the top."

"Hey, you have a fridge! That's handy. I didn't get breakfast toda—"

"Don't touch that."

I paused with my hand inches from the handle.

"That's not a refrigerator," she said. "It's an incubator."

"Oh." I pulled my hand away. "So how did it go?" I asked. "Everything went okay?"

Emma finally looked up at me. "I don't normally work with human tissue. I had to lean on one of the grad students from anthro to get me the primers I needed. Fortunately, the grad students are in here all weekend."

The lab was empty now, except for the two of us.

"Are you supposed to be wearing a white coat or something?" I asked.

Emma glanced up at a sign over the doorway. "This is a Biosafety Level Two lab. So yeah, I'm probably supposed to be wearing a lab coat. You too."

"How do you know if there's a match?" I asked. "Does something light up?"

Emma peered into the monitor.

"Not exactly. I sequenced the meat and a sample from the toothbrush separately. Then I fed the two sequences into this program. It's comparing the two sequences. Aaaaaand—"

She slumped in her chair, looking crestfallen.

"Not a match." She shook her head. "Huh."

"What about the fine muscle fibers?" I asked.

"I don't know," she sighed. "It must have been just a smaller animal. Maybe even a piglet."

"So then the meat is just pork?" I asked.

"I don't know. I guess so."

I sighed and sank down onto a lab stool, immensely relieved.

"So is there any left," I asked, "or did you have to use it all up?"

Emma shot me a look, and I didn't pursue the question any further.

"Oh, while we're on the subject," I said, "let's not mention to Donnie that we tested his potluck dish for a murdered man's DNA. Okay?"

"This was a *lot* of work." Emma glared at me. She seemed annoyed at Donnie for disappointing her.

A muffled jingling sounded in my bag.

"What happened to 'O Fortuna'?" Emma asked as I pulled out my phone.

"It went off in class and one of my students kind of freaked out. Oh, hi *Donnie*! Yes, I am feeling much better, thanks. *Much* better," I repeated, directly at Emma. "In fact, I'm back on campus today. Right now? Oh, nothing. Just hanging out with Emma. Listen, you want to hear something funny? Hang on, just a minute."

I walked outside and closed the door behind me. The sun was up now, and the air felt surprisingly warm for so early in the day.

"So Donnie. I was looking up information on covenants not to compete, you know, for my class?"

"I'm familiar with those."

"So in the search results, I happened to see a news article about you."

"Oh?"

"It said that Merrie Musubis was suing Donnie's Drive-Inns, over a noncompete agreement."

I paused, but Donnie didn't say anything.

"For a huge amount of money," I added.

Another few seconds of silence. Finally, Donnie said, "M-hm. That was a pain in the okole."

"Is it still going on? The lawsuit? Jimmy Tanaka's death didn't change anything, right?"

"As far as the lawsuit? No, not really."

The lab door opened and Emma came out to join me. We

started walking together toward my office.

"Right, because it's Merrie suing you, not Jimmy Tanaka as an individual. So where does it stand now?"

"We're working on a settlement. Just to avoid having to go to court. Greg doesn't think the case has any merit, but it's not worth the humbug."

"Was it because you started selling musubis?"

"They can't stop us from selling standard musubis. Even convenience stores sell them. It was our Loco Musubi. With the beef patty and the gravy."

"Ooh, I've never tried those," I said. "They sound good. Anyway, I couldn't believe the amount they were asking for. I didn't think there was that much—"

I was about to say that I didn't think there was that much money on the whole island, but I realized that that might sound kind of condescending.

"You didn't think there was that much what?" Donnie asked.

"Uh, competitiveness among the local businesses. I thought you guys tried to work together."

"Most of the time we do," Donnie said. "Jimmy can sue for any amount he wants. That doesn't mean he's going to get it."

"Jimmy? You mean his company, Merrie Musubis, right?"

"Yes, that's what I meant. Listen, are you going to the Business Boosters installation this weekend?"

"I probably *should* go."

"You should. Quite a few of the members were at your potluck the other day. They'd notice if you weren't there."

"Really?"

"Why don't you come down and we can drive over together."

"Come over to your house?" I said. "Sure, okay. Why not? That sounds good."

I'd stopped walking as I talked, and was now standing in the middle of the pathway blocking the flow of between-class traffic. Student bodies jostled around me, and Emma had gotten ahead of me. I hurried off the phone and dodged through the crowd of students to catch up to her.

"What was that about?" Emma asked.

"The lawsuit. They're settling. It's no big deal. Just like I said."

Emma was still sulking.

"Fine," she said. "Donnie might not be a cannibal. That doesn't rule out his being a murderer. I wouldn't spend any time alone with him if I were you."

"Don't be ridiculous," I said.

I started to put my phone away when I saw that I had missed a call from an on-campus number. I also had a new voice mail.

"Go ahead and check it," Emma said. "It might be important."

The message was from Officer Medeiros. He had some news for me about the classroom tapes, and could I please call him back at my earliest convenience?

Finally. We were getting somewhere.

Chapter Forty

I was alone in one of the Student Retention Office lounges. The door must have been propped open. One of the Student Retention Officers had come in without my noticing. She was pushing an AV cart.

"Molly! I'm glad I found you here. You need to take responsibility for these students."

She lifted the top skull from the pile on her cart, and placed it carefully on a table.

"Wait a minute," I objected, as she continued placing the skulls, one per chair, on the round tables, facing inward.

I picked one up and peered in through an eye hole. "These are empty skulls! There's nothing inside!"

Now Bill Vogel was there too, and Vogel and the Student Retention Officer were batting the skulls around, as if they were playing beach volleyball. The skulls hovered in the air like balloons. I had to get to my class, but I couldn't leave. My feet were stuck. I tried to cry out, but I could barely breathe. Bill Vogel turned to me and let the skulls float to the ground. "Head count," he said. "We need to maximize our head count."

"No excuses," the Student Retention Officer added. "You don't have the luxury of academic rigor." She made air quotes with her fingers when she said this.

Bill Vogel snorted. "*Rigor.* Like 'rigor mortis.' " Then he said, "We'll be keeping an eye on your student satisfaction reports, Molly."

"No!" I cried. "Student satisfaction reports? Come on! How are they supposed to fill out student satisfaction reports? This is impossible!"

Clearly the Student Retention Officer thought I was being difficult. "As we have told you people many times, a dedicated teacher doesn't know the meaning of the word 'impossible.' For your information, Dr. Rodge took them out for night golfing." She smiled proudly. "They glow in the dark! Can *you* do that?"

I could hear my heart pounding. I forced my eyes open as the infuriating dream thinned out and faded away.

You didn't have to be an expert in dream interpretation to figure out that the Jimmy Tanaka murder had been bothering me. Pat was as close to the police as anyone, and as far as he knew, they weren't making any significant progress on the case—or if they were, they were keeping it quiet. The tip line hadn't yielded anything substantial. Stephen couldn't remember anything, assuming there was anything for him to remember. I wondered if Nate had ever called in to report the voices he'd heard. I had been leaving messages for Officer Medeiros to see what his news was about the class recordings, but he wasn't answering his phone, and he hadn't called me back.

I had fallen asleep on my kitchen counter with a stack of ungraded papers in front of me. I noticed with alarm that it was already four in the afternoon. I didn't have much time to get ready to meet Donnie for the Business Boosters event. I rushed through hair, makeup, and wardrobe in under two hours (which included about twenty minutes searching for a particular pair of shoes that I finally remembered I had stored in an unused area of my kitchen).

I parked down the street from Donnie's house and checked the time. I was a few minutes early. I decided to give Officer Medeiros's direct line one more try. This time he did answer. He had wanted to talk to me in person because what he had to tell me was confidential.

"There are no recordings," he said. "This is very disappointing."

I spotted a smudge on the center of the steering wheel, on the clear half dome with the tiny thunderbird embedded within. I rubbed it with my thumb.

"You mean someone destroyed the tapes," I said.

"There was never any tapes," he said and paused. "There are no recordings from that classroom at all."

"What?"

" 'Cause of the budget cuts. They installed part of the lecture capture system, but there was no money to install the rest of it."

"What about those cameras they have hanging from the ceiling?" I asked.

"Yeah. Expensive, those things. But they're not connected to anything."

"Great," I said. "I've been suffering from stage fright for nothing. Were they going to tell us at some point?"

Officer Medeiros was quiet for a moment. "No. They didn't even want to tell me about it. And they don't want to let this get outside the university. Would be too embarrassing."

I assured him that I would not say a word. The administration had already asked us not to make public statements about the effects of the budget cuts. Such information might shake the public's faith in the university, frighten away potential students and make the legislature even more disinclined to invest in us. The problem was that when we put on a happy face and kept our suffering to ourselves, the legislature concluded that we hadn't been punished enough and that they still had leeway to cut some more—and so they did.

I put away my phone, locked up my car, and approached Donnie's house cautiously. To my great relief Donnie's yard was silent and hellhound-free. As I stepped up to his front door I realized that I was shielding my throat with my hands and quickly let go.

This time I had worn platform mules with bare legs. This time, I wasn't going to go plodding around Donnie's house in my stocking feet like a dork. When Donnie opened the door I slipped my shoes off and walked in barefoot. My feet stuck to the hardwood floor and with each step I took I could hear a little pop. I wondered if I should have worn stockings.

"It's so nice and quiet," I said.

"Davison is out hunting this weekend, so he took the boys with him."

"The boys. Oh! Right. Cerberus and company."

I looked around the living room. It was as perfectly arranged as I remembered it. This evening the jade green vase held a turgid, bright red anthurium.

"How was your Saturday?" Donnie asked. "Did you do anything fun?"

"Not very eventful. I was trying to get some grading done, but I fell asleep in the middle of it, and then I had this weird dream! I was being forced to teach a room full of empty—" I realized that describing my dream might not make a very good impression on the father of one of my students. "Actually, I can't remember all of it now. You know how that is, with dreams. How about you? Saturday is your busiest day, isn't it?"

"Business is good. I can't complain. What would you like to drink? Wine? Guava juice? Coffee?"

"Coffee sounds good, if you don't mind. If the speeches last as long as they did last year I might need some help staying awake."

"That's true," he said.

At that moment I remembered where it was that I'd first seen Donnie.

"Oh! I wasn't talking about *you,* of course. I thought *your* presentation was really good last year!"

Donnie smiled. "Fortunately for everyone, I won't be speaking this year."

I opened my mouth to say something, but then I decided that for the rest of the evening, I should probably speak as little as possible.

CHAPTER FORTY-ONE

Donnie disappeared into the kitchen. I made myself comfortable on the genuine Sottsass sofa and imagined what it might be like to live in Donnie's lovely house. I heard the whirring of a coffee grinder, and then quiet. A few minutes later Donnie returned carrying two thin-walled white china cups on saucers. He seemed to have the correct vessel for every possible beverage: coffee cups, tea cups, red wine glasses, white wine glasses, port glasses, sherry glasses, highball glasses and who knows what else.

"So your son is out with his friends," I said.

"Until tomorrow night."

"That's good. I mean, to get his mind off of things. How is he doing now?"

"Am I allowed to answer that question?" Donnie asked. "I thought we weren't supposed to discuss Davison."

"I can't tell you his grades, or how he's doing in my class or anything like that. But I'm asking as a person, not as his professor."

I had been feeling slightly more tolerant toward Davison recently. He had been attending class fairly regularly, and turning in original, if not stellar, work. He was making an effort. More importantly, I was really starting to like Donnie, and the cognitive dissonance of disliking his son at the same time was starting to wear on me.

"He'll be okay," Donnie said. "He's strong."

"So, it's just you and Davison living here? No one else?"

"Just the two of us."

I paused to let Donnie elaborate, which he did not. I had so far resisted the temptation to find out more about Donnie's background by asking around. Mercedes would surely be able to tell me anything I wanted to know. But the coconut wireless transmits both ways, and I had no doubt that any inquiries about Donnie's personal life would get back to him. I didn't want him to think I was snooping.

"Do you have any cream for the coffee?" I asked, more to break the silence than anything.

"If you like. But taste it first."

It was inoffensive, thin and mild.

"It's Kona," he said.

"You're right," I said. "It doesn't need cream." I wasn't really in the mood for coffee; I would have preferred something with a robust ethanol content. On the other hand, I did have a long night of speeches and ceremony in front of me. Also, drinking coffee probably made a better impression. I didn't want Donnie to think I was a lush.

Donnie quietly placed his arm on the backrest of the couch behind me. His eyes met mine.

"Donnie," I blurted out, "would you mind showing me around the outside? I'd like to see it before the sun sets. I didn't really get a chance last time." I still had no idea whether he was divorced, or widowed, or what. I had to find out before things went any further.

Donnie sighed and pulled his arm back.

"It's not anything to write home about," he said. "Davison and I have an agreement. The front and the inside are mine. Davison and his dogs have the backyard. I make no promises about what you'll find back there."

"I was just thinking, we're going to be sitting for a long time at this dinner. It might be nice to walk around a little now."

I hurried to the front door to retrieve my shoes, then padded barefoot to the back door with my shoes in my hand. I placed the shoes outside the back door and wiggled my feet into them. Then I realized that the sun was low on the horizon and I needed my sunglasses, so I slipped back out of my shoes and went back into the living room to retrieve my purse. After a few trips back and forth I was finally in the backyard, wearing my shoes and my sunglasses and carrying my little red brocade clutch, the one that went so well with my vintage Lilli Ann dress.

Donnie was right about the aesthetic appeal of the backyard, which was mostly an expanse of patchy lawn. Hibiscus bushes covered some of the chain-link fence. A shed in the far corner had a white corrugated roof to match the one on the house. A long kennel, a concrete pad enclosed with tall chain-link walls and roof, occupied the center of the yard. Chewed-up sticks and bone splinters littered the grass, and patches of bare dirt marked where the dogs had been digging.

"How many dogs are there?" I asked. I guessed two dozen, at least.

"Six," Donnie said. "No, five now. Ku, Kaupe, Milu, Kanaloa, and Kukailimoku. Pig hunting is dangerous. Those tusks are like daggers."

"The backyard looks nice and clean, considering."

Donnie squinted at the rubble heaped along the fence. "This looks clean to you?"

"Well," I said, "compared to what you'd expect from five dogs. We had a Golden Retriever when I was a kid. She was a big floppy dog, really friendly and sweet. But walking out onto the lawn was risky. Kind of like an Easter egg hunt, in a bad way."

"Do you like dogs?" Donnie asked.

"Sure. I mean, I like some dogs. I judge them on their individual merits. I don't have any pets. Geckos don't count, right?" I wondered if I was sounding like a heartless pet-hater. "I don't have anything against pets," I added. "But if you have them, you have to take care of them. It's hard on pets when you have to travel."

"You have to travel?" Donnie asked. "Why?" He sounded surprised.

"I go to conferences in my field to put my research out there, and get comments and criticism, preferably the constructive kind. Then I work on it some more, and send it out to get published. I have to publish to keep my job."

"That must be where the saying 'publish or perish' comes from."

"Exactly."

"How often do you need to go off-island?" he asked.

"Couple of times a year. I have a conference coming up in San Francisco pretty soon. I'm still putting the finishing touches on my presentation."

"That's a long trip," he said. "Who's going with you?"

"No one. With the budget cuts it's hard enough to get travel funds for one person, let alone two. It would've been nice to have Betty come with me—she's my coauthor—but only one of us can go."

Donnie stopped walking.

"You should be careful," he said. "A young woman traveling alone. When is the conference?"

Was he thinking of flying out to join me? Stephen never would have done that. I told him the dates of the conference and the name of the hotel, making sure to repeat the information so he wouldn't forget.

Chapter Forty-Two

I inhaled the cool evening air and felt warm inside. Donnie was actually planning to take time away from Donnie's Drive-Inn to be with me in San Francisco. Naturally I would insist on his taking a separate room. Donnie impressed me as somewhat old-fashioned, and I didn't want to scare him off by appearing too brazen.

"Davison has an aunty in the Bay Area," Donnie said. "I can arrange for him to visit her, and while he's there he can check in on you too."

"What? No! I mean, no, don't go to all that trouble. I'll be fine. I'm just going straight from the airport to the hotel. It's very safe."

"It's no trouble at all. I can't get away from the restaurant, but I'd feel better knowing someone was watching out for you."

"I appreciate the thought, really—"

"Let me know the flight times and record locator numbers, and I'll set it up. Maybe Davison can even fly over with you."

"I don't remember the exact numbers right now," I said.

"You can email me your itinerary."

"Sure. I could do that."

Donnie brushed my shoulder with his fingertips. "I'm glad you have such a good relationship with Davison. That's important."

"Yeah," I said.

We strolled side by side around the perimeter of the expansive backyard. The temperature was dropping, and the gentle evening breeze was refreshing. This seemed as good a time as any to ask nosy questions.

"So Donnie."

"M-hm?"

"Are you married? Or what?"

He paused for a long time before he spoke.

"The last time I saw Davison's mother was when Davison was eight years old."

"Oh."

That didn't exactly answer my question.

"So you're divorced now?" I asked.

Another pause. Why was he pausing?

"I could have filed for divorce after three months."

"*Could* have filed?" That came out sounding more confrontational than I had intended. But I was a little startled to find that no, he's not divorced. I could imagine the conversation with my mother: "Molly, a divorced man?" "Well, Mom, the good news is, he's actually *not* divorced . . ."

"On the grounds of abandonment," Donnie said. "She left us."

"I'm sorry to hear that."

"You probably want to know why I didn't file right away."

"Probably. I mean, yes, I do."

"I wanted to keep her on my insurance," he said. "She wasn't well. In case she decided to get treatment, I wanted the option to be there for her. Wherever she was."

"But that was . . . what, eleven, twelve years ago?" I said.

"Yes. It's been a long time. A long time. Davison was a little boy when it happened. He's a man now."

I would never have described Davison Gonsalves as a "man." A "guy," or a "dude," maybe. A "bro," certainly.

"But Molly, I want you to know something."

Now what? What kind of married-man excuse was he going to come up with? She doesn't understand me. We have an open relationship. The divorce isn't quite final.

"I have filed the paperwork. It's in process now."

"Oh. So you're saying the divorce isn't quite final."

"It'll be another two months, give or take."

I wanted to ask when he filed the paperwork. But that would sound like I was fishing around to find out whether the decision had anything to do with me. There was no way for me to ask that question that wouldn't make everyone feel uncomfortable.

"Do you know where she is now?" I asked.

"Somewhere on the mainland, last I heard. I never tried to look for her. I don't really want to know. When you care about someone it's hard to watch them self-destruct."

I watched my feet as we stepped over the uneven lava rock. The conversation about Donnie's wife (wife!) hit close to home. I understood what Donnie was saying about watching someone self-destruct. I wondered about Stephen. Whether his rehab was going as well as he claimed. Whether he ever did succumb to the urge to strangle Isaiah Pung. How Jimmy Tanaka's disembodied (not decapitated) head managed to find its way into his prop room. What Stephen remembered about any of it.

"Are you okay, Molly?"

"Yes. I'm just thinking about what you said."

Something on the ground caught my attention. There, sitting in the rubble of the sticks and bones and leaves piled at the base of the chain-link fence. I did a double-take and then looked away quickly.

Donnie was on my left. We were walking counterclockwise around the property so I was between him and the fence. I closed my eyes briefly and tried to think. My first impulse was to point it out to Donnie and demand that we call the police immediately, but then I reconsidered. How well did I really know him? I didn't even know he was married (married!) until two minutes ago. At that moment, I didn't trust him.

But I had an idea.

I clapped my hand over my right ear.

"Oh, no!" I exclaimed, trying to put exactly the right note of dismay in my voice, "I think I dropped an earring."

"I'll help you look."

"Hey, do you have a flashlight?" I asked casually, as if the idea had just occurred to me. "It's starting to get dark. If we shine a flashlight across the rocks, maybe we'll see it reflect the light."

"Sure. I have one in the kitchen."

Luckily I had worn fishhook earrings, the kind you can slide out quickly with one hand. By the time Donnie came back out with the flashlight I was crouched down examining the ground, wearing only one earring. I hoped Donnie didn't notice the uneven bulge in my little red evening bag. Donnie shone the flashlight along the ground. The silver and marcasite sparkled, and he quickly reached down and recovered the earring for me. Normally I would find this gesture gallant, but now I resented him for being such a control freak. Why couldn't he let me pick up my own earring? Calm down, Molly. There's probably a perfectly good explanation for all of this.

I thanked him and asked if I could use his bathroom before we left for the dinner. I spent a long time in Donnie's immaculate bathroom, washing my hands.

Chapter Forty-Three

Every woman in the Maritime Club (where the Business Boosters held all of their major events, including tonight's installation dinner) was wearing either a knit suit or a flowery muumuu. The men, of course, all wore aloha shirts and black dress slacks. I knew I looked out of place in my beloved lipstick-red vintage Lilli Ann tweed coat dress, but that was the least of my concerns at the moment. I stowed my little red purse under my chair and scanned the room for Mercedes Yamashiro. I saw her in the entryway, magnificent in a tiered lavender and green muumuu, her hair (now a glossy blue-black) cut in a sassy bob. She caught my eye and glided over to our table. I exhaled with relief. Mercedes would keep the conversation going. All I had to do was sit and listen.

Mercedes did not disappoint. She had some interesting news, she said, and shifted to what was intended to be a conspiratorial whisper. A nice group of young people had come to volunteer on the small organic farm connected to the Cloudforest B and B, she told us.

"I remember Iker Legazpi telling me about that," I said. "That's working out?"

"Oh, the young people are always so nice, Molly. But this time, one of them was someone I had already met. I didn't recognize her at first. And guess who she was!"

"One of my students?"

"No!" Mercedes exclaimed. "The former wife of Bill Vogel, your *dean*!"

"Bill Vogel's ex-wife is still around?" I said. "So Vogel's not keeping her head in the freezer after all?"

My hand flew to my mouth. Why did I say that? That was not at all appropriate dinnertime conversation. Out of the corner of my eye, I thought I saw Donnie give me a strange look.

"Oh, Molly," Mercedes said. "Anyway, she wasn't wearing any makeup, and her hair was in those kine snakes, those dreadlocks." Mercedes made expansive gestures around her own sleek hair. "Still a pretty girl, though."

I nodded quietly, not trusting myself to speak.

"And that's not all!" Mercedes stage-whispered, gesturing toward her abdomen. "Hapai!" Then she added, "Oh, that means pregnant, Molly."

I already know what hapai means, but I just smiled agreeably. I knew that Bill Vogel's wife had been out of the picture for at least a year. The former Mrs. Vogel had apparently moved on. I wondered where Donnie's wife was.

The evening proceeded uneventfully, if you don't count the fact that my heart felt like it was going to pound right out of my chest and shoot across the dining room. From time to time I glanced uneasily at Donnie. I'm pretty sure I managed to hold up my end of the dinner conversation, although I don't recall being particularly brilliant. I remember Donnie saying something about the rice not being left to settle long enough in the cooker, which was why it tasted spongy. We probably talked a little about my upcoming conference presentation. But all through the Business Boosters anthem, the wait at the buffet line, and the speeches, my mind kept wandering back to the bag under my chair.

During a short break between speakers I excused myself to the ladies' room and texted Emma.

RU there i need 2 talk important!!!

No reply. I texted again:

emma answer me

Nothing. I called her. No answer.

Seconds later my phone buzzed with this reply text:

CALL ME 2MORROW HAVE FUN 2NITE

Pat lives way up the mountain, where the phone coverage is intermittent at best. I tried to call him anyway, and got the usual error message. I considered calling the police, but decided against it. I still wasn't sure what I had, and chances were that it was nothing. I'd just be wasting their time and embarrassing myself in the process. No, Emma was the one I needed to talk to.

Donnie seemed relaxed and cheerful on the drive back to his house. Either I was hiding my stress well (unlikely) or Donnie had decided it had nothing to do with him (wrong). I did not want to *HAVE FUN 2NITE.* I wanted to get away from Donnie and back to the safety of my house as quickly as possible.

I was out of Donnie's car almost before it stopped moving. I hurried around the back to the driver's side, as if the Lexus were a horse that would kick me if I lingered back there too long. I waited for Donnie to step down, gave him a quick, halfhearted hug and thanked him for a lovely evening. I couldn't read the expression on his face, and didn't want to stick around and puzzle it out. I fled down the dark road toward my car.

I pulled up into my carport, let myself out of the car, and sucked in a big lungful of the cool night air. The individual coqui frog chirps from earlier in the evening had massed into a wall of noise whose volume was somewhere between a vacuum cleaner and a Black Flag concert. I locked up the car and carried my misshapen purse into the kitchen. I opened a drawer and dispensed a length of wax paper, then snapped off a paper towel and went directly to the dining room table. Using the paper towel, I pulled the thing out of my little red purse and set it down on the wax paper. That purse wasn't going to get used again until I had it professionally cleaned. Who was I kidding? I'd never use it again. Might as well donate it to the St. Damien's rummage sale.

Maybe I was overreacting. I hoped so. I had to make sure. I went online and searched for images of cow and pig skeletons. I found some good high-resolution pictures, mostly line drawings, but also some photos. I examined the images carefully, especially the leg bones. Nothing on those pictures matched what I had picked up from Donnie's yard. I searched for illustrations of human anatomy, just to be sure.

There was no doubt. Sitting on my dining room table was a human elbow joint, with stubs of two slender bones—the radius and ulna—protruding from it. The ends were jagged and chewed.

I didn't sleep well that night.

Chapter Forty-Four

The sky was still gray when I woke up, but I knew I wouldn't be able to get back to sleep with a human elbow joint sitting on my dining room table. It was too early to call Emma. I would drive over to her house instead. I sent her a text to let her know I was coming. The facility on campus wouldn't be officially open today, but I hoped Emma had a key. I didn't want to wait until Monday.

The front door cracked open as soon as I pulled up. Emma shuffled out into the cool morning, unsmiling and bed-rumpled. She gripped a weathered blue travel mug from a few PBS pledge drives ago. She yanked open my car's passenger door and crawled in.

"Hey, thanks for getting up," I said.

She clutched her coffee cup silently as I backed down her driveway and out onto the road.

"I got your text," she said. "It made my phone buzz. Woke me up."

"Oh, sorry about that," I said, unremorseful. I was glad that she was awake and ready to go.

"I think Yoshi slept through it, though. Probably for the best. He's such a pain when he doesn't get his eight hours."

"You have all your keys, right?" I asked. "You can get into the lab?"

She turned to squint at me.

"Molly, what on earth is going on?"

"Look in the back seat."

She did.

"What's inside the box?"

"Do you still have the sequence from Jimmy Tanaka's toothbrush?"

She held up her keys. An enameled USB drive with the logo of a biotech company dangled from the key ring.

"Right here," she said. "We won't need it until after we sequence whatever is in that box back there. That's what you want me to do, right?"

"Yes! I knew I did the right thing getting hold of you, Emma."

"We have to set it up first. It'll be done by tomorrow morning. Then it'll be really quick to compare the two sequences."

The sky was beginning to lighten when we arrived at Emma's lab. I carried the towel-wrapped bone, which was squashed into a plastic Ziploc bag and sitting inside a cardboard box. As Emma was about to insert her key into the lock, the door opened. A hollow-eyed young man drifted out, rubbing the stubble on his cheek and staring straight ahead. He looked as if he hadn't slept in a week.

"Grad student," Emma whispered to me.

There were two more of them inside, young and sallow, hunched over a small tray on the counter. They didn't even glance up as we entered.

"Okay, let's see that," Emma said.

I handed it over and let her unwrap it.

"Aah! Geez, Molly, where did you get this?"

The two grad students perked up. I glanced over and they quickly averted their eyes. I hopped onto one of the rolling stools and slid it right next to Emma, and in the quietest voice I could manage, I told her the whole story. She burst out laughing at the part about the earring. I didn't think it was funny at all.

Then she lowered her voice to match mine.

"Why didn't you just leave it there and call the police later?"

"Think about it. What would I say when I called in? Hi, go look in the backyard of one of the most successful and respected businessmen on our island. Pick up every bone splinter on his three-acre lot and see if anything looks funny to you."

"Maybe they would've . . . nah, you're right," she said. "They woulda thought you was lolo."

"Besides, Emma, this is all because of you."

"What? How is this my fault?"

"Remember Trivia Night at the Pair-O-Dice? You were explaining about the bones of the arm, the radius and the ulna, how in four-legged animals those bones are fused together to support the body weight, but in humans the bones are separate like two sticks."

"I said that?"

"Yes, you did. So I saw this on the ground, with the two bone pieces sticking out like two sticks, and I remembered your explanation."

"Oh. Well, I must be an amazing teacher. I managed to teach *you* something about human physiology."

"So was I right? Is this really a human elbow?"

She poked at it with some sort of stainless steel implement.

"Sure looks like it. Did you actually pick this up with your bare hands?"

"Yes. I did." I winced, recalling it. "And then I put it in my bag. The red clutch with the gold clasp."

"Oh, the one that goes with that cute red dress?"

"Yes, and that dress is really hard to crouch down in, it turns out."

"The coat dress? I thought that used to be loose on you."

"Anyway, I scrubbed my hands in Donnie's bathroom afterward for about ten minutes straight. I probably used up half of his L'Occitane verbena soap. Then we drove to the Business Boosters event in his car and I ate dinner next to him with the bag sitting under my chair the whole time like the Telltale Heart."

"Why didn't you point the thing out to Donnie when you saw it on the ground? You don't trust him now?"

"I don't know. His backyard is really big. The neighbors are pretty far away. It was just the two of us back there. No one else was around. Maybe it was a dumb thing to do. I should have just let the police do their job."

"Well, what's done is done." Emma had gotten past her sleepiness and seemed invigorated by her new task. "Now this first part will take a couple of hours."

"A couple of hours? That seems like a long time."

"Yeah. That's just the DNA extraction. Then we wait overnight to get the sequence."

"Let me go get you some breakfast."

"How about some coffee from your office? That would be awesome."

She took one last gulp and handed over her freshly emptied travel mug.

"With cream," she added. "Plenty cream."

I got Emma her coffee and left her in her lab. I managed to make it to early Mass and then spent the remainder of the restless day at home, trying to finish up my grading. I missed a call from Donnie. I didn't return it. I was going to wait for Emma's results to come back before I talked to him.

Pat had spent the entire weekend up at his house fixing his water pump, so on Monday morning I had to catch him up on the weekend's events while we shared a coffee break in my office and waited for Emma. Emma didn't want us to meet at her lab. "I'm not really supposed to have looky-loos hanging around contaminating things," was her gracious explanation.

"It doesn't matter if Emma finds that it's a match, or what she finds," Pat said. "You messed up the chain of custody when you took it from the scene. It's not admissible in any court of law."

"I know that, but what were my options?"

"You should've called the police."

"Yeah, I'm sure they would have taken me seriously."

"You should've called me."

"I *tried* calling you."

"Doesn't matter anyway," he said. "This is going to turn out the same as when you guys tested that pork dish. You're going to get all excited, and then it'll turn out to be nothing."

"I was not *excited* at the thought of Donnie serving up Jimmy Tanaka at my potluck," I said. "How did a human bone get into Donnie's backyard in the first place? Maybe the dogs found it, on one of their hunting trips?"

"Already thinking up excuses for Donnie?" Pat said.

"Mercedes has that goat-slaughtering operation. I know Nathan and Margaret use it. Maybe her organic farming interns . . . she said Bill Vogel's ex-wife was one of them."

"My guess?" Pat said. "It's not a human bone at all. You two are just letting your imaginations run wild."

My office door flew open.

"And here she is," Pat said.

Emma pulled the door shut behind her, sat down, and closed her eyes. We waited.

She opened her eyes. "Well," she said, "it was a match. Now what?"

Chapter Forty-Five

"So Donnie did it," Pat said. "The elbow joint in Donnie's backyard matched the DNA from Jimmy Tanaka's toothbrush."

"That can't be right," I protested. "Donnie didn't have any rational motive for murder."

"Yeah, speaking of irrational," Emma replied, "Molly, *you* were the one who asked me to run the test! Now you don't wanna believe the results?"

"Pride and spite are pretty common motives for murder," Pat said.

"Donnie has too much to lose," I objected. "He wouldn't do something stupid and life-ruining out of spite."

"Oh, and don't forget denial," Emma added pointedly. "Something else that supposedly rational people do."

I tried to remember what Donnie had told me about his mysteriously absent wife. He claimed that she had left years ago, just disappeared, and he hadn't pursued her. Did I still believe that? I felt wobbly on my yoga ball and gripped the edge of my desk to stabilize myself.

"You should call the police tip line," Pat said.

"Does Molly have to give her name?" Emma asked.

"No. It's anonymous. There's a third party that assigns a random ID."

"Well," I sighed as I picked up the phone. "I guess *that* was too good to be true."

Pat and Emma stayed with me through my office hours,

which I appreciated, even though it cost me a lot of coffee. We hunkered down to our respective tasks, none of us in much of a mood to talk. Emma had her chair pushed back against the wall and was studying an article reprint. Pat hunched over in the cracked plastic chair doing something on his phone.

"Pat, you're not writing about this, are you?" I said.

He shook his head no. "Normally I'd post it as a blind item, but I don't want to tip Donnie off that you were the one who ratted him out. You're in enough danger as it is."

"Wait, danger? Why?"

Pat just shrugged, and I went back to trying to complete my report for the Student Retention Office.

My Teaching Philosophy for Week Five: In light of the fact that my life has just fallen apart, I will drag myself to class and go through the motions. What more do you expect from me, you heartless monsters?

I didn't have it in me to concoct a fresh and enthusiastic-sounding teaching philosophy. I pulled up my Week Four form and copied and pasted the Statement of Teaching Philosophy from there. If the SRO didn't like that, I'd hear about it soon enough.

Rodge Cowper poked his head into my office.

"Hey Molly, ya going up to the parade? Oh, hey, Emma Lou, didn't see you there. Hey, bro."

Emma didn't acknowledge Rodge's greeting. Pat gave him a curt nod.

"The parade?" I asked. "Oh, that clapping thing?"

Today was the grand opening ceremony for the Student Retention Office's new Student Explorations Lounge. Faculty members were instructed to line up on either side of the walkway and "clap in" the students as they walked into their new space. They would raffle off a new tablet with an Internet connection (which the winner would most certainly use to goof off during class). Refreshments awaited students inside the lounge, but of course faculty members were not allowed to enter. We were supposed to remain outside, clapping in the blazing sun.

"I don't think I'll be able to make it," I said. "I was really hoping to go, but I have so much to do. Are you going?" Rodge said he was, and made sure to make some not-worth-repeating pun involving the phrase "clap in" before he left us. When she was sure he was out of earshot, Emma made a rude guttural noise.

I must have made it through class that afternoon, although I don't remember anything about it. On the way back to my office I felt my phone humming in my bag. I pulled it out to see a new voice message. The caller had managed to leave the message without activating the ringer. I dialed voicemail and listened as I walked.

"Hi, Molly, this is Donnie. Listen. Some things have come up. I'm going to be very busy and—you'll know more about it soon, I suppose. I'm very sorry, Molly. Take care."

I felt a brief pang of guilt, and had to remind myself that this wasn't my fault. Human elbow joints don't just turn up randomly in people's backyards. If this was all a misunderstanding, or some kind of bizarre coincidence, it would get straightened out soon enough. I trudged up the stairs and down the hall to my office. The door was ajar, and I pushed it open. Emma and Pat looked up quickly, as if I had caught them talking about me.

"Hey, you guys," I said, trying to sound chipper.

"I just got back from the police station," Pat said.

"You mean you left Emma here unsupervised?"

Emma didn't retaliate with a barb of her own, a sure indicator that something was wrong.

"Your tip was a big break for them," Pat said. "They acted on it right away. I was kinda surprised to see them move that fast."

"Fantastic," I sighed.

"Molly, maybe you should sit down." Emma's uncharacteristic gentleness rattled me more than if she had punched me in the arm.

I seated myself on my yoga ball. "You know what I forgot to tell you?" I said, "I guess this slipped my mind with everything else that was going on. Donnie's married. Or was. You guys already have your coffee?"

They nodded.

"One for me then." I pulled a new box of coffee pods from my drawer, opened it, and set it up.

"He's married?" Emma asked.

I told them the story as Donnie had explained it to me.

"I wish he'd been a little more forthcoming about that," I said. "He doesn't really volunteer much information, unless he's talking about work. Then I get to hear all about the shelf life of cooking oil and how to keep sliced potatoes from turning brown."

"I think Donnie Gonsalves's interpersonal communication style is the least of your worries right now," Pat said.

"What is it?" I asked.

Pat and Emma looked at each other.

"I'll tell her," Pat said. "Molly, they found blood in Donnie's car."

"His Lexus? With the leather interior? I can't believe that. He keeps that car spotless!"

Pat and Emma watched me quietly, looking concerned.

"I was just in that car," I said. "I hope I wasn't sitting on any horrible stains."

"Not unless you were lying down in the back," Pat said. "That's where the blood was."

"That was so fast," I said. "We only called in the tip this morning."

I had a flash of hope.

"Now wait," I said. "They found blood in the car, right? But they haven't ID'd it, have they? It could have been from something else. It might not even have been human. Maybe he bought hamburger meat at the grocery store and it leaked through the bag."

"No, Molly. Donnie confessed."

Chapter Forty-Six

I shook my head. "I don't understand."

"I know," Pat said. "This is hard for you to process. But Donnie Gonsalves confessed to murdering Jimmy Tanaka."

Emma was avoiding eye contact with me.

"Molly," Pat said, "you should be proud of what you did. They never would have thought of looking at the Gonsalves place if it weren't for your—*Ow!*"

Pat rubbed his shoulder. "Geez, Emma, what's wrong with you?"

"What's wrong with me? What's wrong with you?" Emma punched the same shoulder that she had just pinched. "You trying to make Molly feel even worse about this?"

"The guy's a confessed murderer! With blood in his car! And human bones all over his backyard! Why should she feel bad?"

"Yeah, what do I have to feel bad about? I should be feeling great right now. Did you say they found more bones?"

"Looks like it," Pat said. "Sorry about that, Molly."

"Do you think Donnie killed his wife too?" Emma asked.

"I'd bet money on it," Pat said.

"Well. I can take comfort in one thing," I said. "At least this day couldn't get any worse."

Then my office phone rang.

The call was from Dan Watanabe, my department chair. He had something important to discuss with me, and could I come down to his office as soon as it was convenient? I hung up, picked up my bag and my coffee cup, and went down the hall to Dan's office, wondering what particular flavor of pie Fate was going to squash into my face now.

Dan was in the middle of a meeting with a student when I walked up. He saw me and quickly brought the meeting to an end.

We watched the young man slouch out of his office.

"*Locus* of control," Dan said once the kid was out of earshot. "A *locust* is an insect. Why do I have to explain that every time? Anyway. Thanks for coming down. Have a seat."

I dropped glumly into a chair.

"This is it, Molly," he said. "It's happening. You're on."

"What am I on?"

"You're taking over as Interim Chair. I'm moving to Interim Dean."

"Wait, what?" I cried. "That's not possible! He confessed!"

"What are you talking about? Who confessed?"

"Are you telling me Bill Vogel was the murderer?"

"Molly, what are you talking about?"

Dan wasn't following very well. He must have a lot on his mind, I thought.

"Bill Vogel must have murdered Jimmy Tanaka," I said. "That's why he's not going to be dean anymore, right? Because he's going to jail. Everyone suspected it was Vogel all along."

Dan looked completely nonplussed.

"How on *earth* would a rumor like that get started?"

Now that I thought of it, maybe the only place that that rumor had gained traction was among Emma, Pat, and me.

"Oh. I don't know," I said. "I guess people can be really irresponsible with their gossip."

"Molly, I'll be the first to admit that Bill Vogel has his faults, but he's not a murderer!"

Dan had a point. Bill Vogel's wife had turned up safe and

sound at Mercedes's place. Donnie's wife, on the other hand, who knew where she was? If Donnie had murdered his wife . . . I supposed my mother would be relieved to know that at least I hadn't been dating a divorced man.

". . . starting next Monday," Dan was saying.

"Sorry, what?"

"You'll be starting next Monday. That gives you almost a week to get up to speed."

"So I'm really going to be department chair? Even though I don't have tenure yet?"

"*Interim* department chair."

I sighed. "So why *is* Bill Vogel going out on leave? Can you tell me?"

Dan nodded. "Sure. I guess so. This is from back when Bill Vogel was provost."

"Oh! That situation with the student?"

"I'll tell you what I know. You know that the provost, as the chief academic officer of the university, is responsible for signing off on degree completions."

I nodded.

"You also know that our legislature has started to fund us based on our completion rates. How many of our students graduate with a degree. I know, it's a classic case of 'rewarding A while hoping for B,' and I wish I could make everyone in the Ledge read that. Anyway, as provost, Bill Vogel was supposed to oversee academic quality, but in practice he was only rewarded for quantity."

"So what was he doing?" I asked. "Was he just handing out degrees?"

"It was a little more subtle than that. He'd let students make substitutions so that they could graduate faster. If calculus was too hard, he let them take history of mathematics instead. If they had trouble with that, they could substitute a photography class. Students were receiving degrees based on . . ." Dan grasped for the right phrase ". . . a dog's dinner of random courses."

The phrase "dog's dinner" made me wince.

"Bill might lose his job over this," Dan said.

"So it's still possible to get in trouble for cheating," I said. "I'm kind of glad to hear that."

"Not everyone's glad. Some people around here are complaining that the student whistleblower cost us a lot of money."

"Seriously?"

"Our completion rates are sinking again with Bill out of the provost's office. Bill was well on his way to meeting our Stretch Goal graduation numbers. If he'd succeeded, the Ledge would have given us funding for deferred maintenance."

Dan gestured up at his ceiling, where a rotted-out acoustic panel revealed the raw framing and ductwork above it.

"That's happening in my office too. Pat says I should just take down all the ceiling tiles and act like I'm going for some kind of industrial aesthetic."

Dan shook a small pile of antacid tablets into his palm, then offered the bottle to me.

"Sugar-free," he said.

I followed Dan's example and popped three in my mouth at once. I instantly regretted it.

"There's enough evidence now to place Bill on administrative leave," Dan said. "Which brings us to where we are now. Molly, are you okay?"

"I don't like these," I said, wrinkling my nose as the cloying chemical odor permeated my sinuses. "They taste like what a gas station bathroom smells like."

"I know. But that's the only flavor they have that's sugar-free. Listen, do you have a few minutes?"

"Right now? I guess."

"Sure this is a good time? You seem a little preoccupied."

I gulped down the last chalky fragments of the antacid tablets.

"I'm not going to be any less preoccupied tomorrow," I said.

"Good. I can start catching you up on the department's active grievances."

Dan wheeled his chair over to the putty-colored file cabinet that occupied the entire back wall of his office.

"So this drawer contains all of the grievances filed *by* Hanson Harrison . . ." he began.

Chapter Forty-Seven

I knew I should be preparing for my new duties as interim department chair, but I wasn't even sure I could manage to get through class. I felt weighed down with regrets. I believed that if I hadn't picked up that bone in Donnie's backyard, life would have gone on as normal. I knew that made about as much sense as when a dog hides its head under the couch and thinks it's invisible. I tried to remember what Dan had told me yesterday, but very little of it had stuck. I remembered talking about stretch goals and completion incentives and active grievances. There was also something about an entire file cabinet devoted to Rodge Cowper.

The class was starting in two minutes and most of the students were already seated. There was one thing I had to take care of before I started my lecture. I made my way to the back row, where Joshua Benson was plugged into his phone.

"Hello, Joshua," I said. He looked up, startled. I waited until he pulled out one of his earbuds.

"Are you ready to do your makeup assignment? It's scheduled for today." I had already told Bill Vogel that I would schedule a makeup assignment for Joshua's missed points. Whether Vogel was leaving or not, I'm not one to break my word.

"Um, yeah," he mumbled. "Couldn't I just take a quiz or something?"

"No. Dean Vogel suggested, and I agree with him, that one of the innovative activities recommended by our Student Retention Office would be more appropriate for your makeup assignment. Don't you remember that from the email he sent to me? You were on the distribution list."

"I dunno. Whatever."

"So. Are you ready for your spoken word performance in front of the class on the theme of the Basic Accounting Equation?"

"I don't have anything ready," he said.

"You can perform extemporaneously, if you prefer. Improvisation can make for a more dynamic and entertaining delivery."

I gestured to the front of the room.

"Never mind," he muttered. "I'll pass."

"Are you telling me that you don't want to do the makeup assignment that you requested? You'll forfeit the points?"

"Yeah, I'm good."

"Fine," I said, and returned to the front of the room.

I started the discussion with something to which I thought my students could relate: "How many of you have ever had something stolen?" I asked.

There were some grumbles of recognition, and a few hands went up.

"What was it? Backpack? Laptop?"

"My stash!" said a sleepy voice in the back.

"How about a bicycle?" A few heads nodded. "Say your bike is stolen. You don't want that to happen again. So what do you do next time?"

Hands went up.

"Buy a lock!"

"A lock like this one, say." I pressed a button on the display console and the website for an as-seen-on-TV bicycle lock appeared on the projection screens.

"But what if the thieves break that lock? Then what? You buy a stronger, more expensive lock, right?"

I had a series of advertisements lined up showing increasingly elaborate and expensive bicycle locks. When we had made our way up to a lock and cable apparatus that cost more than most bicycles, I said, "You can't have perfect enforcement. Someone is always going to figure out a way around the rules. You have to balance oversight with trust. Otherwise, if everyone's always policing everyone else, people are always looking over their shoulders, society can't function at all . . ."

I realized I could probably go on for hours about honesty, and trust, and especially about the cost of doing the right thing.

"What you need to remember," I said, "is that when we're able to trust, we don't have to spend all of our resources on surveillance. But you can't be *too* trusting. As a manager, you have to consider where to strike that balance."

We went on to discuss the new self-checkout lanes at Mizuno Mart, the honor system coffee urn in the student lounge, and Disneyland's old coupon books that were phased out in 1982 but left us with the expression "E-Ticket." I asked the class for examples of oversight costs.

Honey Akiona raised her hand. "Parking at the airport," Honey said. "If you tell 'em you lost your ticket they only charge you for one day, even if you was there for more days. How do they know you're not lying? So that's a good example, yah?"

"Okay," I said. "So do you think they need more oversight, to ensure compliance, or do you think they're already overspending?"

"I think it's good how it is," she said. "You spend too much money on security, no guarantee you gonna make it up in extra fines or whatevers."

"Exactly," I said. "You have to balance the cost of additional surveillance with the increased revenue you'd get from catching the people who are going to try to get past the nine dollar a day—"

"Ten dollars," Davison Gonsalves interrupted. I hadn't expected to see Davison in class today. He was sitting off to the side, not in his usual front-and-center seat.

"Is it ten dollars now?" I didn't chide him for interrupting. He had given me an idea.

I didn't stick around after class. I ran up the stairs to my office and pushed the door open. I was relieved to see Emma and Pat there.

"What's the hurry?" Pat asked.

I raised my hand as a signal that I needed to catch my breath. "I don't usually . . . run up the stairs," I gasped.

"Or anywhere else," Emma added gratuitously.

I staggered to my desk, sank onto my yoga ball, and spent the next few moments wheezing, Sydney Greenstreet–style.

"So what's going on?" Emma asked.

"I need to talk to the detective. On the Tanaka case."

"Detective Silva?" Pat asked.

Now I was confused. "What? Nehemiah Silva? The ex-cop? He's back on the force now?"

"No." Pat said. "They're not even related. I wondered about that too, but Silva's a really common name. A Silva on the police force here would be like an O'Brien in Boston."

"I think Donnie's confession might not hold up," I said.

"Oh, Molly," Emma said pityingly.

I glanced up at my open door. Pat reached a long arm behind him and pulled it shut. I leaned across the desk so that I could speak quietly. I didn't want my voice to carry through the wall to Rodge's office.

"We were talking about SOX in class," I said.

"Socks?" Emma said.

"The Sarbanes–Oxley Act of two thousand two," Pat explained. "Accounting reform. Its nickname is SOX."

"Exactly. I used it to start a discussion about the costs of monitoring. So someone brought up airport parking. Listen. Donnie was in Honolulu during the time Jimmy Tanaka was murdered, right? That's where he bought the truffle oil."

"According to him," Pat said.

"He told me that he flew back the morning of the breakfast, and then he drove right over to campus after he landed. Anyway, if he drove right over to the breakfast, then he had to have parked at the airport."

"Even if he went to Honolulu like he said," Emma said, "he could of come back in between. On a private plane or something."

"Those flights all have to be logged, though," Pat said. "Someone could check that."

"I'm actually thinking about the parking. There's a record of people who drive out of the parking lot, right? I know I've seen that lady at the booth writing down everyone's number. If Donnie's car was *in* the airport lot, there would have to be a record of it driving *out* of the airport lot."

"Sure," Pat said. "But you can walk in and out of that lot without anyone seeing. Donnie Gonsalves could have put the car in the lot as if he was headed for a flight, and then he could've walked out. From there he could've taken a cab or hitched a ride—"

Emma had started bouncing excitedly in her chair. "But Pat! Molly's right! The problem is that there's blood in *that* car! In Donnie's car. If *that* car, Donnie's car, was at the airport, then Donnie's car was involved in the crime at the same time that it was supposedly sitting at the airport. Or something. Wait."

"Or the car got involved later," Pat countered. "Maybe when Gonsalves was moving the body. Molly, you said that Donnie was worried about some truffle oil in his car going bad in the heat, right? Maybe it wasn't truffle oil he was worried about. Maybe the rest of Jimmy's body was in Donnie's trunk."

"I don't have it all figured out, I admit," I said. "But Pat, I was just hoping that you could ask Detective Silva to check on Donnie's trip to Honolulu. And the cars going out of the airport."

"You're a tax-paying citizen," he said. "You could ask her."

"She can't be the one to ask," Emma said. "I'm sure everyone down there knows that she's involved with Donnie."

"Yeah, that's true," Pat said, "They do. Okay, I'll ask about it."

"Can you ask her to get the license plates of the cars that drove out of the airport lot during the time that Donnie was in Honolulu, too?" I asked.

"I'll do what I can," he said. "But I wouldn't get my hopes up."

"Molly," Emma said, "if you're right, it seems like it would be so easy for Donnie to clear himself. So why doesn't he?"

"Because he can't," Pat said. "Sorry, Molly, but you know it's true."

Chapter Forty-Eight

I had been looking forward to this conference for months. Betty Jackson and I had been thrilled when my professional organization had accepted our paper, and I was able to put one of my field's most competitive conferences on my CV. And now that I was finally here in San Francisco, I couldn't wait to get back home to Mahina.

Pat had promised to follow up on my questions about the airport parking and about Donnie's trip to Honolulu, but I hadn't heard anything from him. I was starting to doubt that he'd ever followed up at all. What kind of reporter was he, anyway? Maybe after getting laid off from the *County Courier,* and then trying to make a go of his own newsblog, *Island Confidential,* he was just burned out.

The coltish young fellow working the A through M side of the registration table had urged me not to miss the networking cocktail hour in the Coral Ballroom. I thanked him politely for the invitation. I had no intention of going anywhere near the Coral Ballroom. I was tired and stuffy-eared from the flight, and wanted to review my presentation and go to bed early.

The first thing I did when I entered my hotel room was roll my suitcase into the marble-tiled bathroom (hotel carpets can harbor bedbugs). Then I pulled the bedspreads off the two double beds, piled them both in the farthest corner, and then went into the bathroom and washed my hands in the hottest water I could stand. I remembered watching a news report where the crew went into different hotels and shone an ultraviolet light around the rooms. The bedspreads lit up like Las Vegas. One glowing wall stain had looked like a map of Hawaii. I pulled out an antibacterial wipe and wiped down the doorknob, TV remote, and room phone. Then I opened my suitcase on the cold marble floor and started to unpack.

As I hung up my clothes, I mentally reviewed the logistics of Donnie's alleged trip to Honolulu. I should have tried to call Detective Silva myself. Could I do it now? It was two hours earlier there. Or was it three? California has Daylight Savings Time and Hawaii doesn't. In any event, what could I say that wouldn't make me sound like an adoring girlfriend in denial? I decided it wouldn't do any good to call.

I was hungry, and not in the mood to go out and dine by myself. If I went downstairs to the networking event I might get two drink tickets and microwaved pizza puffs, but at the cost of my privacy and peace of mind. Room service sounded like the best option. I was about to pick up the room phone to call in my order when it started to ring.

It was my mother, checking to make sure I had arrived safe and sound after the long flight. We chatted about airplane food and security lines and the airline's scandalously lax safety standards, and then she asked, "So what is the latest with your new beau? What was his name? Dexter?"

Boy, did I not want to talk about that. It was bad enough when I thought I'd have to tell her was that he was divorced. I decided to rip off the bandage quickly.

"His name is Donnie," I said. "*Not* Dexter. Donnie. It turns out that he's married."

"Oh!" my mother said.

"But he claims he's getting a divorce."

"I see. Well, I hope you don't believe—"

"And there's something else. He just confessed to a murder.

You might even have read about it."

"You know I don't follow that sort of news. Did you say murder? What is that all about?"

"Well, you remember Stephen Park?"

"Yes, I do. Another testament to your unerring judgment, dear."

"For some reason the skull turned up in Stephen's prop room. But then Donnie confessed because I found an elbow joint in his backyard. I knew about that 'cause Emma was showing off at trivia night. But Donnie and Stephen don't even know each other. Well, they might, but as far as I know they don't. Anyway, he doesn't know I'm the one who found it because I called the anonymous tip line."

"You're rambling, Molly."

"Sorry. Anyway, a guy got murdered, Donnie confessed, and things are on hold for now. With Donnie. Because he's a murder suspect."

"This is America, Molly. Your friend is presumed innocent until proven guilty."

"I guess that's—"

"You know, it's nice that you have high standards and everything, but at your age, beggars can't be choosers. And you really need to learn to get to the point when you tell a story."

As soon as I was off the phone I closed my eyes and did some of the Lamaze breathing exercises that Betty had taught me. Then I arranged my toiletries on the bathroom counter, realized I had forgotten to pack dental floss and went downstairs to buy some in the gift shop. While I was there I picked up a bottle of Sauvignon Blanc.

On the way back I peeked in on the networking event, which was now in full swing. They were playing one of these inoffensive baby boomer hits that they always break out at corporate events after everyone has cashed in their drink tickets and is ready to party. In the center of the darkened hotel ballroom I glimpsed shirt-sleeved arms doing fist pumps from the dance floor. I turned away and hurried back to the elevator and up to my room, to review tomorrow's presentation in grateful silence.

I showered, dressed for bed, opened the wine, and was about halfway through my slides when my cell phone rang. The caller ID showed Pat's number, but it was Emma's voice I heard first.

"Hi, Molly!" she called from a distance. Then, closer to the phone, "We miss you!"

"Hey, Emma! Where are you guys?"

"We're in my office," Pat said.

"In *your* office? Are you sitting in those hairdryer chairs from Tatsuya's Moderne Beauty?"

"Yes!" Emma said. "And I keep bumping my head on that hood thing every time I stand up."

"It's a bonnet, not a hood," I heard Pat say. "Hoods are soft, bonnets are rigid. Hey, Molly, I wanted to let you know I finally got through to Detective Silva for you. I asked her to look at the airport parking logs and double-check Donnie's flights."

"You did?"

"You probably thought I forgot."

"I would never think that! I knew you would follow up! So is there any news?"

"Not that anyone is telling me. With the confession from Donnie, I'm not even sure they feel like they need to follow up."

"But shouldn't they at least—"

"I don't know what they're going to do," Pat said. "But how many prosecutors do you know who get a confession in a high-profile murder, and then go out of their way to find evidence that contradicts it?"

"I don't know any prosecutors. But I see your point."

"Did what could," Emma added.

"Yeah. I know. Thanks. Hey, can I ask you something? Do you think I look old?"

"What?" Emma said.

"Like if you saw me walking down the street, would you describe me as old? Am I too old to get a husband?"

"Molly, you know better than that," Pat said. "The capitalist patriarchy wants you to keep you perpetually discontented so that you'll keep buying products to fill the void. I know you've read your Eisenstein."

"Sergei?" Emma asked.

"Zillah," Pat replied. "And Molly, once they've got you spending your time and money in your endless quest to be young and thin and perfectly dressed, that keeps you too busy to compete with men."

"You're right," I said. "Forget I asked. My mother just called, that's all."

"Ah," Pat said. "Alles klar. What, you want me to ask her now?"

"I'll ask her," Emma said. "Molly, there's this wine you have to get, from this little winery close to where you are. Hagiwara's distributor doesn't carry it. You gotta get a dozen bottles so you can get the case discount."

"Emma, I can't bring wine in my carry-on. They'll make me check it."

"So?"

"You know there's two types of luggage, right? Carry-on and lost. Plus there are all those baggage fees."

"And get some sourdough bread too," Emma added. "For Pat."

"Well, I'm not going shopping now. My presentation's tomorrow morning and I still have to go over it. Oh, hang on, someone's at the door. Must be room service."

As I opened the door, I remembered that I had never completed the call to room service. But it was too late.

Chapter Forty-Nine

"Eh, Aunty!"

He squeezed me a little too tight for a little too long, and finished up with a stubbly, boozy kiss on my cheek.

"Davison! Wait. Don't move."

I carefully disentangled my hair from his earring and stepped back.

"Well!" I said. "This is really a surprising . . . surprise. So. Your dad sent you?"

"Business class!" he exclaimed. "Only way to fly. They never even card me!" I watched him stride uninvited into my room and sit down on my bed.

"You get one big bed, Aunty!" He bounced a few times. "Nice and firm too."

"How did you know where to find me?" I asked. I was still holding the door open. His eyes traveled down to my bare feet and back up to my wet hair.

"Eh, you wearing Hello Kitty pajamas?" He grinned. "Aw, da cute!"

He flopped back on my bed and ran his hand over his stomach, pulling up his tank top to expose his elaborately tattooed abs. I wondered how many thousands of dollars Donnie had paid for all of that ink.

"Well, that was very nice of your father to have you stop by," I said. "And now you can tell him, mission accomplished. I have to get ready for this presentation tomorrow, and I'm sure you can't wait to see your family, so—" I gestured at the doorway with my free hand.

"Yah, Dad really wanted me to check on you," Davison said, to the ceiling. "Make sure you okay and everything."

"Oh. Your dad. That's right." I hurried over to the upholstered chair next to the bed. I scooted it back until it touched the wall and then sat down. "How *is* your dad doing?"

"Young, single woman, all alone. That's what he said, Aunty. My dad acts like you one delicate little doll. Kinda funny, cause mosta your students think—"

"Your dad," I interrupted. "What's going on with your dad? How is he?"

"Cannot tell you, Aunty. Not supposed to say nothing to no one."

I wanted Davison off my bed and out of my room. But I really wanted to find out how Donnie was doing.

"I understand you need to respect his privacy," I said. "Is there anything you *can* tell me?"

"He's working wit' his lawyer. He said everything's gonna be okay. That's all."

I thought about the paper I was going to present the next day. Rapport and Relationship Building. I had never tried the techniques in real life. But this was my only chance to find out what was really going on with Donnie.

I remembered from my review of the literature that one method used by police interrogators was to make sure the suspect was sitting in an uncomfortable chair. Unfortunately, Davison was already sprawled quite comfortably on the hotel bed. Another tactic was to offer the suspect a glass of water. This established the interrogator as sympathetic and trustworthy.

"Uh, Davison. Um, can I get you a glass of water?"

"Nah," he said to the ceiling. "I'm good."

Well. *That* didn't exactly unleash a flood of information. The overall goal was to get the target talking. The idea was that once you start talking, you tend to keep on talking. The topic didn't matter, as long as the words flowed. "Davison," I said, "you know, I meant to ask you. Let's see. That smoked meat that you brought to my office was very good. Could you tell me how that was prepared?"

That turned out to be a good opening, as it allowed Davison to brag about his pig-hunting prowess. From his supine position on the bed, Davison lectured me on the superiority of the bow and arrow to firearms, which he considered noisy, dirty, and unsporting. (He didn't actually use the word "unsporting," but that was the idea.)

I saw no physical signs of stress. Davison wasn't tapping his fingers, moving his feet, or anything like that. Those kinds of movements would indicate that he was uncomfortable and wanted to leave. No, Davison seemed very comfortable indeed. I had apparently succeeded in coming off as nonthreatening—an objective I feared was made all too attainable by my Hello Kitty pajamas.

Davison went on and on about his powerful truck, his favorite hunting bows, and the music he listened to as he made the long drive up to the hunting areas and back. (I didn't recognize any of the musical artists he mentioned. I probably wouldn't like any of them.) Finally, I decided we had done enough bonding. Time to move to the next stage.

"Davison," I said. "Your dad travels a lot?"

"Sometimes."

"Right before Jimmy Tanaka was murdered, your father drove to the airport and flew to Honolulu. Remember that?"

Davison struggled to a sitting position on the edge of the bed.

"Aunty. I like that glass of water, yah?"

Now we were getting somewhere. It was working! I returned from the bathroom and handed him the glass. He sipped and made a face.

"San Francisco tap water." I shrugged. "I think it's supposed to taste like that."

I sat back down in the chair. A few strands of my hair, still stuck in Davison's earring, glinted in the fading light from the sliding glass doors that led to the tiny balcony.

"Davison," I said, "Let me ask you something."

Here it was. The big bluff. I prayed that alcohol and travel fatigue had lowered his defenses.

"You know, Davison, people talk."

"Yeah."

"Can you think of any reason why people might say that they saw your father's car driving around? While he was supposed to be in Honolulu?"

I saw Davison's feet jittering on the floor now, as if he were running in place. He was nervous. He stared at his lap. "I dunno."

"If there's anything you know about this, you should tell me. Now is the time to tell me."

More than three out of four suspects waive their right to remain silent. The urge to unburden is stronger than the drive for self-preservation. The fact that Davison had indulged in unlimited business-class booze could only help. Or so I hoped.

He was quiet for such a long time that I wondered if he had passed out in a sitting position. But then he said, "Okay, Aunty. I tell you. You cannot tell nobody, but."

Chapter Fifty

"You know Jimmy Tanaka was suing my dad?" Davison said.

"Yes," I said. "I read about that."

He jerked his head up and looked at me. "We woulda lost everything."

Davison was wrong about that. Donnie was only at risk of losing assets from the business. His personal property would be shielded. That's the whole point of limited liability. Davison would have known that if he'd paid attention in class.

But I said none of that. I listened.

Davison's voice trembled with suppressed fury: "My dad, he was just gonna lie down and take it. He was gonna let that—"

He breathed hard, struggling to get himself under control. "He was gonna let Jimmy Tanaka destroy us."

I hadn't seen Davison lose his cool before. It was a little scary. I gave a noncommittal nod and glanced at the door. It must have closed by itself. I was about to get up and prop it open but then Davison said, "I saw the invitation."

He was about to tell me something important.

"The invitation?" I prompted.

Davison gulped the last of the water, got up, and refilled his glass from my open bottle of wine. He walked back over, sat on the edge of the bed, and leaned close enough for me to get a whiff of hair gel, body spray, and sour alcohol sweat.

I glanced at the closed door again. For the first time, it occurred to me that I might be in danger.

"I told my dad, don't go!" he said. "I said to him, eh, where's your pride?" He chugged the full glass of wine and went for a refill. "An invitation to a breakfast in *honor*"—he mockingly stressed the word—"of Jimmy Tanaka. How could he *honor* Jimmy Tanaka?"

Davison sat back down on the bed, splashing wine on the sheets as he gestured. Good thing I'd chosen a white.

"And you know what Dad says, Aunty? He says"—here Davison deepened his voice in imitation—"this is a small community, Davison. We all have to work together."

Davison drained the glass a second time and set it down on the floor.

"You know what?" I started to rise from my chair. "I'm going to go downstairs and get some bottled water. It'll just be—"

Davison reached out and grabbed my hands. "No, Aunty. Don't go."

I looked down at the huge, tattooed hands grasping my own. This was a bad surprise. Did this ever happen to real police interrogators? I suspected not.

"Why don't you come with me?" I suggested. "A walk will be nice. Won't it?"

"Don't leave me, Aunty!" He blinked. His eyes were shining.

I glanced at the closed door again. Davison's grip tightened. He leaned forward and held me in my chair.

"Listen to me, Aunty."

"Oh, I'm listening," I said.

"It was like fate, yah?" Davison stared into my eyes.

I had not intended to build *this* much rapport. I wondered if I could dial it back somehow.

" 'Cause Dad had to travel off island right when Jimmy Tanaka was coming! And I knew exactly where Tanaka was gonna stay too. Inside the invitation, was one paper, a list of everything Tanaka was gonna do and what times."

"An itinerary," I suggested.

"It was all there. So. Was up to me now."

I considered snatching my hands away and bolting for the door, but Davison was holding on too tightly. He was angry now, but at Jimmy Tanaka. Or his father. So far the anger wasn't directed at me, and I wanted to keep it that way.

"So what happened?" I asked, to keep him talking.

"So I get Dad's spare keys," he said. "Then me and Isaiah park at the commuter lot, you know the one? Right next to the airport. And then we walk over to the airport lot. On the way in I press the button to get a new ticket. We find Dad's car. Small lot, yah? Doesn't take too long to find it."

"Why your father's car?" I asked. "What about your truck?"

"Eh, everyone knows my truck. Dad's Lexus, it's a businessman car. Nice ride, low profile, yah?"

I nodded. Where had I set down my phone when I answered the door? If I could get to my phone . . .

"So we drive out, pay the parking. Not too expensive 'cause it looks like we was there less than one hour. 'Cause I got the new ticket when we walked in."

He hesitated, as though he regretted telling me about his parking stub scam.

"What happened next?" I prompted.

"Isaiah and me, we wen' drive down to the Cloudforest to wait for Jimmy Tanaka. I wen' park behind one bamboo stand, across Tanaka's cabin. I know the dean's taking him to dinner, 'cause it said on the, uh . . ."

"Itinerary."

"Yeah. So we go right after sunset an wait. Around ten o'clock a car drives up, and Tanaka gets out of the car."

I spotted my phone on the night table. Well out of my reach.

"I see his bald head and his skinny monkey body and right away I know it's him. Then the car drives away. He gets to his door and looks like he had a few drinks 'cause he's fumbling his keys. I'm already out of the car, all set up, waiting. So I call out, kind of medium yell, not too loud: 'Mr. Tanaka!' He turns his head and looks right at me but he cannot see me 'cause I'm in the shadows. But his body still sideways, cannot get a good shot. So I call again, just a little louder. 'Mr. Tanaka!' This time he turns his body all the way, swinging his head around but cannot see nothing, like one blind dog. So I pull back . . ."

Davison mimed pulling back an arrow, drawing my left arm toward him.

"An boom! First shot. The arrow pin him to the door, just for a second. He kind of slumped down a little, yah? Then pop! His weight pulls the arrow out of the door and he falls down. Clean shot."

I shuddered, remembering the tiny, splintered divot in the door that had caught Mercedes's attention. Davison's wolfish grin made me feel a little sick.

"Isaiah, he's in the car the whole time. I never tell him the plan in advance. So Isaiah helps me move the—move everything to the back of Dad's car, and we go back to my house and take care of things."

"Take care of things?"

"Yeah. We done the butchering in the shed. Like we do with the pigs. Ku an the boys, you know my dogs, happy to help us get rid of the evidence. Give 'em a few hours, they grind up one whole pig. You seen my dogs, yah?"

My vision wavered and went gray around the edges. Take a deep breath, I told myself.

"Your dogs. Yes. I have seen your dogs. Very impressive."

"Yeah! So then Isaiah and me, we cleaned up the Lexus and drove it back to the airport."

"And you pulled another parking stub to get your dad's car back into the lot?"

"Yah, but we just threw that one away. Dad could use his original one. That way he'd never know nothing. So then we just walked back to the commuter lot, got in my truck, and drove away. Dogs took care of Jimmy Tanaka. What was left of him. Well, except one thing. The skull. Someone walks by, sees chewed-up bones in the backyard, there's dogs, eh, no big deal. But a human skull in the backyard, too promiscuous."

I decided not to question his word choice. "But how did you get the skull so clean overnight?" I asked.

"Easy. You gotta boil it for one hour at least, soften things up, then use one power washer to blast everything off the bone. Make sure you wear safety glasses when you do that. You don't want none a that junk shoot you in the eye."

"That's handy to know," I said, feeling quite ill.

"So Aunty, after me and Isaiah was done, was early morning, yah? So I bring the skull into the prop room. I know it's never locked so I walk right in, see one fake skull on a shelf, grab it and hide it in my backpack, then I put mines down where the other one was, yah? Like switch 'em, no one gonna know. I get outta there quick, still get one skull in my backpack, except this time it's one plastic one."

"What did you do with that one?" I asked. "You threw it away in the classroom?"

"Yah, was me. Dad told me about how someone found it the day he talked to your class." He smirked. "I hadda try act surprised."

"But *you* didn't put the skull in the food tray," I said. Honey Akiona and her comrades must have raided the prop room later that morning, after Davison's switcheroo but before the breakfast.

"Nah!" Davison frowned. "Wasn't me. I didn't have nothing to do with that. Terrible, that thing. Waste of good food."

"Right. What kind of sicko would do something like *that.* So what about Isaiah? What happened to him?"

Davison's grin faded. He took a deep breath.

"Accident," he said. He shook his head as if he were refusing something. "He wasn't cool with what we done. Isaiah, he always had my back when we was kids. But wasn't like that no more. He said he was gonna tell someone. He said he wanted to tell *you,* Aunty."

"Oh," I said. I wished I hadn't put Isaiah off until my Monday office hours. Monday was too late.

"So we was arguing about it, and it turned out bad. I cannot remember all the details."

Davison's bulky shoulders sagged a little. "Wasn't supposed to end out li' dat," he said.

I nodded and glanced over at my phone. The red battery warning light was blinking. It was going to shut down in a few seconds.

"So anyway, I thought everything was cool, yah? But then, one day I come home, my dad, he's all mad. He wen tell me the police found blood in his car. I say eh, not possible, cause we cleaned it up real good. *Then* he jus snap and starts yelling and grilling me."

Davison scowled.

"So I got mad too. I told him what I did. He didn't do nothing to protect us from Jimmy Tanaka, so I had to step up. Me. And you know what, Aunty? No gratitude."

Davison was squeezing my hands so tightly I could feel my bones sliding around.

"After all that, and Isaiah gone and everything, he doesn't think about *my* feelings or nothing, he told me just shut up and don't say nothing to no one. He can't tell me to shut up!" Davison was shouting now. "He can't tell me what to do!"

"Your father took the blame for you," I said quietly.

Davison opened his mouth to say something, but he was

interrupted by the sweetest sound I've ever heard: loud banging on the door and shouts of "Police! Open up!"

I realized that Pat and Emma deserved as much Sonoma wine and sourdough bread as I could carry, baggage fee or no baggage fee.

Chapter Fifty-One

I'm going to be department chair (sorry, *interim* department chair) for a while. The university auditor found that Bill Vogel had falsified records, and then retaliated against the student worker who reported him. Vogel resigned and accepted a position with a small college in the Midwest. Our administration sent him off with enthusiastic recommendations. Getting rid of Vogel probably saved our accreditation. Good luck with your new Chief Integrity Officer, tiny heartland college.

Rodge Cowper didn't get the teaching award, but the mere fact that he was nominated was an affront to our two most senior professors. I keep explaining to Hanson and Larry that I can't force Rodge to "maintain academic standards worthy of our university" (Hanson's words) or "teach a real college class and knock off that feel-good bullshit" (Larry, naturally). In the end, the teaching award went to my coauthor Betty Jackson in the psychology department. I told her how happy I was for her. She didn't seem very happy for herself. She said that this just meant that she was going to keep getting stuck on those "work–life balance" panels to serve as a role model for the rest of her natural life.

Stephen Park looks healthy and well rested after his Southern California rehab. His skin is smoother than I've ever seen it, especially around the forehead. He claims it's because he cleaned up and adopted a healthy diet, but I noticed when I was talking to him that his eyebrows were strangely immobile.

Emma's husband Yoshi still doesn't have a full-time job, but he's started doing freelance artwork. He had been sitting in Kahuna's Coffee down on the bay front, waiting for Emma to finish her shopping. She hadn't wanted him to get bored while he waited, so she left him there with an old Student Retention Office publication she had found in her bag. A local clothing designer who was sitting at the next table spotted the embellished picture of a horned and flaming Bill Vogel, and immediately offered Yoshi a commission for a t-shirt design. As Yoshi had been adding a blacked-out tooth to the picture at the time, he didn't see the point of denying authorship. It turns out that Yoshi is a decent artist, and Emma is thrilled that he's working.

Pat and Emma had not only heard Davison's confession over the phone, they had had the presence of mind to record most of it. So you're probably thinking at this point that Davison Gonsalves is serving two consecutive life sentences in some maximum-security prison. That's not quite how things worked out. Donnie hired a hotshot legal team, which included a jury selection specialist. Davison was convicted only of the involuntary manslaughter of Jimmy Tanaka (although it seems pretty clear to anyone who was paying attention that there was nothing involuntary about it) and got a suspended sentence. *Island Confidential* ran a photo of the jury foreman, former police officer Nehemiah Silva, reading the verdict.

The day after the trial ended, I gathered my courage and showed up at the Drive-Inn to confront Donnie. He'd obstructed a police inquiry, he'd deceived me, and he'd almost let Davison get away with murder.

Donnie sat down with me at one of the Drive-Inn's spotless outdoor tables, and heard me out.

"You're right," he said matter-of-factly, when I had finished. "But wouldn't your parents have done the same for you?"

"Well, yes," I admitted. "But they would have, well, they would have had the decency to make me feel bad about it!"

Davison finished out the semester as something of a local celebrity. Jimmy Tanaka really was not well liked on this island, and the fact that Davison had lost his best friend Isaiah in an apparent hunting accident got him a lot of additional sympathy. When the semester ended, Donnie arranged for Davison to transfer to a prestigious private liberal arts university in Southern California. On an archery scholarship.

I guess you could say that Donnie and I are an item now. He still doesn't know who tipped off the police to search his house. Couples don't have to tell each other everything, right? Now that his divorce is final, he seems to be thinking of me as a possible "good maternal influence" on his son. He's welcome to think that all he wants, as long as Davison stays on the other side of the Pacific Ocean.

On the first day of class this spring semester, I started off with the usual review of the syllabus for the students, but after I covered the section on plagiarism I was able to add something new: "Last semester," I announced, "I had two students hand in identical papers."

Naturally someone asked, "What happened?"

"Well, since you asked. One of them was arrested. The other one is dead."

Which was true.

ABOUT THE AUTHOR

Like Molly Barda, **Frankie Bow** teaches at a public university. Unlike her protagonist, she is blessed with delightful students, sane colleagues, a loving family, and a perfectly nice office chair. She believes that if life isn't fair, at least it can be entertaining. In addition to writing murder mysteries, she publishes in scholarly journals under her real name. Her experience with academic publishing has taught her to take nothing personally.